THEir BOY

THE GAME SERIES

BOOK 2

CARA DEE

Their Boy
Copyright © 2019 by Cara Dee
All rights reserved

Edited by Silently Correcting Your Grammar, LLC.
Beta read and proofed by Eliza Rae Services and Tanja.

ARE YOU READY FOR THE GAMES?

The Game Series is a BDSM series where romance meets the reality of kink. Sometimes we fall for someone we don't match with, sometimes vanilla business gets in the way of kinky pleasure, and sometimes we have to compromise and push ourselves to overcome trauma and insecurities. No matter what, two things are certain. This is not a perfect world, and life never turns out the way you planned.

Their Boy is the second book in The Game Series, and it's been written so it can be enjoyed as a standalone, but characters do cross over in several titles.

1.

Kit Damien

Oh no, the jogger was gonna trip. I paused with my ice cream cone in midair and watched the man and woman wrap up their conversation. I came to the Reflecting Pool on the National Mall every Sunday to get a glimpse into other people's lives, but sometimes there were mishaps. The man was going to trip; I was sure of it. The shoelaces on one of his shoes had come undone, and they were pretty long. It could get ugly.

When the man looked like he was about to continue his morning exercise, I didn't think. I made a move to get up and warn him about his shoelaces, but I was stopped. Vincent put a hand on my leg and let out a sharp whistle to get the man's attention.

He looked over, confused, as did the pretty woman he'd been chatting with.

Vincent jerked his chin at the ground near the man's feet. "Don't make it an obstacle course, son."

I grinned quickly and licked my ice cream. Vincent had the wittiest way of phrasing himself.

Crisis averted. The man retied his shoe before running off, and the woman went in the other direction.

I relaxed on our bench and squinted at the sun. It was a good day to people watch in DC. Early summer brought tourists in droves from all over the world.

"You always gotta rescue someone." Vincent brought out his pack of cigarettes from the inside of his suit and lit one up. "So what if he'd tripped?"

I shrugged and bit into the waffle cone. "He was attracted to the lady. You could tell. We don't want to make fools of ourselves in front of people we desire."

Vincent nodded at a spot a few paces away on the path, then blew out some smoke toward the sky. "Maybe he had it comin'? He almost ran into a woman with a stroller over there and got cunty about it."

Oh. Vincent was good for me. He often gave me a new perspective to consider.

"If we'd let him trip because he was rude to someone else, it would mean we judged him," I said. "More than that, we'd have doled out a punishment."

Vincent chuckled and gave my neck a gentle squeeze. "We always judge, kid."

I tried not to, though. It wasn't my business. I only wanted to be part of something.

Glancing over at the Lincoln Memorial, memories filled me —memories of better times. Of when I was part of a family. All the times my mom and dad had brought me here, the anecdotes they'd shared about our country's capital, legends, history... I let out a breath and eyed my ice cream, then stood up as my stomach revolted, and I threw the cone in the trash can.

"I think I'm ready to go home now." I tugged at the bottom of my shirt to smooth it down, and I brushed a finger over a button that was coming loose. Maybe Rosa could help me reattach it after lunch.

"All right." Vincent stood up and threw away his cigarette.

I stepped on it as we started our walk to the car.

***

Perhaps it was time to give Vincent a position in the company instead.

We stopped at a red light, and I looked out at all the people crowding the sidewalk. It was where Vincent should be, with family or friends, enjoying the lovely weather and a day off. Instead, he was here with me, in a black car with tinted windows, drumming his fingers on the wheel as if he had no cares in the world. But I knew better. I knew he was hiding. He was hiding from the very thing I craved.

I sat in the back, where I only had to look chipper when Vincent checked the rearview mirror.

A woman about to cross the street dropped one of her shopping bags. She picked it up and shared an "oops" laugh with her friends. She could've been Vincent's girlfriend, I thought. Maybe they'd have a few kids. I could visit them.

He'd been with my family since I was little. Back then, I didn't think it was weird for him to work basically all hours of the day. Most twenty-five-year-olds in bigger cities were career-driven and hungry for that next step on the ladder. My father had promised Vincent many great things, most of all, the position as head of security.

That ladder was gone now, and Vincent wasn't getting any younger.

He *had* to be hiding from something.

I'd thought he would leave when my parents died. Most of the staff had.

"You turn forty soon," I noted.

"Whoa." Vincent gave me an incredulous look in the rearview. "Can I turn thirty-six first?"

I smiled crookedly and shrugged.

He had a massive family up in Jersey. Brothers, sisters, nieces, nephews, his father—he'd lost his mother to cancer a couple years ago—aunts, uncles, et cetera. If Vincent didn't want to start his own family, then at the very least, he should spend more time with the family he already had. He shouldn't spend every hour of the week at my constant beck and call just in case I wanted to go somewhere.

If he continued this way, his next birthday just might look like my twenty-second one last week.

I'd spent it with Vincent—for all intents and purposes, my driver—and Rosa, the woman who'd cooked all my meals since I was in diapers. Diapers that she'd changed.

I didn't mean to be ungrateful to them. I loved them very much. Hell, it was why I urged Vincent to get away. Or, I wanted to urge him. I *would* have, had I not been so terrified of losing him.

Rosa had a husband, kids, and grandkids to come home to every day.

"Don't you want children?" I wondered. "A wife?"

I wasn't a complete fool; I knew his job came with perks many would only dream of. His pay was substantial, and my father had given him his own condo across the river in Arlington. He had access to our summer residence and Dad's cars there that I didn't know what to do with. And so on, and so on.

However, he rarely took the time to enjoy those perks.

"There's time," Vincent replied with an easy smile. "You know what I see when I drive you around? I see people rushing through life like it's some fucking contest they gotta win. And the price? Death. I'm good, thanks."

"Hm." I glanced out the window again, not sure I agreed with him. Yes, people were often rushing—toward goals and happiness. Wasn't that the point? Because, why drag out the stuff we didn't like?

Anyway... I shook my head and tried to clear it. The end of May was approaching, and I was looking forward to my one and only social event. The munch two subs hosted for my BDSM community once a month.

Okay, it was a bit bold to call it *my* community. I'd only attended a handful of kink events in the past three years, and I couldn't seem to form lasting connections anymore.

I used to have a lot of friends.

These days, I'd dare say I had two—outside of my online life. And it was just my luck that Abel, whom I knew best, lived across the country. He was from the Seattle area and had only been out here because he'd played hockey for Pittsburgh.

Because of his NHL status, he'd wanted to keep a low profile with kink, hence making trips to DC for that.

He was visiting me in a few weeks, and I couldn't wait.

He was my age, yet he'd already found the love of his life. They were engaged now.

I should suggest he bring his Daddy Dom. Then we could attend an event together, and I would feel braver. Hopefully brave enough to approach another Dominant and possibly even play. My heart rate kicked up a notch at the mere thought of it. I hadn't played in over a year, and it'd been a disaster.

As soon as we crossed into Georgetown, the familiar unease settled in my stomach. It was a nice area with picturesque town-houses and a lot of history, but I didn't see the beauty anymore. My street was just off the tourist path, though many still came here to take pictures of the old houses. They were all narrow, three-story homes painted in different colors.

When my parents bought our house, they'd renovated it and Dad had jumped through bureaucratic hoops to get the permit so Mom could have the house painted dark blue. It'd been her favorite color, and Dad hated saying no to her.

She'd dedicated her life to helping others, he used to say, so it was his job to make sure she got whatever little she wanted for herself.

Our home made me nauseated.

It'd once been my favorite place on earth. Now, it was dead. Like a light had been flicked off, even as the interior was well-maintained and you hardly ever found a speck of dust. It'd been repainted last year too. The white paint that covered the stoop and the concrete wall around the property, as well as framed the windows, was blinding in the sun.

All I saw were childhood memories being peeled off the fucking walls.

I left the car in a depressed mood and trailed up the steps, passing the flower beds Rosa took care of for Mom's sake, and I unlocked the door.

In that second, right as I stepped inside, I could almost believe Mom and Dad were alive. Mom's perfume still lingered, and Rosa wasn't the type of person to switch brands on fabric softeners and cleaning supplies. All of it combined simply smelled of warmth and family.

It was fake.

It was a lie.

A museum was what it was, managed by Dad's best friend, Richard.

"Is that you, Kit?" Rosa called from the kitchen.

"Yes." I took off my shoes and joined her. She was by the stove, humming to the song playing. My Spanish wasn't very good, so I didn't understand much of it. I appreciated the food a lot more. Rosa was from El Salvador and cooked like a goddess. "It smells good."

She threw me an infectious grin over her shoulder. "How was the outing today, *mijo*?"

Same as every Sunday. I got to look into people's lives. It was a constant reminder that I was on the outside. "It was nice. Did you make it to church?" Because when she did, she stopped by the market near her church, where she picked up treats from her country for me.

She chuckled. "Maybe. I might have left you something in the fridge—no, no! You stay there. You're gonna eat a meal first."

Damn it.

Vincent joined us soon enough, and he reminded me I had an extra appointment tomorrow.

I nodded. I already knew. It was that other thing that happened once a month. A meeting with Richard, who, besides making sure this household still ran like it did when Mom and Dad were alive, also managed their money. Or my money. Whatever. I didn't like thinking about it.

It brought me some strange sense of giddiness to hate Mondays. It was something I had in common with others. On Monday morning, for instance, I could go on Twitter, post a meme about how much Mondays sucked, and I would get tons of likes and retweets. It was like being part of the gang for a minute.

It was nice.

After that, it was all suffering.

My meeting with Richard went as expected. He gave me his monthly report, his concern, and his advice. While he transferred funds to this and that account, he told me—again—I should visit more often, but I shook my head. It was too painful.

Our families had spent so many holidays together that everything had shattered when Mom and Dad died. There was no recovering. Every conversation was stilted. Richard's two daughters tiptoed around me. We couldn't speak about anything outside of boring current events. There were too many memories. And two empty seats at the table.

I saw Richard once a month, and I saw Linda, his wife, whenever she needed help with a new fund raiser she was organizing. That was enough.

I made it through the meeting and breathed a sigh of relief when I was back in the car. Next stop, the spa, which was anything but enjoyable. My skincare treatment was an itchy, tickly affair. But if I skipped an appointment, I suffered even more. Something I'd learned from experience.

The only funny part about my session at the spa was the banter between my dermatologist and my tattoo artist. Sometimes, I didn't know if they were out to murder each other or fuck.

"Stop scratching," Vincent reminded me before I got out of the car.

I huffed and smoothed down the sleeve of my button-down.

The facility I went to across the river in Alexandria was big. Health club, fitness center, clinic, spa, cosmetic surgery—all wrapped up in one. Thankfully, my surgery days were over. I hadn't needed laser treatments in a while either.

Supposedly, I was almost done healing.

Vincent waited in the car as usual, and they called my name after a short wait.

Dr. Cohen was a nice woman, and she had the best treatment room I'd ever been in. It faced the building's courtyard and had one-way mirrored windows. So my view was of a sliver of nature that belonged in the tropics while Dr. Cohen and Kirk —if he'd get here already—worked on my upper body.

Dr. Cohen checked her watch and rolled her eyes. "Why is he always late?"

I kept my smirk to myself.

She offered an apologetic smile and gestured at her examination table. "We might as well start. You can remove your shirt and take a seat there."

I left her office chair and unbuttoned my shirt. These days, it didn't bring me as much pain to show my body. It was why my last play partner hadn't wanted to continue, because I'd refused to be shirtless—unless the light was off.

A mirror on the wall waited for my flinch, but it didn't come. I carefully draped the shirt over the examination table and side-eyed my reflection. I'd always be slight and short, and my hair would never be tamed, but the scars...I'd done something about the scars.

I had no recollection of that part of the accident. I only knew I'd flown through a window at a high speed, and the glass had shattered, leaving my upper body riddled with cuts and scrapes. The smallest ones had faded in the first year.

What I did remember was waking up to blistering heat and the smell of gasoline and fire.

I swallowed uneasily and closed my eyes for a second. *Don't think about it. Don't go there.* The bigger scars, the ones skin grafts couldn't fix completely, from sharp edges of glass and metal, as well as from the burns...they weren't going anywhere, though Kirk had done an amazing job at covering them permanently. My entire torso, arms, back—all of it—and even a bit of my neck, had been his canvas.

He'd taken my favorite places, memories, fantasies, quotes, tributes, symbols, and lyrics and used my body as my own personal photo album. But due to the scarring and slow healing process, I had to come here to Dr. Cohen once a week for her to check my progress. I also had to have Kirk fill in the ink where the skin was particularly angry.

It'd been a long year since I got the first tattoo.

"Your back looks much better, Kit." Dr. Cohen came over and inspected me as she reached for a pair of gloves. "Is it still itching?"

"Not as much," I replied. "My elbows, though. I think I scratch them in my sleep."

She hummed and lifted my arm. "They're a little dry, but that's normal, especially with the seasons changing. Just keep using the creams."

God forbid I forgot.

There was a knock on the door, alerting us to the arrival of the other half of my dynamic duo. Tattoos basically went against everything Dr. Cohen believed in for this type of recovery, although she'd softened her approach a lot from the first time I'd mentioned wanting the cover-up. Meeting Kirk and seeing how professional he was had changed her mind some, I was pretty sure.

That said, she still enjoyed pointing out that I had been "almost healed" before Kirk started working with me.

"You're late," was all she said this time.

"Lower your expectations," Kirk replied. He walked over to us and gave me a grin. "How's my favorite client?"

He was incredibly attractive, all ink and steel. It was impossible not to smile. "Better, I think."

He wasn't here for every appointment. In fact, I'd probably go to his studio next time I needed him. The last tattoo was in place now, and he only showed up to check the progress and if I needed touch-ups. I'd needed more than a few already, because tattooing scarred skin wasn't the easiest.

I shuddered as Dr. Cohen drew her fingers over a sensitive

spot on my arm. A contrast to the spots where I felt close to nothing.

She was unhappy about something. It was always the same thing. Slow-healing, dry skin. She'd wanted me to wait much, much longer before I got inked.

She didn't understand that I'd rather take a slow healing process than another minute of what I used to see in the mirror.

Kirk did his own thing, checking on the last part of my back piece.

"I'll need to fill in a bit here," Kirk murmured. "We'll get you a session soon. Won't take more than half an hour."

No problem. It was an opportunity to leave the house. "Are you coming here, or do you want me to come to the studio?" Either was fine.

"Up to you, buddy. I don't mind coming here."

I pursed my lips and looked away. Of course he didn't mind coming here. It was where Dr. Cohen worked.

I hoped they got together before my sessions were over.

"Do you have a treatment scheduled for today, Kit?" Dr. Cohen wondered.

"Yes, ma'am," I replied. Same building, just across the courtyard. It was some hydration therapy for my skin, and I hated it. It itched like crazy.

I suppose I should be grateful. Not too long ago, my doctor's appointments had involved surgery and skin transplants. Lotions that itched were nothing in comparison.

"Seriously, look," Kirk said. "Look what a fucking master I am." He turned me around, to Dr. Cohen's dismay because it interrupted her exam, and gave me a smaller mirror. "Have you really looked at the artwork?"

Of course I had. "What do you mean?" I angled the mirror to see what he was talking about. The cathedral across my back came into view, along with a Latin quote, two dates, and the shadowy pews at the bottom where a few silhouetted forms had their heads bowed in prayer.

"You can't see the scars," Kirk responded smugly. "Look closely, Kit. You're as self-conscious and insecure now as you were when we first met. But it's time you quit hiding in those shirts. Next time we see each other, I wanna see you in a vintage tee and jeans."

"Now he gives fashion advice too," Dr. Cohen muttered under her breath.

I grinned unsurely and eyed the mirror. Maybe he was right. Not about the clothes. I hadn't owned a pair of jeans since before the accident, and my mom hadn't liked the look. But perhaps I appeared more normal than I'd thought.

I did agree with him on the master part. The placement of the ink was perfect. Where the skin had recovered or never been damaged, he'd gone easy on the shadowing, giving the heavier work breathing room in between the dark contrasts.

I had to admit the idea of wearing a T-shirt this summer was appealing too.

Meeting Kirk's grin, I felt a boost of confidence.

"You got this," he said with a nod. "You've been to hell and back, and the ink isn't about hiding from it. It's about choice. You choose when to reveal whatever you feel insecure or vulnerable about. You've taken back that control."

I swallowed hard as his words reverberated inside of me.

Even Dr. Cohen looked a little taken aback in the corner of my eye.

Kirk was right, damn it. He was right. It was my choice.

2.

Kirk gave me a similar boost the day he touched up my ink. And the day after, I went out and bought a T-shirt. I wouldn't part with my chinos and dress pants and get jeans, but the tee was nice. It was faded gray, ridiculously soft, and had the silhouette of an F-22 printed across the chest. It wasn't my favorite fighter jet, though it was certainly close.

I spent the morning in front of the mirror doing double-checks, only to make sure you couldn't see the scars at first glance.

You couldn't, but that didn't stop me from being nervous as hell when Vincent drove me to my munch. I felt naked and exposed wearing so little.

We arrived in Logan Circle and at a pale-green-painted corner rowhouse that had been turned into a popular brunch place. The second floor had big windows, and the third was the rooftop terrace where the munch was hosted.

"I'll be back to pick you up in three hours," Vincent said, looking at me in the rearview. "Don't let anyone take advantage, ya hear? I'll drop-kick a fucker."

I snickered and opened the door. "Thank you, Vincent. I'll be careful. Would you like me to bring you back some eggs Benedict?"

"I'll never say no to those."

I smiled and nodded, then got out of the car and put on my sunglasses.

It was a good day for nervousness and brunch with fellow kinksters. Nervousness was nothing new; I usually shook it off by the time food was served, but today was different. The buttoned-up shirt with long sleeves had been replaced by something much more casual.

Mom had accepted T-shirts somewhat, so I didn't feel guilty wearing one. That was nice.

I could see the hostess's gaze lingering on my neck, where some of the ink peeked out, and then down to my arms. Then she cleared her throat and checked the bookings.

"Oh, here we go." She found Ivy's last name. "You're on the terrace. Drinks will be brought to you soon."

"Thank you." I stuck my hands down into my pockets and trailed up the spiral staircase. What I liked most about this place was that I didn't have to struggle to fit in, because everyone fit in as much as no one did. Jamaica met DC chic, with colorful walls and picnic tables against fancy silverware and black-and-white photos of actresses from Hollywood's golden era. The servers here were cheerful, and there was good music. I liked that. The place was simply alive.

Ivy and Gretchen hosted the munch every month, and the two subs greeted me warmly with hugs when I reached the terrace. The red canvas ceiling moved in a slow wave with each breeze, and the flowers that sat atop the stone wall around the entire terrace reminded me of my mom. She used to love tulips. "We wake up with the tulips in spring," she used to say.

"Oh my God, I love your tattoos," Ivy gushed. "Are they new? I don't think I've ever seen you without a button-down."

I grinned hesitantly and eased back some. While I appreciated the compliments, I didn't want them touching my arms. "Thank you. Yes, they are kind of new."

"Well, they're amazing," Gretchen said with a smile. Then she nudged Ivy and nodded at someone behind me, so I moved out of the way. They had more people to greet, and I spotted a handful of people I wanted to call friends.

The picnic tables had been pushed together to form two long rows of seats, and I bypassed the first one without giving the men and women there a single glance. I didn't know if it was like this in other kink communities, but Doms and subs naturally gravitated toward their own "type" here. It was a big community, and many who were paired up sat with their partner. Though, for the most part, it seemed the munch drew the subs together for gossip, and the Doms made evil plans. Sadistic, twisted, evil plans for play parties and stuff.

Plans that never included me.

Cameron, the other one of my two friends, theorized that one of the reasons we split up into Doms versus subs for munches was because many of us were heavily into Daddy/Little kink. And a munch was the perfect spot for Littles to "go play."

I couldn't see Cameron here today...

Reaching the end of the table, I put a smile on my face and said hello to Ella, Sandra, and Shay.

Shay was kind of new in our community, reserved but nice. "Well, hell. Welcome to the club?" He smirked lazily at my arms, making me remember the damn T-shirt. Perhaps I shouldn't have strayed off the beaten path. Shay had no issues putting his tattoos on display, but he'd gotten them because, per his words, it made him hard to get inked.

Ella and Sandra chimed in with their own surprise, and by the time they'd asked all sorts of questions about the tattoos, I was vowing to cover up for the rest of my damn life. Their attention was a little much. Their interest was...new.

I did my best to laugh it all off, and I sat down next to Shay like I didn't have a stick up my ass. Or a care in the world.

Our preordered drinks arrived approximately when Cameron did, and I was thankful he wasn't as exuberant about my body art as the girls. I breathed a sigh of relief and took a sip of my Coke.

"Did you guys hear that Master Lucian is single again?" Cameron asked and raised his brows. "Just saying his name gets me hard."

I withheld my grin and bit into an ice chip.

Shay looked over his shoulder to see the table behind us. "Who's that? Is he a Sadist? I need to find a Sadist."

"You want the twins," Ella said with a wink. "River and Reese play on another level."

River and Reese were also the ones who'd started this community, along with five or six others. Together, they were often referred to as the Founders.

Cameron and Sandra were happy to point out where these Sadist twins sat, and I followed their subtle pointing and nodding—only to get stuck on Colt Carter.

The man was indecently attractive, in a rugged, dirty way. He smirked cockily at whatever someone across from him said, and then he scratched his scruffy cheek and replied. I couldn't hear over the din. Everyone was talking. The terrace had filled up.

It was my turn to sigh when he grinned and leaned over to the man next to him for a quick kiss. Lucas West, Colt's partner. Or husband. Their gold bands glinted in the sun. They were founding members as well.

I did my best to avoid looking at those two, though obviously

I failed from time to time. Last munch had been particularly difficult, because they'd caught me staring three times.

I was always going to be the people watcher, it seemed. The guy looking into other people's realities to get a glimpse of life.

Colt laughed at something. He shrugged. Lucas shook his head in amusement. Then Colt took a swig of his beer and—shit. He saw me. Turning around again, I fiddled with my napkin and tried to pay attention to what Sandra and Shay were arguing about.

Halfway through brunch, I had to hurry down to the second floor where the bathrooms were. That's what I got for chugging two Cokes.

I wanted to get back quickly, because Cameron and the others were discussing a kink event coming up. If there was the slightest hint of an invitation to join them, I had to take it. I could not chicken out, and blaming the stupid accident was no longer a viable excuse. I was here, out in the open, wearing a *T-shirt*. No more hiding, scars or otherwise. The munches clearly weren't enough to gain more friends.

After relieving myself, I zipped up and went to wash my hands. Then I grabbed a paper towel and rushed toward the door—and I crashed into someone.

"*Oomph.*" Eyes screwed shut, I flew back a foot or two and rubbed my nose. "Sorry." Ouch. It actually hurt. What the hell had hit my nose? I cracked one eye open, and the first thing I saw was a dog tag glinting in the light from the ceiling.

Crap.

It was a freakishly tall man... A freakishly tall Colt Carter.

"I'm sorry," I repeated. Picking up the paper towel from the floor, I avoided making eye contact and sidestepped to the trash can.

"No worries." His voice was a low drawl that drew my gaze to him whether I wanted to or not. I swallowed hard. Seeing him up close for the first time was heaven and hell at once. He was dangerously sexy and daunting. Much older than me. Cutting features, trimmed beard, green eyes that looked too calculating for my liking.

Abort, abort!

I looked away again and fidgeted, wondering how to get past him. He was blocking the exit.

"You buy clothes just because you think they're cool, don't you?"

Well, they should be functional too...

I furrowed my brow, and I made the mistake of looking up once more.

He folded his arms over his chest, causing the fabric of his tee to stretch around his biceps, and nodded at my chest. "Why else would you choose a design with that jet on it?"

I glanced down at the print on my T-shirt, then up again. "The Raptor is an outstanding fighter," I told him matter-of-factly.

He cocked a brow. With a shake of his head, he left the doorway and walked over to the urinals. "Outstandingly expensive, sure. Most of the time, they collect dust while someone else's gotta do the work."

What was his problem? This was a sore topic for me. We all had our hobbies, and he'd just kicked the door into mine.

"Doesn't erase the fact that it's the king of the sky," I replied.

He had his back to me where he stood, so I couldn't see his expression. I heard his snort, though. "King of the sky," he muttered, seemingly to himself. "Maybe not the best thing to say around F-16 pilots—you know, the real kings up there."

I sucked in a breath. The F-16 was my favorite plane in the whole world, but this wasn't the best place to have that conversation. I was in the way. He was relieving himself. If he wanted to chat about fighter jets anywhere else, I'd be happy to. Perhaps he was a fellow military nerd like me. I could talk about planes and tanks for ages in my online community.

"I didn't say the Raptor was my favorite plane," I said stubbornly. "Have a good day."

My hand was on the door when he spoke up again.

"Which one would that be?"

I suppressed a sigh, flustered and uncomfortable. "The F-16."

"Now *that* is a great thing to say around F-16 pilots."

Okay, now he was irritating me. I was not having a discussion about fighter jets in the men's bathroom with a man who could probably crush me like a bug.

"I'll make sure to do that if I meet one," I replied curtly and walked out the door.

I heard his chuckle right before the door closed behind me.

"You just did, kid."

I froze in place and widened my eyes. Oh God. *He* was a fighter pilot? Oh God, oh God. Mortification flooded my face, and I felt my cheeks flame. I'd just been rude to a pilot. Last time I met one, when I was ten years old, I'd asked for an autograph. My dad had taken me to an air show. I'd stuttered like an imbecile.

"Oh God, oh God," I whispered under my breath, hurrying up the stairs.

How had I not known Colt Carter was in the Air Force? Or so I assumed; it was the only military branch that still flew the F-16. Oh, *God...* How had I not *known?*

Should I leave? Perhaps that was best. One thing was certain—I could not face that man again. I was a fucking fool. A moron. A bumbling idiot who'd seriously tried to come off as someone who knew more than he did. An actual pilot.

I'd gained my knowledge from articles online and books and building model planes and listening to Dad's stories. Colt Carter had been through years of training, and then, well, he'd flown the planes.

I couldn't believe myself.

Someone had joined my table when I got back to—motherfucker! It was Lucas West. He sat right there next to Cameron. Across from my seat.

I almost turned around right away, but Cameron called my name.

Fuck my life.

I sat down again, mumbled a hey, and gulped some more Coke. I felt Lucas's eyes on me, which I studiously ignored; it was as if he could sense I'd just offended his husband. Thankfully, Ivy and Gretchen asked for our attention, giving me an excuse to look the other way.

They stood between the two long tables and explained that the restaurant was launching their summer menu before the next munch.

I scrunched my nose. I very much liked the menu they had now, and I preordered the same meal before every munch.

On the other hand, given what I'd just done, I shouldn't come next time. Or the one after that.

"Hey, Kit, didn't your dad work in real estate?" Cameron asked.

Don't make me face you, I whined internally.

"Sort of?" It was the short answer.

Cameron nodded at Lucas, and I had no choice anymore. I had to act cool.

Lucas had removed his suit jacket from the last time I'd

gawked at him and Colt. He'd folded up the sleeves of his pristine button-down too and put on his shades.

Anxiousness flowed freely in my veins, and I swallowed nervously and glanced toward the stairs. It was only a matter of seconds or minutes before Colt returned, I was sure of it.

Damn it, I was missing out on what Cameron was saying. Something about pulling strings. I furrowed my brow in confusion. He knew my dad was dead.

"I'm sorry." I interrupted his explanation. "I'm not sure what it is you need...? My dad dealt primarily with companies."

Companies wasn't entirely accurate, unless you counted the ones contracted by the military.

"Not me—Mr. West." Cameron gestured at Lucas again. "I could've sworn you told me about your dad renting out apartments for short-term leases..."

"For private contractors, sorry," I answered. I gave Lucas an apologetic look. "Are you looking for housing?"

"Temporarily. We're doing renovations at home over the summer." He extended a hand across the table. "I'm Lucas West."

Yeah, I know.

"Kit Damien. Nice to meet you." I shook his hand. Lucas was as attractive as his husband, but in a different way. Lucas was clean-shaven, sleek, and appeared to work in a very nice office. His hand—Christ. Piano fingers that were well taken care of. He definitely didn't bite at his cuticles like I did.

"You too, Kit." Lucas offered an eye-catching smile.

I wished I could see his eyes. I'd only seen them from afar before.

"Anyway," Cameron said. "Sorry to drag you over here, Sir. I thought—never mind. I made a mistake."

"No problem, dear, but I do believe I came over to say hi without any dragging involved." Lucas gave Cameron's neck a quick squeeze. "We don't mind staying at a hotel for a while. It's only another couple of months."

Was there something between them? Given that both Lucas and Colt were Daddy Doms, it was likely that they invited submissives to play with them. A spark of envy flared at the thought of Cameron getting to experience that with them. He was gutsy. I'd lost my balls somewhere approximately three years ago.

"I can ask around," I blurted out. Holy crap, what was wrong with me? I suddenly had all eyes on me, and I almost squeaked. Almost. But to hell with it, right? Even though my dad wasn't around, his company was. And I did love helping others. It was selfish of me; helping out tended to provide me more interactions with people. "I can ask Richard—he ran the company with my father. I'll ask him. He might know someone."

Something softened around the corners of Lucas's mouth. "You don't have to do that, Kit. We knew what we were getting ourselves into when we planned the renovations so late."

Right, but if I were able to help out, maybe a certain fighter pilot wouldn't think I was an idiot any longer.

I was going to help. I insisted.

"So they gotta be super hot, yeah?"

I shot Abel a look in the webcam, at which he laughed.

"Oh, come on, Kit! You've talked about them nonstop for twenty minutes." He was way too amused. "If you haven't had their dicks in your mouth by the time I visit, I'll be disappointed."

I shook my head and carefully attached the sidewinders to the plane I was working on. "Prepare yourself to be disappointed, then," I said with a sniff. "Fuck." I got glue on my fingers.

FaceTiming with Abel through my computer was always fun, but when was I going to learn that I shouldn't work on my model crafts at the same time? Last time we talked, I'd completely destroyed the blades on a Blackhawk because Abel distracted me.

Then again, it was either this or spending the next hour fidgeting and scratching.

Lucas was coming over then because Richard was a godsend. It'd taken him less than an hour to email me a listing of short-term leasing options.

If I'd interpreted Lucas correctly on the phone, he was stopping by *alone* after work, meaning it would be the second time I successfully dodged his man. It'd been a miracle that Lucas had returned to his table at the munch before Colt had come back.

"You can't tell me you don't wanna play with them," Abel stated. I glanced up at the screen to see him leaning back in his desk chair and twisting his cap backward. "It's been forever since you got any action, and it's not the first time you've mentioned these two."

Of course it'd been forever. In fact, my entire life in BDSM had been plagued by breaks and disasters. The fantasies had been with me for as long as I could remember, and I'd attended my first munch—with Abel—a couple days after I turned eighteen. Months later, I lost Mom and Dad, and I'd spent enough time in the hospital to call it my second home.

My comebacks into the kink world after that had been brief and fraught with anxiety. Kirk had given me some confidence since then, though. I did love my ink. It felt like an armor.

I was ready for more. I longed for it, but that didn't mean I had the guts to approach not only one but two Doms. Jeesh. Besides, they were way out of my league. Cameron had told me some things as we'd left the munch. First of all, he'd found it hysterical that I'd managed to miss out on the tidbit about Colt being in the Air Force, because apparently "everyone" knew that.

Everyone also knew he was a Sadist.

They had a line of subs wanting to be with them, and Lucas and Colt did play with quite a few at events, though it was rarely sexual. I'd asked if Cameron was in that line, to which he'd said, "Been there, done that." He'd received a couple beatings from Colt, and Lucas had tied him up a few times. From the sound of things, it'd been nonsexual.

"Even if I did, they wouldn't be interested," I muttered, scratching the glue off my fingertip.

"You're a blind fool, Kit," Abel said. "You know my thoughts on this."

I nodded once and kept my gaze stuck to the plane. Carefully running my knife along an edge, I scraped off the excess glue and scrambled for a topic change. I knew I sold myself short sometimes; I was working on changing it. I was just...so incredibly tired of my own baggage. It weighed me down.

I wasn't always like this. So pathetic.

"Anyway," I said and cleared my throat. "Did you tell your man he's welcome to visit too?"

"Hell yeah." Abel's grin lit up the screen. "He's in. He's already looking for kink events for us."

Nervousness crashed into me, though I couldn't contain the smile that walked hand in hand with the butterflies. I'd hoped for this.

"I can forward the newsletter Ivy sent out this week," I said. "There's a whole new schedule."

"Fucking A. We're gonna have a blast, Kit. *And* we're gonna get you laid."

Good luck with the last part.

3.

My heart was pounding and my hands had become clammy by the time I surveyed the kitchen one last time. Lucas was due any minute, and Vincent and Rosa had just left. Vincent, reluctantly so. He was protective of me.

Rosa had given me a wink.

I scratched the back of my neck and swallowed anxiously. The cookies I'd requested were plated on the kitchen island. Everything was spotless. The listings Richard had provided were next to the cookies, and the coffeemaker was ready in case Lucas wanted a beverage.

I could do this. It was only a meeting—of sorts. I was helping out. If I got lucky, we'd find we had something in common, and maybe it would turn into some chatting and having cookies.

When the doorbell rang, I stuttered a curse and took a shaky breath. Great start, stuttering before I'd even opened the door. This could only get worse. I skidded out of the kitchen and ran a hand through my hair. Then I adjusted the collar on my shirt—crap, should I have put on a tie? No, this was casual. I was pretty sure. Fuck.

"Please like me," I whispered, reaching the entryway. After wiping my hands along my thighs, I opened the door. And my heart stopped. *No, no, no, no!* Why was *he* here? Why, oh fucking *why?*

I barely registered the polite smile on Lucas's face. I was stuck on the damn fighter pilot. Colt stood there, with a freaking USAF ball cap on, and he was eating sushi from a to-go container.

My cheeks felt like they'd caught on fire.

Lucas snagged my attention when he removed his sunglasses, and then I was kind of trapped in his steely gray eyes.

Shoot me.

"It's good to see you again, Kit." Lucas flashed that infectious smile I remembered from the munch, and I swallowed dryly.

"Y-you too," I stammered. *No, seriously, shoot me!* I took a breath and stepped to the side so they could enter.

"I hope you don't mind I brought Colt," he replied as he passed me. "He was curious."

I gnashed my teeth and mustered a tentative glance at Colt, who flashed me a faint smirk and chewed on a piece of sushi.

"I had to see the Raptor kid again." His smirk turned wolfish, and he walked past me too.

I was toast. This was *not* what I signed up for.

My hand was literally trembling as I closed the door. Uncomfortable and unnerved, I left the entryway and joined Lucas and Colt in the living room. They were both so tall. Even when waiting for directions or a cue, they looked at ease and perfectly chill. I envied that.

"Very...New England." Colt was eyeing the seating area.

I cleared my throat and gestured for the kitchen. "I thought we could, um, sit in the kitchen...?"

They ignored how that came out as a question, and Lucas inclined his head and took the lead.

"You have a beautiful home," he mentioned on the way. "I love Georgetown."

Colt grunted. "Price tag is less desirable."

He'd said the exact same about a certain plane.

"Don't mind him, dear," Lucas told me, rounding the kitchen island. "His favorite pastime lately is to find something to complain about."

I looked down at my feet and withheld my smile.

"Look at this place, baby," Lucas murmured. "They don't build houses like this anymore."

Following his gaze, I tried to see my home through his eyes. To me, nothing stood out. I'd lived here all my life. I'd heard my mother sigh about the size of the kitchen, and that was about it. It wasn't huge, though we had a dining room next to the living room. Only I ate in the kitchen. Well, with Vincent. There were four stools around the island. I didn't exactly need more than that.

Since my parents had died, I'd eaten in the dining room once. It was only me at a table for twelve.

Never again.

Lucas shifted his gaze to me as I sat down on one of the stools, and he tilted his head slightly. "And you live here alone."

Ah. I cleared my throat, a twinge of discomfort hitting me. He'd spoken to Cameron, probably. It was hardly a secret that I'd lost my parents. "Yes, Sir," I replied with a quick nod. In my peripheral vision, I was acutely aware of Colt eyeing me, so I scrambled out of my seat again and aimed straight for the first distraction I could find. "Coffee?" I croaked. Like an idiot. I didn't wait for a response; I turned on the machine and set it to regular coffee. Then I went to the fridge and grabbed some bottled water and sodas. Because for some idiotic reason, I didn't ask what they wanted.

After dumping the drinks on the island, I went back for

another round to get milk and creamer and two mugs. Just...in case.

"Rosa made cookies," I said and took my seat again. "She makes the best ones with white chocolate and macadamia nuts."

Lucas adopted a curious expression and sat down next to me. "Who's Rosa?"

I removed the plastic wrap from the cookie plate. "She takes care of the house. I'd like to call her family." But she had her own. "Anyway. I'm sure you're more interested in hearing about the places my dad's friend found." I slid the printouts to Lucas and explained that the best option was actually on the next street over, but it was a long, long street. I lived in the first block on one end, and they'd be at the other.

Colt opened the cupboards under the sink and located the trash, where he threw away his sushi container. Then he chose to stand rather than sit down, so he stayed on the other side of the island and leaned over the countertop, his forearms hitting the marble surface.

"This is an awfully big property for the two of us," Lucas said pensively, reading the first page.

"It's a two-story version of this house," I confirmed. Securing housing for out-of-town clients was only a small part of what my father used to do, and the number of private contractors who arrived with their families was even smaller. Therefore, the few houses and bigger condos the company had on hand were usually the ones that stood empty.

"This was a done deal the second you heard the house was nearby." Colt quirked a wry smirk at Lucas. "You can't resist this neighborhood."

Lucas chuckled and turned the page. To me, he said, "My grandmother on my father's side lived in Georgetown. I loved visiting her as a child, and I stayed in the studio apartment in her basement all through college."

I smiled. We had a basement like that too. "Where did you grow up otherwise?"

"Bethesda," he replied. "Colt's a Texas boy."

I half glanced at Colt to see him tipping his cap at Lucas.

They were sweet together. I bit at my thumbnail and caught the soft smile on Lucas's face before he refocused on the documents, and my heart made an extra thud. Would I ever have what they had? Would I ever belong to someone?

To be honest, love was the last thing on my mind. It was a distant dream. I'd be beyond happy to make some local friends. I missed playing too.

Colt turned to me, instantly putting me on edge. "So, if the place we're movin' in to is a smaller version of this one, mind giving me a tour?"

I certainly would mind. "No, Sir. I can do that." I prayed I didn't sound as nervous as I suddenly felt.

Lucas would join us, right? He felt safer. In the presence of Colt, I'd already made a fool of myself once. Oh God, what if he brought it up?

Colt was the picture of casual as I slowly shifted off the stool, stalling an extra second to see if Lucas would spare me any agony. But he was immersed in the paperwork. I was a goner. He wasn't tagging along.

I swallowed hard and left the kitchen with Colt in tow.

"You've, um, seen the living room." I cleared my throat and gestured to the room past the living room. "The dining room is over there—"

"Where's your room?" He glanced up the stairs, then cocked his head at me.

My jaw tensed. I didn't want him to see my rooms. Well, the bedroom was safe, but he'd have opinions about my hobby room.

"Third floor," I muttered.

His eyes glinted with amusement. "You know I gotta see it, kid."

Heat flooded my cheeks, and I sort of wanted to kick him in the shin. "I know nothing of the sort," I replied in a clipped tone.

He flashed a grin at that and entered my personal space. I instinctively took a quick step back, but there was the wall. Shit. I almost gulped, and my heart rate kicked up.

When he hooked a finger under my chin to lift my gaze to his, my eyes widened. Definitely gulped this time.

He had some silver in his scruff. Beautiful laugh lines around his mouth. Crap.

"I make you uncomfortable," he murmured. *Bastard.* A smirk tugged at the corners of his mouth. "There's a streak of defiance buried somewhere, though. I can see it."

I scowled, embarrassed and flustered, and moved away. The stairs were the inevitable next route, so I began heading up. All while cursing a fighter pilot to the fiery pits of hell. I remembered Cameron telling me Colt was a Sadist, and that was becoming abundantly clear.

"One more thing," he said, following me. "I assume you know you don't have to call Luke and me Sir."

"Don't take it personally," I blurted out irritably. "I call a lot of people Sir."

He laughed. "There might even be a brat in you."

He frustrated me so much!

Gritting my teeth, I reached the landing and didn't even bother pointing out the rooms on this floor. I had a feeling he didn't give a crap. I took the next set of stairs instead and didn't stop until I was outside my bedroom.

I opened the door, revealing a tidy room in blue and white. Rosa had made the bed and removed the bowl of grapes I'd had on my desk.

"Okay, now you've seen my room," I said. "Would you like to see the basement?" I figured that was as far away as one could get from my rooms.

"Hold your horses." Colt entered the room, looking around with a pensive expression.

I scratched my arm absently and waited. He studied my school pictures on the wall, then looked over at the shelves above my desk. I saw his eyes narrow at the one model plane I had on display on the top shelf. A beautiful F-15 fighter jet I'd spent two weeks painting to perfection. It wasn't often I was so satisfied with a project.

"You built that?" He nodded at the plane and walked closer to my desk.

I bit my tongue and made a conscious choice to refrain from calling him Sir. "Yes."

It was difficult not to fidget when he merely stood there and stared at the plane, hands clasped behind his back. His posture screamed of his profession. I'd never met anyone from the armed forces who didn't stand in a certain way. Feet aligned with their shoulders, back straight. Definitely no fidgeting.

Growing up, I suffered through a lot of banquets and functions with my parents. I hated those. What I loved were the private dinners they'd hosted at our house. Majors and generals and other military personnel had sat at our table, and I'd always struggled to stop staring. They oozed composure and discipline, two things I'd craved since I was little.

There was a calm to them as well. A straightforwardness. A "what you see is what you get" kind of feeling, with a big side of "but I'm also trained to end you."

"You use an airbrush, I take it?" Colt inquired.

I nodded once.

So did he. "A buddy of mine... His kid brother did this— model craft or whatever. His room was its own war zone—shit

31

everywhere. Paint, brushes, stacks of these things boxed up, glass displays." He slid his gaze my way and smiled. "Somethin's missin' from your room, Kit."

Crap.

I jutted my chin and steeled myself to—

"Show me, boy," he stated. "I tend to get what I want."

Arrogant freaking—*gah*. I was not confident enough to duel him. I could picture it, him in his F-16 and me with a squirt gun.

I deflated with a sigh and gestured down the hallway.

He followed me once more, and then I was opening the door to my hobby haven.

Shelves upon shelves with planes, tanks, submarines, helicopters, my stash of models that were still in their boxes, paint jars, and all sorts of supplies. There was no furniture in here except for a desk that stretched from one end of a wall to the other. That way, I could have more than one station, more than one ongoing project.

"Now we're talking," Colt murmured, looking around. He stopped at the shelves where I kept my books. There was at least one for every model I'd built. "This is how you learn... Interesting."

"Pardon?"

"You learn by doing." He turned back to me. "I'm the same way. The information doesn't stick if all I get is text."

Oh. I hadn't thought of it that way. He was right, though. I loved learning about the vehicles and aircraft armed forces around the world used and produced, but I needed to see them for myself. It was where the models played a part.

It was also the best distraction when one didn't have a life.

I winced at my own bitterness. I actually loved building model planes for several reasons, one being that I found it soothing. It was a wonderful hobby for me, and I was grateful for the people I'd met online who were into the same thing.

Colt chuckled at something and picked a book from the shelf. "This fuckin' guy—you know who he is?"

I frowned at the cover. It was a book about general Air Force history, not a specific craft or anything. "You mean the author? No. I mean, I read the book—it's good. I use it as a source sometimes." I liked adding info about the planes I worked on when I blogged the finished result.

"Arrogant son of a bitch," he said wryly and returned the book.

"I guess it takes one to know one." The words left me before I could think twice, and I felt the embarrassment prickling my skin.

Colt turned to me, a slow smirk taking over.

Oh my God, I had truly done it again. I looked away and stuttered an apology. "I didn't mean to—"

"Yes, you did." The bastard was coming closer. Too close. He stopped right in front of me and lifted my chin like he had before. As if on cue, I broke out in a cold sweat. My pulse went through the roof. I didn't fear what he'd do; it was what he'd say. He could be disappointed or he could call me rude, or, or, or he'd simply leave and never look my way again, and he'd take Lucas with him.

"I'm sorry," I repeated.

He was studying me intently. "I don't want you to be afraid."

"I'm not—"

All he had to do to silence me was cock a brow. "Don't lie to me."

Fuck. Shit. I swallowed hard.

A tightness around his eyes faded. "I think I need to get to know you. Draw the brat out properly."

Hope exploded in my chest, mingling with the fright.

He dipped down a couple inches, and his mouth twisted up

a fraction. "I'm definitely an arrogant son of a bitch, for the record. But the next time you call me that, you'll also call me Sir for the right reason. Are we clear?"

Not at all. "I-I understand."

He laughed under his breath. "You're fun. I'm lookin' forward to seein' more of you."

Holy shit. He had to notice how unsteady my breathing was becoming. It was too much. Too overwhelming. Someone wanted to get to know me, see more of me. *Me.*

"Did you go through a lot of trouble to find Luke and me that house?" he asked. "Be honest."

The topic change threw me for a second. I shook my head. "No, Sir."

"Good. We won't be needing it." He took a step back and scrubbed a hand over his jaw and mouth. My forehead creased. Was something wrong with the house? "I have something else in mind." He smiled a bit and squeezed my shoulder quickly. "You got any plans this weekend?"

Nope, no plans, my schedule was wide open. "No."

Spend time with me, please.

"You do now." He nodded at the door and started to leave the room. "I'm gonna talk shit over with Luke, but you'll hear from us by Friday at the latest."

I followed him down the stairs, dazed and confused, but already excited to tell Vincent that I had weekend plans. Holy fuck. Weekend plans!

"So you're waiting for them to call today?" Abel asked.

I shook my head. I'd abandoned the project I was working on five minutes into my FaceTime call with Abel. Now I just sat there and stared at the screen. "They called yesterday—or Lucas called, but I heard Colt in the background." Colt was a special guy. He'd hollered a lot. *We'll be there at 1200 hours sharp*, he'd yelled to Lucas, who'd sighed in that way—the "I love you, but you drive me nuts sometimes" way.

I snickered my way through the story, and Abel laughed when I explained how Lucas humored Colt with his "Yes, dear" deadpan.

"They seem to have the funniest dynamic," I said with a grin.

Abel smiled and shook his head. "You're finally gonna get laid, buddy. With *two* guys. I'm so proud."

I stuttered a laugh and widened my eyes. "Don't be crazy. I'm barely bold enough to hope for friendship."

"Bitch, please!" He leaned forward in his seat and twisted his cap backward, something he did when he wanted to "give me the business." It was just cute. "Let me ask you this—what're you gonna do? What's the plan?"

"Movie marathon," I replied. "I was told that I'm under no

circumstances allowed to prepare anything. Food or otherwise." It had rattled Rosa almost as much as it had me. I was raised to make sure there was something to eat if I had guests. "They're bringing everything."

Abel was smug about something. "See? They're testing the waters by giving you a rule to follow. And movie marathon? Come on. That's such a Daddy/Little thing."

"Because we are!" I laughed, half frustrated. "You're reaching, Abel. You of all people should know that Daddy Doms and Littles are into that type of stuff even outside kink—and definitely outside of labels."

"So? Either way, you should prepare yourself for the fact that this might be a playdate," he told me seriously. And his tone was enough to give me pause and make me listen. "You've seen how quickly things happen in clubs, and we in the Daddy/Little community don't use that platform as much. But that doesn't mean we don't go from greeting potential partners to fucking them in five minutes sometimes."

I widened my eyes at that last part. "Exaggerate much?"

He shrugged. "Maybe, but you know what I mean. If you all like each other, don't be surprised if they make a move fast."

I nodded once. On that, we could agree. Playtime did occur casually and without much beating around the bush. Even so, I didn't see that happening with Colt and Lucas. I could certainly see me losing my marbles around *them*, however. And I told Abel as much.

"Whatever." He rolled his eyes. "Excuse me for being a romantic and thinking you'll hit it off, you shithead."

I grinned.

He narrowed his eyes. "I can't wait for you to tell me I was right, and I can't wait to rub it in when I get there in a few weeks. My buddy Kit, in a *triad*. That's wild."

Yeah, well. I was hoping I'd be able to tell him in person then that I'd made two new friends. That was all.

"I guess we'll see," I said.

He nodded. "I'm curious about the house, though. Something's missing there. Suddenly, they didn't want a place for the summer?"

I was confused about that too. As Lucas had been when Colt had returned to the kitchen and declared, "New plans, darlin'." The baffled look on Lucas's face had remained there while Colt gestured for them to leave. He'd told Lucas about the plans for the weekend, and then when they got to the hallway, he'd said something about, "Remember when we talked about the exception that proved the rule?" *Then* some understanding had dawned on Lucas. With me, not so much.

"I have no idea," I said to Abel with a shrug. "Maybe they'll let me know tomorrow at *1200 hours sharp.*"

Abel scrunched his nose. "That's noon, right?"

I nodded. "They told me comfy clothes are mandatory. Sweatpants and a hoodie should work, right?"

"The sweats are fine..." Abel cocked his head. "T-shirt or no shirt at all. You'd only wear the hoodie to hide your arms. It's time you show off that hot ink."

"Ugh." I fidgeted with the collar of my button-down. "In my defense, I wore a tee to the munch."

"Then there's even less of a reason to run back into hiding."

He was right; I just hated it. I felt so damn exposed. Especially in the presence of two Doms. At the munch, I'd only had to answer to my acquaintances and their curiosity. I had a feeling Lucas and Colt wouldn't settle for brush-offs or bullshit.

I ran my thumb over the faint scar that extended up my jaw. Would they be close enough to notice it? There were some smaller scars on my face from cuts that hadn't faded either, but you almost had to be nose-to-nose to see them. My thighs and legs had some minor scarring too, and I didn't think I'd ever have the energy to cover those up with tattoos. My torso and arms had to be enough.

"What're you scared of, babe?" Abel asked, concern in his eyes. "The whole point of having friends is being able to share your shit with them. Not being alone, having fun together, helping out—and so on. It's what you want. And you do it just fine with me. Now you just have to stop keeping others at arm's length."

I huffed and narrowed my eyes. "When did you get so bossy?"

He laughed.

I really had to be more meticulous with my skincare. I'd used everything prescribed to me religiously the past three days, and I was reaping the benefits as I woke up on Saturday morning. My skin felt much better, and there was no rasping against the sheets. I rolled over onto my back and stretched out, and then I caught a whiff of the familiar smell of Rosa's baking.

I blinked sleepily and peered over at the alarm cl— "Crap!" I bolted out of bed, only to stop abruptly because I was too disoriented. Hell. Begone, sleep. I rubbed at my eyes and yawned. I was late, damn it. I'd stayed up half the night arguing with some idiot who thought the Eurofighter was a better-equipped plane than our Raptor. I'd been so mad!

I ignored my T-shirt that was draped over the chair by my bed and stuck my feet into my pajama bottoms.

After stumbling into my bathroom, I relieved myself, washed up, and brushed my teeth. I was still squinting when I headed down the stairs, and I hoped Rosa had something that could wake me up properly. Because Colt and Lucas would be here in less than an hour, and I probably shouldn't look like I'd just rolled out of bed then.

Vincent was in the living room, channel-surfing with his leather jacket on.

There was a twinge of discomfort in my chest as he spotted me. My upper body was bare, and I hadn't gotten used to him and Rosa seeing me this way. Despite that they were the only ones who'd seen me, all of me, throughout my recovery.

"Hey," I said. "Didn't I give you the weekend off?" By "give," I meant that I'd told him to take some time to go see his family.

"I'm heading up in a bit," he defended. "I wanna meet your new friends first."

"That's certainly not necessary," I replied, baffled. In the kitchen, I heard the telltale sound of Rosa taking something from the oven. "Come on, let's eat. Then you're going—and I mean that respectfully." I didn't want him to feel like he needed to be my bodyguard.

"I'd feel better if I met them," he said with finality and rose from the couch. "I don't want anyone takin' advantage, and you trust too easily."

Maybe I did. I didn't know.

In the kitchen, I wished Rosa a good morning and asked what she was making.

She had some attitude in her today. "No one told me I couldn't make sure you had some bagels in the house. Men—telling me I can't prepare anything for your movie night? Bah!" She made a crude gesture that made me snicker.

She'd made more than bagels, however. There were three baskets by the stove full of baked goods. Cheese rolls, bagels, and I was pretty sure those were her garlic knots. I *loved* those.

"May I have a garlic knot, please?" I asked.

"No, *mijo*, you want nice breath for kissing later," she

responded. My cheeks flamed with heat, and I dropped my gaze. Vincent chuckled and poured himself coffee. "I'll make you a bagel with cream cheese and prosciutto, yes? Extra tomato?"

"Yes, thank you," I mumbled. "It's not a date. I want to put that out there. Maybe we'll be friends, that's it." I trailed over to the fridge to grab the OJ before taking my seat again. Vincent brought me a glass on his way back with the coffee. "Lucas and Colt are a couple."

"Sí, you tell me," she answered, nodding. Then she waved the knife with which she'd sliced a tomato at me. "You also tell me about this lifestyle—couples with three people or more? And you are a special boy. Kind—big heart." She nodded again, this time firmly. "How can they not love you?"

Warmth spread in my chest, at her acceptance of me and her openness, and I smiled to myself. She'd come far since I'd explained what kind of meetup Vincent drove me to once a month. She had tested the word munch to herself and listened to my stuttered clarification, and after that, I wasn't sure who'd blushed the hardest. These days, she could even make jokes about whips and rope.

"Before we start talkin' about love, I'mma see if they're even good for him," Vincent told Rosa. "We don't know shit about them. They could be players or out to use him."

That dropped a rock into my stomach. I hadn't gotten that impression at all from Colt and Lucas. The opposite, in fact, they seemed genuine and nice. Well...Colt was a piece of work, but he didn't strike me as anything but honest.

Rosa and Vincent began bickering; it was "you have to take chances" versus "welcome to reality, people are scum."

I tuned them out with my bagel in a firm grasp.

If they asked for my opinion, I'd say they were both far off. Of course, I had to take chances, but even when Rosa got heated and switched to Spanish, I could decipher some words, and I wished she wouldn't mention love. Meanwhile, Vincent had a harsher outlook on life, and he said people always looked out for themselves. Probably true to a degree, depending on how you twisted and turned everything.

I was looking out for myself when I wanted friends. I didn't want this loneliness to suffocate me anymore.

Halfway through my bagel, Rosa and Vincent realized they didn't understand each other. Rosa huffed something in Spanish, and Vincent was mostly yelling New Jersey slang and gesturing wildly with his arms.

They were always entertaining to watch.

"Kit has to try," Rosa said firmly. "He has much to offer life, and life has much to offer him. That takes risks and bravery. He has it! You will not hold him back."

"I ain't holding him back," Vincent growled. "I'm protecting him."

"Guys," I interrupted. "I love you both, but you're arguing in circles now. I will do my best to find a balance—" The sound of the doorbell interrupted me, and I froze in horror. It couldn't be them, could it? My gaze flicked to the clock on the microwave. They were way too early! Half an hour early! "I'm n-not ready!" I stammered.

"Could be someone else, buddy." Vincent crammed a piece of bread into his mouth and left the kitchen to go check.

I couldn't think about food. I scrambled off my stool and tried fruitlessly to smooth down my messy bed head.

"Yup, that's them," Vincent announced, returning to the kitchen. "Want me to open, or should we keep quiet until they go away?"

I rolled my eyes, then threw a helpless look at Rosa. "Could you get the door while I put on a shirt?"

She was about to nod; she was *right there*, and then something changed in her eyes. They crinkled at the corners, and she pursed her lips. "Or you rip the Band-Aid, *mijo*. Let them see you. Be proud of who you are."

What? No! No! I couldn't possibly. I was a mess. My hair was all over the place, I hadn't shaved in three days, and my body was still too lean. As soon as my doctors cleared me for heavier exercise than the rehab I'd been through, I'd gone to a gym...once a week. And that wasn't enough. I swam sometimes too. But God, showing up shirtless was out of the question with my scrawny body littered with ugly scars.

I shook my head vehemently and folded my arms over my chest. "Please open the door for me."

"No," she said simply.

Ugh! I looked pleadingly at Vincent. "Can you—"

"Yeah, no." He smirked. "Get the door, or let them disappear."

Anger engulfed me, even though I realized how childish I was being. I loved my tattoos; I knew for a fact that they covered almost all the scars, and I was hardly ugly to look at. It was the vulnerability I feared people would see, and Colt and Lucas certainly struck me as two men who would fish that out quickly.

The doorbell rang again, and I was out of time.

I swallowed dryly and walked toward my doom. My heart rate spiked as I reached the entryway and saw two blurry silhouettes through the frosted window in the door, one slightly taller than the other tall guy. I was screwed. Christ. Okay. Here we go.

Twisting the doorknob, I opened up to see Colt and Lucas— and worse, for them to see me.

"Hi," I croaked. "You're, um, early."

Lucas took off his sunglasses and smiled. "Yes, we are. Hello, Kit."

Colt was more interested in making me uncomfortable than

saying hello. His brows went up a bit, and he gave me a slow once-over that turned my face beet red. I hugged myself loosely, probably failing at coming off as casual.

"Early is on time," he murmured as he made eye contact. One of the corners of his mouth twisted up. "This is gonna be a good weekend." With that said, he picked up a duffel from the stoop and entered the house.

I shivered as he brushed past me.

Lucas picked up something else, a grocery bag. "Don't let him unnerve you, dear."

"Too late," I laughed shakily.

He paused right in front of me in the doorway and tilted his head at me. "Well, if it makes you feel any better, you've unnerved us too."

That didn't compute. "What? How?"

He chuckled warmly and leaned closer. My breath hitched as he cupped my jaw and ghosted his thumb across my cheek. "You're a compelling boy, Kit. That's how."

Maybe I died right there. Or blacked out. I stopped breathing at least, and when I came to, Lucas was gone.

I heard both him and Colt in the kitchen, talking to Rosa and Vincent.

I sucked some air into my lungs and closed the door, only to lean back against it. My heart was racing. Abel appeared in my head, as did his smug expression. But I couldn't believe he was right, not yet. Tell that to my hope, though, because that crashed through the roof. There was a possibility they wanted to...what, play with me? Holy crap. No, wait. He'd only been nice to me, technically. Daddy Doms were often affectionate merely because they were lovely people. For instance, the way Lucas had acted with Cameron at the munch.

There. My head was level again. Sort of.

Deep breaths.

"This is gonna be a good weekend."

We hadn't discussed how long this movie marathon would last. I'd assumed they would leave before the day was over. Now I hoped that wasn't the case. I mean, what if we had a sleepover? I'd read about those! I truly, truly wanted to experience one. They sounded like so much fun. Movies, treats, cozy lighting, blankets and pillows everywhere, and togetherness.

Was there an actual chance I'd be a temporary part of a triad this weekend? Oh my God, was there a chance we'd be intimate?

Filled with nerves and anticipation and foolish hope, I snapped out of my state and headed for the kitchen. I'd already failed to introduce everyone properly; there was no need to worsen things further.

I suppose I wasn't too surprised to see Lucas and Rosa in good spirits. They were chatting about something while Lucas put stuff into the fridge. I also wasn't surprised to see Vincent with Colt on the other side of the kitchen island. I couldn't hear what they were discussing, though.

It was a good place to start. "Everything okay here?" I wouldn't say they were in a stare-down, but there was some tension coming off Vincent's shoulders.

"Everything's perfect." Colt took a step back and offered a dim smirk my way. Not that it cleared the atmosphere one bit. He had his arms folded over his chest, shoulders square, and *that* spoke volumes. I'd picked up a thing or two as a people watcher. "Vinny here's just protective of you. Can't fault him for that."

Vincent narrowed his eyes at him, and I winced internally. He did not like being called Vinny.

"I'm serious, man." Colt loosened up and clapped Vincent on the shoulder. "I respect where you're comin' from, and if Luke and I hurt Kit, you're welcome to have a go at me."

Welp. I could almost cut the testosterone in here with a knife. Thankfully, Vincent relaxed some and was seemingly satisfied with what Colt had said.

Rosa sent me a cheeky grin and said she and Vincent were "just about to leave." A solid instruction for Vincent. There would be no lingering.

She all but pushed Vincent out of the kitchen, but not before kissing my cheek and wishing me a good time. There was a wink too, and I shook my head in amusement and blushed like a dork.

Colt, Lucas, and I stood there in awkward silence—okay, I was the only one who felt awkward, I was sure—while Rosa and Vincent bickered in the hallway. Colt smirked when Rosa told Vincent he tied his shoes too slowly.

"Maybe you need Velcro shoes," she said.

I pressed my lips together to keep from laughing.

"I'm not twelve, woman," Vincent snapped.

"*Dios mio*, you wore Velcro when you were twelve?" Rosa asked, the mirth clear in her voice.

Covering my mouth with my hand, I closed my eyes and giggled as quietly as I possibly could. Poor Vincent. Rosa's wit was sharper than a knife at times.

Soon after, the front door opened and closed, and I cleared my throat and flicked my gaze between two amused Doms.

"So, uh, that's Rosa and Vincent," I said.

Lucas smiled fondly and went back to stowing away groceries. "They seem like lovely people."

They were. My life would be bleaker without them.

Colt hopped up to sit on the kitchen island, and he reached for a bag of apples among the groceries. "You have your own housekeeper and personal driver. Ain't every day you meet someone who has that."

I shifted my weight from one foot to the other, unsure of what to say.

"Colt," Lucas chastised with a frown.

"What?" Colt frowned back. "I'm just sayin'."

"It's okay." I ignored the discomfort and dared to go closer and sit down on one of the stools. "To me, they're family." I paused. "My parents traveled a lot when they were alive, and my mother wanted me surrounded by people I knew well when I couldn't accompany them."

Colt nodded once. "We heard about your folks."

I'd figured as much.

"I hope you don't mind I spoke briefly to Paul." Lucas closed the door to the fridge and placed a few bags of chips next to the coffee machine. "I wanted his two cents even though it's been a while since you two played."

My eyebrows went up at that. Been a while...? Understatement. I'd made such a fool of myself, too. I was thankful he didn't show up at munches often, if ever. I'd seen him there once or twice, but it was a long time ago.

"How did you know we played?" I wondered.

"Well, I remember it." He smiled curiously. "Our community isn't that big."

Wasn't it? Then again, when you were focused on finding hiding spots, you didn't pay much attention to who might be watching.

"I doubt he had anything positive to say." Feeling the need to cover up again, I wrapped my arms around myself and tried to be casual about it.

"What makes you think that?" Colt asked.

I lifted a shoulder. "I couldn't hand over control one bit." I'd kept most of my clothes on, and I'd insisted on the light being off or dimmed low. "I wouldn't, um, undress."

"He mentioned that." Lucas's eyes showed concern. "He

also mentioned it was due to your accident. He spoke kindly of you."

Oh. That felt...strange. I'd been so stupid, thinking I could play without being fully invested in the moment. Submitting without surrendering. I'd been wrong, of course, and he'd seen right through me. I did recall him being patient, but he had his limits. I understood him completely. I wouldn't have played with me either.

Lucas leaned over the island and rested his chin in his palm. "Has that changed? Do you think you'd be able to hand over control now—or try it out?"

I nodded slowly, assuming he meant if I'd like to try in general, not necessarily try for *them*. "I think so. I mean...it's what I ultimately want. I'm stubborn sometimes—and I get scared, but I want to."

He smiled slightly.

Colt picked the little sticker from an apple, then tilted his head at me. "Why wouldn't you undress for him?"

The discomfort grew, and I struggled to maintain eye contact. "I have a lot of scarring," I replied stiffly. "I played with him before I was finished with recovery, though. I've had—" Fuck, I hated talking about this. "Um, skin transplants, and—" I lifted my right arm a bit. "The past year, I've been going to a tattoo artist." My right arm was the one that'd been damaged the most, and my forearm was almost completely covered in dark shadows. Flames that were nearly black.

Colt shifted toward me. "May I?"

I knitted my brow in confusion until I realized he wanted to...get even closer. I did my best to control my blush, and I scooted out my chair a bit so he would be seated right in front of me on the countertop. I coughed lightly and eyed his legs, one on each side of me, and pushed in the stool again.

He didn't seem to think twice about the proximity, or the

fact that he was sitting much higher up than I was. Meaning I only had to drop my gaze a few inches and his crotch was right there. He was more focused on my tattoos, and he brought my left arm—oh God, no, what was he doing? I stiffened. He was inspecting my ink way too closely.

"Take a deep breath." He brushed his fingers over my arm, and I swallowed hard. Nausea crawled up my throat, and all I could do was stare in horror.

I didn't like this. I didn't like it at all, and I wanted him to stop. I wanted it to be over. He would see the ugliness beneath the body art. He wouldn't be fooled by ink.

Breathe—he wanted me to breathe. Yeah, right. I gulped. It was the best I could do. My eyes started stinging, and it was followed by my vision blurring. No, no, no, he had to stop. Panic rose, and—

"You're a strong boy," he murmured. Then he dipped down and chastely kissed one of the tattoos before lowering my arm again.

"No, I'm not." My voice came out strangled and distorted, and I could not feel weaker. Or more pathetic.

"If you wanna be wrong, that's fine." He nudged up my chin and offered a small smile. "This was rough for you, yeah?" He didn't wait for a response. "Come on, let's go watch the first movie."

Lucas inclined his head. "You two go ahead. I'll get us some snacks. But perhaps a blanket on the couch where we'll sit? It's too white and beautiful to get guacamole on it."

5.

I released a shaky breath, glad the ordeal was over, and kept a safe distance as I followed Colt into the living room. Wanting him to pick a seat first so I could sit down farther away, I walked over to the flat screen and fiddled with the PlayStation. I didn't know if they had Netflix or DVDs in mind, but I might as well prepare for both.

"What used to hang up there?" Colt asked.

I looked at him over my shoulder and found him staring at the empty spot above the big couch, and I decided he was too observant. Two screws were still attached to the wall where an enlarged family photo used to hang. I'd had it taken down shortly after the funeral.

"A picture." I grabbed the two remotes from the entertainment center and set them down on the coffee table. Where was he going to sit? The sectional or the armchair? I was sort of hoping he and Lucas would get comfortable on the couch. Then I could drape a blanket around me and keep to myself in the chair.

"Family picture?" Colt guessed.

I suppressed a sigh. "Yes."

"I understand." He nodded at the corner of the sectional. "Wanna set up camp there in the corner with me?"

So much, but hell no. If I'd been a normal guy, maybe I could've basked in the attraction I felt and gotten lost in the hope of playing with Colt and Lucas. But I wasn't normal. I couldn't relax; I couldn't shake the anxiousness. And if I sat next to either of them, they would, in one way or another, rattle me further, and they'd discover what a moron I was. What I needed was composure. That way, they would stay.

Fear struck me when I noticed Colt was watching me. Worse, he was coming toward me, and he came to a stop approximately one whole step after he should have.

What was wrong with me? I couldn't fucking function whatsoever.

"I'm not gonna ask what you're afraid of." His voice was low and warm, carrying a hint of the Texas drawl. "I have a feelin' you wouldn't wanna answer." He was definitely correct. "I'll tell you what I want instead." He placed his hands on my shoulders, causing me to startle, and his mouth twitched. "Sweetheart, I'm not gonna hurt you."

"I'm sorry." I flushed, embarrassed by my stupidity. I wasn't freaking Bambi.

He shook his head minutely, and then he took off his ball cap and threw it on the couch. He then returned his hand to my shoulder—or, no, he shifted both hands down my arms, and I did my damnedest not to freeze up again. God, his touch—I wanted nothing more than to draw pleasure from it. I shuddered and forced myself to swallow before my throat dried out.

"My grandfather used to tell me that the best way to get to know someone was to see how they acted in conflict." He watched me intently and slipped his hands to my sides. "When someone strips you of safety and security, it's only a matter of time before you're willing to change your beliefs in order for the safety to return." He paused, and he drew small circles along my ribcage with his thumbs. "It's the sole reason why you can't push someone too hard in an interrogation. Once you cross that line, they'll tell you whatever you wanna hear, whether it's the truth or not." His green eyes glinted with dark amusement. "But that's a kink for another day."

Kink? No. I didn't believe him at all. The way he reeled me in, with quiet conviction and experience in his eyes, I knew it came from elsewhere—his years in the service. I was sure his knowledge had provided him the best tools to further himself as a Sadist, but I had the strongest gut feeling telling me BDSM was not the platform he'd used for learning.

"Now," he murmured with half a smile, "the situation wasn't as dire the day you ran into me at the munch. You didn't fear for your life, and our interaction wasn't serious." That was the moment he chose to close the distance between us further and bring my hands to his chest. My breath got stuck in my throat, and I stared straight ahead. "That feels nice." He dipped down and rested his forehead to mine. Heat spread across my entire body, and I felt my fingers twitch. Christ, he was solid. Sturdy, broad-shouldered, bordering on stocky. In slow, tentative strokes with my fingers, I traced the muscle underneath his tee. I couldn't help it.

He was perfect. Not all muscle; there was flesh on this man. And chest hair.

"You were intimidated by me, though." His voice came out as a low rumble, and he gripped my hips firmly and pulled me flush to his body. I sucked in a sharp breath, and my gaze shot to his. Holy fuck. *Holy fuck.* He wasn't even hard, and I could still feel the outline of him against my lower abdomen. "I frightened you," he whispered. "And despite that, you held your ground. You spoke of the superiority of an F-22 even though you were almost shaking from nerves, and that's how you got my attention, Kit. That's how you got my interest."

I couldn't respond. He had me captivated by his presence,

and I was swimming in wants.

"Put your arms around my neck," he ordered quietly. My pulse skyrocketed as I complied. Locking my hands around his neck, I noticed both how clammy I was and that I was trembling. Colt drew in a deep breath through his nose. "You're also the sweetest little shit I've ever seen—sexy and adorable—with a brat buried somewhere inside of you just itchin' to be unleashed." He was fucking killing me. "Now you know why I want what I asked, so I'll ask you again. That corner over there—wanna sit there with me?"

Utterly defenseless and seduced, there was only one answer I could form, and it left me in a stuttered rush. "Y-yes, Sir."

"Great response." Rather than letting me go, he slipped his hands to my ass and hoisted me up. I let out a yelp and held on tighter, and he wrapped my legs around his hips. "I think we'll stay like this for a bit. Get to know one another a little better." He walked us over to the couch and sat down in the corner. My stomach flipped at the impact, and I could barely believe what was happening. I'd just been *carried*.

After reaching for a blanket that was thrown over the back of the couch, Colt scooted in farther and got comfortable, me never leaving his lap. The only thing that changed was that I adjusted my legs to not be around him. Then he draped the blanket around me, the soft material sending a shiver through me. Since the accident, I'd replaced everything from blankets and lawn furniture cushions to sheets and pillowcases. All fabrics had to be soft for my scarring, or I'd start to pick nervously at anything that wasn't impeccably smooth.

I had issues...

T-shirt fabric was my favorite. Even my bedsheets were jersey material now, and it was almost as perfect as Colt's tee. His sweats ranked up there as well. The cuddliness factor went up by a hundred thousand.

Colt hummed and wrapped me in a tight hug. "This is nice, innit?"

I nodded against his neck. The comfort was still outside of my reach; this was too new, too unfamiliar, and I didn't know how to get used to his hands on my skin. He had to feel the scars. But I didn't want to move. He smelled amazing, and he was holding me. I wasn't alone.

"Here." He gathered my hands on his chest instead, silently telling me to cuddle up against him. "You're stuck here for a couple hours now, so you might as well get comfortable."

"In ten minutes, you won't feel your legs," I protested.

He shook with a silent laugh. "You let me worry about my legs, boy. You're lighter than a feather."

I was not!

I huffed. "Why do you want me on your lap for so long, anyway?"

I caught his grin before he ducked his head to give my shoulder a playful nip. It was so bizarre, this entire situation. The lines were incredibly blurry, mainly because I'd seen how some kinksters interacted. I'd seen groping and kissing between friends, both at munches and at events.

Did Colt and Lucas want to play with me like Abel was so sure of? Even I couldn't deny that the evidence pointed that way, and if it was true... *Whoa.*

"For one, you're not trembling anymore." Colt brushed his fingertips up my back, but he was nice enough to do it over the blanket. "For two, if you start talking shit about my Viper again, I'll have you right here so I can knock some sense into you."

His Viper...? *Oh.* Of course. The plane—the F-16. And as I understood what he was referring to, I straightened up with a scowl. "I didn't talk shit about the F-16. I told you it's my favorite."

He leaned back against the cushions and folded his fingers behind his head.

"*After* you said that the Raptor was the king of the sky," he pointed out.

"Because it is!" I insisted. How could he not see this? It was absolute madness, and before I knew it, I launched into a rant on why the F-22 was superior. And I was just gone. I drifted into a world of fighter jets and air warfare. Seeing the models I'd built, the books I'd gotten lost inside of, the heated debates I'd crushed people in, I ticked each item off my fingers, from the stealth technology that was so advanced they didn't even allow other countries to purchase the plane, to the multipurpose features that'd been upgraded to the extremes. For goodness' sake, the Air Force didn't even buy the F-16 anymore because newer, far more advanced planes had been produced.

At the end of my rambling, I sucked in some much-needed air, and I blinked. I wasn't in my room. I wasn't arguing with people online. I wasn't surrounded by my models.

Colt was watching me with eyes lit up with amusement.

The bastard! "Are you provoking me?" I demanded.

That made him laugh, and he leaned forward to hug me again. "You're fun to rile up."

Without thinking, I smacked his arm and—that was it. The hug ended abruptly, and Colt grabbed my jaw. My stomach somersaulted. I forgot how to breathe. Despite the lingering mirth in his eyes, there was an underlying threat clouding the green, and it shot my nerves straight to hell.

"Did you just hit me?"

I started shaking my head, but, oh God, that was a lie. "I'm sorry."

He narrowed his eyes.

"Sir," I added nervously. "I'm sorry, *Sir*. I'm very sorry."

He thawed out slowly, too slowly, but eventually, he gathered me in his arms again. "We're gonna work on your fear." He hummed. "It might take all summer."

What—

"What might take all summer?" That was Lucas. It seemed for one reason or another, my heart was going to race all day. How on earth would I ever relax around these two? "Aren't you cute together?" Lucas smiled and set down a tray filled with snacks and candy, then found his own seat next to us.

"The cutest," Colt agreed and gave my cheek a loud kiss.

I flushed like the useless idiot I was.

I hadn't foreseen how absolutely frazzled I was going to be. My existence consisted of monotony and occasionally venturing outside to see how others lived their lives. Now, I had two out-of-this-world handsome Doms in my house. There was no protocol, no cues, no lines, no guarantees, no safety net.

"I was telling Kit we're gonna work on his fear," Colt said. "It might take a while—and what do you think you're doin', darlin'? *You* said we had to be in comfortable clothes for this. Go change."

I pinched my lips together as Lucas looked down on his own shirt and tie. His chagrined smirk was endearing.

"I suppose you're correct," he replied with a sigh. "I will be right back."

"There's a half bath under the stairs," I offered.

"Thank you, dear."

Lucas walked off again, but the second I turned my head to face Colt, he gripped my chin and held me in place.

"Look at that ass," Colt murmured. Pardon? He wanted me to stare at Lucas's butt? As if I hadn't seen it already... He wore suits like he was born to do it. I watched as he bent down slightly to grab the duffel bag from the bottom of the stairs. "When he bottoms for me...there are no words."

Oh. "He's a switch?"

Colt shook his head. "Not at all. I'm the only one he bottoms for." He chuckled under his breath and released my chin as Lucas disappeared into the bathroom. "Ain't that a kick in the head? I fell for a stubborn paper pusher who gets off on setting up rules."

"I like rules," I mumbled unthinkingly.

"Of course you do." Colt smiled at me. "I prefer to break them."

I dared a small smirk. "Of course you do."

He let out a carefree laugh and touched my cheek. "You're fucking cute." He stopped me when I ducked my head, and he inched closer. "No. Don't hide from me." He cupped my jaw, and he seemed to like what little scruff I had. A three-day-o'clock shadow. "You know we wanna play with you, right?"

I drew an unsteady breath and struggled to maintain eye contact while hope exploded within me. "I-I d-didn't want to assume."

He chuckled and leaned back once more. At the same time, I heard a door open, and Lucas was back.

They wanted to play with me! I had it confirmed!

I found a way to relax when the curtains were drawn and the living room was blanketed in mostly darkness.

With Colt sprawled out in the corner, me sitting next to him, and Lucas on my other side, the tension started to leave my body halfway into an action film. Okay, maybe it helped that Colt was dozing on and off. He was just so... I didn't know how to put it, but it was like he never let down his guard. He could be perfectly at ease and still catch every movement around him. Not now, though. His light snores were music to my ears. They let me know he wasn't observing me, *and* they provided a reminder that my home wasn't empty. I was watching a movie with two men who weren't on my family's payroll. There was snoring, there were chuckles, there was a film running, there was motion.

There was life.

Lucas, I was discovering, exuded the kindest aura. He'd changed into a white tee and blue pajama bottoms, and everything about him screamed of comfort. Of course, I'd blushed when he placed his arm behind me, along the back of the couch, but that was all he did. He wasn't like Colt. I could already tell Lucas had the patience of a saint.

I mean...you kind of had to if you were with Colt, right?

I snickered to myself at the thought.

They were so different. There was Colt to my left, sleeping, one arm thrown over his face, one leg hanging off the edge of the couch, the other pulled up slightly. And then Lucas to my right, unquestionably comfortable in his own way—or so I assumed. Leaning back, that arm so close to my shoulders, one leg folded over the other. Colt was the brute, the bull in the china shop.

It was Lucas's china shop.

I snickered again, unable to help it.

"That's the second time you've found humor in a building blowing up on the screen."

Oops.

I met Lucas's curious smile with a sheepish look, and I fumbled my way through my explanation about the china shop.

He found it funny, thank goodness.

"Does that make you the china?" His eyes glinted in the dim light, and I knew he was joking. It was humorous, but also thrilling. Anticipation kept growing inside of me. I had no idea what to expect from these two. "Funnily enough, when Colt and I met, I was the bull in the china shop. I'd had the worst week, and then I made a colossal fool of myself in front of him."

That must've been a sight. Lucas struck me as so composed and graceful. And warm and kind and encouraging.

"Will you tell me about it?" I asked, hopeful. "Have you been together long?"

"I'd be happy to share the story." He reached for the remote and lowered the volume a little. "A fair warning, I was in a bad place when he and I met, so karma had her way with me, and Colt got a good laugh." Lucas angled himself a bit more my way, and I mirrored his position, intrigued. "It was about nine years ago, so I was..." He squinted at nothing. "No, wait—eight years ago. I was twenty-nine and angry."

I grabbed my soda and took a big gulp.

"I was driving back to DC after a week of meetings in Atlanta," he went on. "I was hungry, I hadn't slept well, and I was infuriated with myself because I was nowhere near reaching the goals I'd set out to accomplish before I turned thirty." He shook his head to himself, appearing to be lost in an inside joke. "As if this weren't enough, a storm rolled in and turned day into night right before I reached Richmond. Hail the size of golf balls, thunder, lightning—and before I know it, my windshield looks like a spider web, and there's a ball of ice stuck in the glass."

"Christ." I'd seen videos like that on YouTube. "You didn't get hurt, did you?"

"No, but I couldn't drive very well," he chuckled. "I was stuck on the side of the road until the sky had stopped firing bullets at the ground, and then I did something stupid. I stepped out of the car and tried to remove the hail. Of course, this left a hole in the middle of the window, right in front of the wheel." He scowled playfully when I laughed. "I was soaking wet in two seconds, and once back in the car, I drove into Richmond at a snail's pace—with the rain spraying through the hole in the window." He shuddered. "The bus station wasn't far away from where I was, and I knew I would find auto shops there, so that's where I headed."

I couldn't help but grin. It had to have been where he met Colt.

"Only one auto shop was still open by then," he said, a rueful smile on his face. "I didn't care about the cost. I was so done—and happy to hand over the keys. I was still stuck, but at least I wasn't on the side of the road in the middle of nowhere." He paused for effect, probably seeing the anticipation in me. "I was about to call a cab to take me to a hotel, when I saw a bar across the street."

So *this* was where he met Colt. Right? Right?

"Alcohol had never seemed like such a brilliant idea as it did then," Lucas laughed softly. "I stumbled inside, and the first thing I did was knock someone over." He narrowed his eyes at my snicker. "You think that's funny? Just wait, little one. It gets worse." How was that even possible? Also, it was seriously hot when he called me little one. "There I stood, soaked to the bone, angry, hungry, out of breath, with a dozen men and women staring at me. And there was a young woman on the floor by my feet giving me a death glare—the girl I'd accidentally knocked to the ground." He blew out a breath and groaned. "Turned out she was there with her family, and she had a handful of brothers who weren't too happy about me."

"Oh no!" I cracked up and fell back against the cushions, and I covered my mouth with my hands. That was too funny!

"He looked like a drowned kitten," a sleepy voice rumbled behind me. Next, Colt's arm snaked around my waist, and I shivered as the chuckles died down. "I knew right away—"

"That you were going to fall in love with him?" I scooted closer to the edge so I could peer down at Colt.

He smirked. "No, that I was going to fuck with him."

Both Lucas and I huffed, which made Colt chuckle.

"You always were a menace," Lucas drawled.

"Mm, but it worked out, didn't it?" Colt shot him a wink. "Besides, I saved you from getting your pretty teeth kicked in."

Lucas conceded there. "You did."

They were so sweet. But it must be an interesting tale. Two dominant men...?

"Was it tricky finding your way in kink when you're both Doms?" I asked.

Lucas gave Colt a look filled with both affection and amusement. "It definitely offered a few hurdles, but I think we handled them fairly well."

"Absolutely." Colt had as much love in his eyes as Lucas did, and it stabbed me with envy.

They were lucky. I could only pray to find something like that one day.

"Thank fuck you're a slut for cock, though," Colt said and sat up. I almost choked at his statement. "Easier to handle your bossy attitude when you bend over so eagerly."

Lucas didn't look impressed. He merely sighed and reached for the bowl of popcorn.

I furrowed my brow.

I turned to Lucas. "But you're not a switch, Sir?"

"Don't confuse bottom for sub." He tapped my nose, and I smiled sheepishly. He had a point. "My God, you're adorable, Kit." He shook his head and cupped my cheeks, which were already heating up. I wouldn't be me otherwise. What had I done to deserve their company? They were so nice to me.

Before backing off, Lucas pressed a kiss to my forehead.

I wanted more. Much, much more. I was beginning to burn for it.

Colt declared he was hungry when the first movie was over, so I accompanied him out to the kitchen to show him the drawer where I kept all the takeout menus. It was the one place in the kitchen Rosa wouldn't touch.

"What're you in the mood for?" Colt asked as I splayed a bunch of menus on the island. "Too bad you don't have a grill. I'm a barbecue master."

"I have a grill." I scrunched my nose. "I've never used it, but it's in the backyard."

"You have a backyard?" That seemed to surprise him.

I nodded, confused. "Didn't you look out the window last time you were here?" My backyard wasn't big by any means, but I did have a barbecue area and a small pool. It'd been Dad's slice of heaven.

"*Huh.*" Colt frowned. "In my defense, the only backyard I was focused on last time we were here is in your pants."

I coughed and spluttered on my own saliva.

Colt found that amusing. "You can't be this innocent." He stepped closer with a look I could only describe as predatory, and he caged me in. "Does everything shock you?"

I shook my head stubbornly. I wasn't some scaredy-cat! Well, I didn't want to be. I didn't *use* to be. "You're very blunt, and I'm not used to anyone wanting me." I spoke with as much conviction as I could muster.

"Hmm." He dipped down some and let our foreheads touch. "I think you're blind. Something took a whack at your self-esteem, and now you don't see your own appeal. That's fine. I like a good challenge." There was no opportunity to respond before he closed the last bit of distance and covered my mouth with his own.

I'd half expected fire and explosions. Instead, I thought I was going to melt. I turned liquid in his arms, and it was good he grabbed on to me. He wrapped me in a tight hug and deepened the kiss. While my bloodstream turned into a lava field of lust, I stopped thinking. I couldn't. I didn't decide to throw my arms around his neck; it just happened. I didn't plan on kissing him back with all that I was; that just happened too.

I didn't know where my bravery came from, but before I knew it, I was clinging to Colt and tasting his tongue along my own.

Fuck me.

His kisses were goddamn seductive. Slow but hungry, deep and sensual. He was fully in charge, and I was desperate to be along for the ride.

"Jesus, boy," he whispered roughly. Then he picked me up to place me on the counter, and he stepped between my legs. *There* was the fire... Oh God, I felt him. He was hard. Heat pummeled through me, and I whimpered. "I reckon it's time to set some ground rules." He grabbed my jaw and angled my face so he could kiss my neck. I panted and squirmed. "Can we trust you to speak up if things are going too fast or if there's something you're not comfortable with?"

"Yes, Sir," I moaned.

"Promise me, Kit." He locked eyes with me, and the severity mingled with barely restrained desire. It was so heady that I got goose bumps all over. "Luke and I can be greedy bastards, and it's been a long fucking time since we found someone we were interested in. We need to know that you can speak up. Saying no or asking for slower is never wrong, but a lot of subs struggle with it."

I swallowed hard and forced my brain to kick-start itself. And I had to admit, I might very well be one of those subs, the ones who pushed themselves a little too hard only for the sake of not disappointing their Top.

"If you promise I won't be a disappointment if I need a break," I said, my voice cracking embarrassingly. Thankfully, he didn't react to it. "I'm a pleaser through and through, but I have a lot to learn. I won't be perfect."

He offered half a smile and touched my cheek. "Perfect is boring as hell. All we demand right now is honesty."

I released a breath. "I will be honest, Sir."

He kissed me. "Whenever this pretty little mouth calls me Sir, I wanna bend you over and fuck you into next week."

I sucked in a breath and gathered my hands over my crotch.

His faint smirk told me he knew what he was doing to me. "We'll revisit that idea soon." One more swift kiss. "Pizza today. Tomorrow we're spending the day in your backyard." At that, my eyes widened, and he rumbled a laugh. "Yeah, I'm gonna let you interpret that however you want." He nodded at the doorway. "Go to Luke. I'mma get us some pies before I take you right here."

Information overload. Joy flooded me first and foremost, because they were spending the night. I mean, they had to. At the very least, they were returning tomorrow, and that made me so, so, so happy. I slipped down from the counter with a grin.

I made him hard.

"By the way," Colt said, clearing his throat. "Protection. Luke and I are clean, so it's up to you. We haven't had sex with anyone but each other in over a year."

"I...I'm virgin-clean at this rate," I confessed.

"Fantastic. Any allergies?" he asked.

How could he flip it to casual so quickly?

I shook my head. "No, Sir. But I'm not super fond of seafood and fish on pizza."

Anchovies, yuck.

"Good to know."

Giddy and horny, I darted out of the kitchen and into the living room.

6.

"Hi." I almost jumped onto the couch, and I found my place next to Lucas. "Colt said you're gonna be here tomorrow too." I smiled widely.

He mirrored my expression. "Something good must've happened in the kitchen. I didn't think you could get any sweeter."

My excitement was nearly out of control, so I could only lower my gaze to make it less visible. "Yes, Sir. He, um, kissed me. And we talked a little about play rules and safety. That we're all clean and stuff."

"Wonderful." Lucas wrapped his fingers around my wrist. "Come here, please."

I looked to him quizzically and let him guide me until I realized he wanted me on his lap. Fuck, here we go again. I wasn't going to be able to hide my hard-on if this continued. I exhaled unsteadily and straddled Lucas's thighs, to which he hummed with approval.

"Is this okay?" he asked gently.

I nodded quickly. "Very, Sir." But about that... I cocked my head, curious. "You're both Daddy Doms. How do you work out the titles in a relationship with a sub? If you don't mind my asking, of course."

"You can ask whatever you want, dear," he reassured me. "Neither Colt nor I are strict on titles. We enjoy Sir, we identify as Daddy, but if we're in the same room and you wish to address one of us, you can mix it up with our names." He started rubbing my thighs slowly. "A title or name carries as much significance as you give it. That said, we do take the responsibility of being Daddy Doms seriously, so we prefer to wait with that title until a relationship is more established."

I nodded, processing. It made sense to me.

"What did you enjoy most in the kitchen?" Lucas wondered. "There was a skip in your step. And I know he's an intoxicating kisser, but..." He smirked slyly.

I laughed lightly and pinched my lips together. I could still taste Colt—and the candy he'd eaten earlier. "It made me happy to know there's a tomorrow with you," I admitted. "I like knowing. If I have to wonder a bunch, I get anxious."

"I'm glad you told me that," he murmured. "Making you anxious is the last thing we want." He was great at making me hornier, though. His hands were traveling higher up in the most unhurried way, and I was doing my best not to squirm. "In the interest of being as transparent as possible...Colt and I hope to build something with you. We're in no rush to set things in stone, but it's not every day we stumble upon a boy we both want to play with. We're actually very picky, even with the most temporary of play partners."

Could this day get any better? I was *not* going to get teary-eyed. Holy smokes, though, what he said went straight to my chest. I couldn't believe it. And I refused to get pessimistic and say I was going to change their minds sooner or later, but I did wonder why. Why me? They hadn't seen much yet. Lucas less so than Colt.

"May I ask what it is about me?" I had to be honest in the

end. "I mean, we haven't spent much time together, and if you're picky..." I trailed off when Lucas chuckled.

"It's a chemistry thing," he said with a smile. "The second you sat down across from me at the munch, there was something. The way you spoke, how you carried yourself. You're timid, yet hungry for something. You were so eager to lend a helping hand to two strangers, and that matters." He leaned forward and cupped my cheek. "You're also incredibly gorgeous. Just those blue-green eyes are enough to make Doms line up, I bet." He truly didn't know me, not that I would tell him that. "I've been watching you a while now. Paying attention. Wondering..." I couldn't form a freaking word. "You have the cutest freckles."

"Just—just in the summer." I fumbled with my words. "Thank you, Sir—for saying such nice things."

He grinned and inched even closer. Our noses almost touched, and it caused my heart to race once again. "You haven't stopped blushing since we arrived, little one."

"I *know*." It came out as the complaint it was. "It's horrible."

Lucas shook his head slightly and brushed his lips to mine. "Quite the opposite, I'd say."

He was wrong, but whatever. I licked my lips and kissed him back—finally. It was the warmth all over again; Lucas radiated comfort and stability, and it showed in the way he kissed me too. Our tongues met tentatively at first, until he made a sound of pleasure and pulled me closer to him. Lust ran through me at the feel of him, and he kissed me harder.

Or maybe I spoke too soon. "Oh God." I gasped, feeling his hand covering my crotch. I hadn't expected that, but now that it was there, I had to have more. I rolled my hips into his touch and locked one arm around his neck. "More, please."

Lucas cursed under his breath. "I'm trying to take things slowly, Kit."

"*No...* Colt already said you could be greedy. I like greedy."

Speak of the devil...I heard Colt behind us.

"Pizza will be here in twenty." Next, he weaved his fingers into my hair and yanked my head back, effectively breaking my kiss with Lucas. "Are you actin' desperate already, boy?"

He didn't allow me to answer. He leaned down and kissed me instead, a hard, hungry kiss that stole my breath and made me hornier than ever. I was officially tenting my bottoms, and there was nothing I could do about it. I moaned at the sensations; suddenly, there were hands everywhere. Lucas kissed my neck, my shoulder, while he teased my nipples and rubbed my dick through my clothes. Colt had a tighter grip. Rougher hands. Fingers in my hair and his free hand snaking itself around my throat.

"I need a taste," Lucas said. "I've waited long enough."

Colt ended our kiss and gave me a predatory smirk. "You're about to discover what a slut Luke is for cock."

"It's true. Up you go, dear." He patted my thigh. "Let me have a look."

I would have tripped if Colt hadn't been standing behind me. With trembling fingers, I pushed my pants down past my thighs, and then Lucas took over. My pajama bottoms pooled around my feet in the end.

At least I wasn't self-conscious about my dick. It was completely average, not big, not small, not thick, not slim—plain average and the only thing about me that was straight. I didn't have much hair, which was something I had never heard complaints about from Doms.

"God." Lucas wrapped his fingers around me, and I shivered. Colt chose that moment to hook his hands where my arms bent, and he pulled them back so I couldn't move much. "You're absolutely perfect. Look at him, Colt. So smooth."

"Trust, I'm looking." Colt pressed a kiss to my shoulder.

I swallowed a moan as Lucas gently cupped my balls and caressed them.

"There's something you need to know about Lucas." Colt spoke in between kisses to my neck and shoulder. "When I say he's obsessed with cock, I mean it. He'll want to touch you all hours of the day, whether it's a discreet pat at the store, a blow job in the car, or a long fuck before bed." Just then, Lucas took me into his warm, wet mouth and sucked me hard. My knees nearly buckled, and Colt tightened his grip on my arms. "Sometimes, he'll want our sweet boy to take his ass brutally. Sometimes, he'll wake you up by pushing inside your fuckable little ass."

I whimpered and bit down on my lip, my mind swimming in freshly made fantasies.

I'd never fucked anyone. I'd never topped.

Lucas hummed and swirled his tongue around me.

"But make no mistake." Colt nipped at my earlobe. "He'll never let you question who's in charge."

I didn't doubt that for a second.

Holy hell, Lucas sucked me like he was born to do it. How would I ever measure up?

There was no way to withhold the sounds anymore, even less so when Colt got started. He managed to lock one arm under my elbows, holding me in place, while he stroked my ass with his free hand.

It was going to be dizzying what with there being two of them, I realized, as Lucas produced a small bottle of lube for Colt. I hadn't noticed squat. How could I, when my cock was rubbing against the back of Lucas's throat and Colt's fingers were teasing my butt?

"It's been—I-I might need," I stuttered. "Oh God, fuck—"

"I'm not gonna fuck you," Colt reassured. "I need to warm you up, though."

"Hnngh," was my intelligent response. My body broke out in a feverish sweat, and my head lolled back to Colt's shoulder. It felt so good, all of it. Two slick fingers circled my bottom, Lucas kept sucking...hell, they could do whatever they wanted with me.

Colt pushed his fingers inside me in one smooth stroke, and pleasure exploded within me. I gasped and bucked into Lucas's mouth. I'd missed this so much. I loved fingers, I loved being played with, but I hadn't experienced nearly enough of that.

"Jesus, you're tight," Colt muttered.

"Please," I panted. I didn't know how long I could last. With four hands on me, fingers buried inside me, a mouth on my dick, I was fighting a losing battle, and I was going down fast. "I'm so turned on," I groaned. "I want to come."

Lucas gripped the base of my dick and stroked me quickly. "Give me every drop, Kit."

I let out a loud moan and pushed back against Colt's fingers. A tight ball of need dropped lower and lower, and I surrendered to it. I welcomed it. I let go of everything and obeyed my body. I fucked Lucas's mouth as much as he allowed, I begged Colt for more, to be fucked, to hurt—I loved the sting—and then I was flying. I hauled in a deep breath and held it as the orgasm crashed down on me.

There was instant tranquility and euphoria. I lost all strength and didn't care one bit. Everything slowed down. One shiver set off another, and several ropes of come rushed up my cock and shot into Lucas's mouth. His tongue caressed me, his lips were tight around me, and he swallowed and swallowed and swallowed.

Colt brushed a finger over my prostate, and tears burned behind closed lids. It'd been too long since I'd experienced anything remotely close to this kind of pleasure.

"Oh God..." The words left me in a shallow breath, and

then Lucas caught me as I fell forward. Listless and shaking, I could do nothing but collapse in his arms.

"This is gonna be quick." Colt's gruff voice pierced the haze I floated in, but I didn't move until I felt Lucas leaning forward again. With me in his lap, he took Colt in his mouth too. And Colt...didn't mess around. He grabbed Lucas's head and fucked his throat raw.

Wanting to please Colt, I scrambled out of Lucas's grasp and kneeled on the couch.

"You can be rough with me, Sir, I promise." I could tell he was close, and that he didn't want to slow down. But he didn't know I loved being used that way. Okay, it had only happened twice, though it'd practically made me religious.

"You sure, boy?" Colt grunted.

"Use me, please," I replied. "I want it."

He quirked a smirk. "How can I resist?" He withdrew his cock—sweet Jesus, his very large cock—and angled himself close to me instead. "Pinch my thigh if you reach your limit."

"Yes, Sir." I placed my hands on his thighs and leaned in, opening my mouth for him.

"That sight," he murmured, threading his fingers into my hair. "Even your tongue is cute. Lick me with it."

More than happy to. I licked him from root to tip and swiped my tongue over the slit, tasting his pre-come. Excitement built up rapidly, and I really wanted to show him I loved to suck cock. Even though I wouldn't be a natural like Lucas. Closing my mouth around Colt's thick shaft, I sucked him in strongly and hollowed out my cheeks.

My fingers met an uneven surface, the kind I was painfully familiar with, and I knew instantly it was scarring. I hadn't noticed it before, but now it was impossible not to. Around Colt's hip was a big area that whispered of suffering.

I didn't know how or why or when he'd gotten the scars, but

it made me want to please him even more. And one day, maybe he'd tell me about them.

"Exquisite," Lucas whispered. "Those sweet lips belong wrapped around a big cock. You're fucking beautiful."

They were going to make me hard in no time if they kept up that talk!

Colt exhaled a low groan and pushed deeper until I choked. Out, then in, out, then in. He quickened his pace pretty fast, and I sensed his urgency to get off. To spur him on, I shifted one hand to his sexy butt, and I pulled him in. He seemed to love that. He relaxed some and went harder. I choked, and my eyes welled up, but I wasn't going to give up. An emotional surge swept through me, and I put all my focus on him. On pleasing him.

Lucas rose from his seat and pulled out his cock too, and he stroked himself while watching us. It was such a turn-on, and an unfamiliar need struck me hard. I wanted to be seductive.

They'd accepted the part of me I loathed, my upper body. They hadn't reacted badly to the scars. They had barely acknowledged them. I could do this.

I positioned myself on all fours along the couch, my head turned to Colt so he could use my mouth and throat. Flashes of panic whooshed by every few seconds. I couldn't breathe. I couldn't do anything. I choked and choked, over and over. But I didn't pinch Colt's thigh, and I forced myself to pay attention to them. I heard Colt's curses, his heavy breathing, and sensed he was letting go. He was fucking my throat the way he liked it. And I felt Lucas. I felt his hand caressing my ass, and I listened to his husky whispers.

"Such a lovely little boy..." Lucas drew a finger over my opening and stroked his cock faster. He wasn't as long as Colt, but he was thick. So thick. I couldn't wait to suck on that too.

Saliva pooled in my mouth, and the taste of Colt exploded on my taste buds.

"His face," Colt gritted, out of breath. "Look at those lashes. I can see the tears, boy." He shoved his cock down my throat, and everything went black. "Perfect little cocksucker." Squeezing my eyes shut, I felt two tears roll down my cheeks. "Fuck—now."

He stayed buried. My face was smashed against his pelvis when I felt heat flooding my throat. Colt groaned loudly. His thighs tremored with how much he tensed up—thighs that were rock solid.

A sob wanted to rip itself from my chest, but it got stuck. Panic rose again, and I counted—one, two, I could do this, three, four—

Colt pulled out, and I gasped for air. Or, we both did.

Stars filled my vision.

"Fucking hell," Colt wheezed.

Panting and regaining my control, I hurried myself into position in front of Lucas. It was his turn. I felt bolder and braver, not to mention proud and super-happy that I could give Colt what seemed to have been a good orgasm.

"May I suck your cock too, Sir?" I rasped.

Lucas touched my cheek affectionately. "You may, sweet boy."

Yes!

I wasted no time. I took him deep, glad I was able to take every inch of him, and sucked him for all I was worth. He didn't go nearly as rough as Colt had, though I loved it just the same. Lucas gave me deep thrusts and let his sounds tell me what I did to him. It was all I wanted. Or, rather, it was all I wanted right now, because I couldn't lie. I couldn't say hope hadn't consumed me to the point where I wondered what it would be like to call these two men Daddy.

It was a farfetched dream so far, but maybe one day...

Lucas didn't take long either, and after a couple of minutes of my worshiping his thick cock, he jerked irregularly into my mouth and came in three hot bursts.

I was in heaven. Colt had come far down my throat, preventing me from getting much of a taste. Lucas thrust upward with a groan, coating the roof of my mouth with his orgasm. I slid my tongue around him and swallowed his entire release, and I drew pleasure from how he shuddered.

I got to pick the movie when we ate pizza and whatever side dishes Colt had ordered. I usually loved action and war movies, but I was in the mood for a comedy this afternoon. *Pirates of the Caribbean* was a great pick, if I did say so myself.

"I'm so full." I fell back against the cushions and patted my stomach. "Thank you for dinner."

Colt was still scarfing down slices.

"Sweetheart, you haven't touched your vegetables," Lucas told me. Then he handed me a Styrofoam container with a salad. I scrunched my nose.

"No one orders salad with pizza," I muttered.

"We do," Colt said around a mouthful of pizza. "Eat up, baby. We're not asking."

Jeesh. I grabbed one of the plastic forks and stabbed a cherry tomato. But I couldn't deny I was a grinning sap on the inside. They were bossing me around, and I loved it. I *loved* obeying. I loved rules and being held accountable.

"If you think about it," I said, "I had a healthy appetizer."

Colt choked on his pizza, and Lucas let out a loud laugh.

I giggled and stuck some boring salad into my mouth.

After dinner, I got to cuddle with the sexiest men on earth. I had my head in Colt's lap, my legs draped over Lucas's thighs. I hadn't been allowed to put my PJs back on earlier, but Lucas had tucked me in with the softest cotton blanket I owned. It felt wonderful against my skin. So did his hand under the blanket. With his gaze and attention glued to the movie, he played with my cock absently, and it was a lovely mindfuck. A turn-on, a comfy snuggle, a reminder that he took what he wanted. He was a Daddy who just loved to play with his little boy's cock.

God, I wanted to be theirs. I wanted a chance to call them Daddy. I could already predict how effortlessly I'd go there. It wasn't a role for them; it was who they were, and even when they wanted to hold off with such titles, everything about them screamed Daddy, in two different ways.

"Stop squirming." Colt peered down at me with a smirk.

I scowled. "I can't help it. He's touching me."

"You can definitely help it." His fingers disappeared into my hair and scratched my scalp. I hummed and closed my eyes. "You're a delightful little cuddle slut, aren't you?"

"Mmm, yes, Sir. I love to cuddle and hug and be close to people."

It was his turn to hum.

I returned my attention to Jack Sparrow and all the other pirates on screen, and I basked in Colt's and Lucas's hands on me.

"I'd make an awful captain," I said. "I don't even like rum."

Colt chuckled. "I'll take the rum. You can be my wench."

Sounded like a plan to me!

"Colt is the one and only Captain, regardless," Lucas added, amused for some reason.

It made Colt roll his eyes and throw a couple kernels of popcorn at Lucas, who dodged the attack and reached for his soda. He also stopped touching me. Temporarily, I hoped.

I turned back to Colt and smiled curiously. "Is that your

rank in the Air Force?" Which reminded me, I didn't know if he was retired. Hell, I didn't know his exact age. I guessed he was in his early forties. "Oh, are you still active?"

He tipped his head, weighing his answer. "I'm under contract, but I'm not involved in day-to-day ops anymore."

"He was a Captain when I met him," Lucas explained. "The nickname stuck."

"Because you insist," Colt replied wryly. "I'd beat your fucking ass if I could, *pretty boy*."

Lucas grinned. "I love you too."

I bit my lip and poked at Colt's stomach. "May I ask what your rank is? I'm very curious about your career."

He offered me a softer smile and resumed scratching my hair. "Colonel Carter at your service."

My eyes widened. "Whoa," I mouthed, completely awestruck. Not to mention impressed. "How old are you? I mean—goodness, to accomplish that—you don't look old."

He exhaled a laugh. "I'm forty-five. Enlisted when I was eighteen and semi-retired last year."

He was a hero. And I was too excited to lie down, so I scrambled up and sat next to him instead. "I have so many questions. Have you flown any plane other than the F-16? Have you seen battle? How many flight hours do you have? Were you ever stationed in Qatar? I've heard horror stories about—"

"Breathe, baby boy." He cupped my cheeks and grinned, then planted a firm kiss to my lips. I huffed and took a breath, but I wanted to know everything! To calm down, I grabbed the candy bowl and jammed a handful of gummy bears into my mouth. They were yummy. "Let's see. Yes, I've flown other planes. I started going through training and logging flight hours with the Eagle before they agreed to my transfer to the Viper. Years later, they wanted me flying Raptors because—"

"Holy crap, holy crap, holy crap." I couldn't even sit now. I left the couch and just stood there like an idiot, and he couldn't fathom the excitement I felt. He'd talked smack about the Raptor! "Oh my God, you've actually—*wow*. I-I don't know what to say. Oh! Can you tell me if—"

"*Hey*." Colt halted me. He looked like he was trying to suppress laughter. And apparently he wanted me to sit, because he yanked me down again. "You're so goddamn cute right now, but slow your roll." He paused and draped the blanket over me again, though it didn't stay on my shoulders because I was almost bouncing in my seat. The blanket pooled around my middle. "We have a saying. The last base you were at is always better than the one you're at now—except if you're at Al Udeid." That was the base in Qatar. I giggled madly at the saying. "Yes, I've seen battle. That's how you skip ranks. And that's enough questions for now." He blew out a breath and pressed a kiss to my knuckles. "I love your excitement, Kit. Do you notice when you regress?"

"I was just thinking about that," Lucas murmured. "It's amazing to witness."

I looked between the two, confused, and swallowed the last gummy bears. "Regress?"

"Mm, not all Littles regress, of course," Lucas explained, "but I'm beginning to wonder if you do. You're...transforming before our eyes, and it's breathtakingly beautiful."

"You're more relaxed now, yeah?" Colt asked me. "You're cheeky and cuddly and—fuck, that giggle of yours. It goes straight to my cock."

I flushed. "I-I don't know if I regress," I stammered. "To be honest, I haven't explored as much as I've wanted to. M-Mostly some casual stuff."

Having gotten to know my friend Abel better since he met the love of his life, I'd received a clearer picture of regression. In the right mind-set, he became a younger version of himself, and it was no act. It happened naturally in the presence of his Daddy. And some of the things Abel had told me...I could relate so well. I lived with the yearning of wanting to let go the way he did.

"You'll explore with us." Colt drew me to him and kissed my neck. "What do you think about that?"

"Yes, please." I couldn't express how much I would love that. "Before you leave tomorrow, can we decide a day we'll see one another again? Just so I know it's going to happen? I...I might worry otherwise that I've done something wrong. I-I fret easily."

"You do more than that." He cupped my cheek, and he furrowed his brow. There was concern in his eyes too. "You're afraid of being left behind."

I took an unsteady breath and nodded hesitantly. I'd promised to be honest.

Behind me, Lucas scooted closer and hugged my midsection. He kissed the side of my head. "We'll be mindful, sweet boy. Of course we can decide on a date."

Colt nodded. "We'll work on that fear too."

I exhaled in relief.

Lucas gave me a tight squeeze. "Thank you for telling us."

Their acceptance made my eyes sting, and I averted my gaze briefly to swallow my emotions.

They were too good to be true, yet I was powerless to doubt them.

At the end of the evening, I looked at the clock more often than necessary. Sleeping arrangements were on my mind, and I had this hope that they would want me with them. There were two—well, three now—guest rooms on the second floor, though I never opened the door to what had once been my parents' bedroom. And then there was my room on the third floor. My bed was big; it was the same size as the ones in the guest rooms. We would fit, I swore it.

I yawned.

Realistically, though, it made sense if they wanted to be alone together. We didn't have a relationship or anything, and it had been a long day. Maybe they needed a break. Maybe they needed privacy to talk or process. I didn't know.

Christ, I was desperate and got attached too easily. It wasn't good being so starved for company. If I weren't careful, they'd find me clingy in no time.

Right then and there, I decided to go full throttle in my friend search. I needed more people in my life. I needed friends. I couldn't put all my energy and focus on Colt and Lucas. They would get tired. Besides, it wasn't healthy.

"Oh—I had no idea it was this late." Lucas was looking at his watch. "Kit, you can go brush your teeth. Colt and I will come tuck you in."

I swallowed my crushing disappointment. "Yes, Sir," I mumbled. Reaching for my pajama bottoms on the floor, I stood up and put them on. "Colt knows where my room is."

Lucas inclined his head in acknowledgment. "And we'll all fit in there?"

My heart jumped, as did my hope. "Yes, Sir," I replied quickly. "You're going to bed also?"

"In a moment," Lucas said with a nod. "We're going to catch up with the news first."

"We're gonna talk about you." Colt smirked and winked at me.

"Colt," Lucas chastised.

I bit my lip, torn between amusement and worry.

Colt chuckled. "All good things, I promise. Go brush those teeth now, boy."

Fine.

Ten minutes later, I finished my bedtime routine, scrolled through my phone a bit, and cranked up the AC in my room before sneaking under the duvet. The colder it was in the room, the closer we would cuddle up against one another.

I was a genius.

With a little squirming, I managed to get out of my pajama bottoms. They landed on the floor just as I heard Lucas and Colt on the stairs.

Anticipation rushed through me, and I pulled up the covers to my chin and waited.

Tonight, the house—this big house—wouldn't be empty. I wouldn't be alone in the deafening silence. There were sounds again.

Lucas appeared first, followed closely by Colt.

"You have a nice room." Lucas smiled.

"Thank you." Few things had changed in here since I was a kid. There were more school pictures and no Legos. My bed had been upgraded a few times, and the walls had been repainted when I was ten.

"You should see his hobby studio down the hall," Colt replied. He went straight for my bed and sat down on the edge. "Did you have a nice time today?"

I nodded and nodded and nodded. "Very much, Sir. I'm glad you came here."

"Me too." He snatched up one of my hands and kissed my knuckles. "Pool fun tomorrow?"

"Yes!" My eyes lit up, and I couldn't freaking wait. "It's going to be good weather. I checked."

"Sounds great." He glanced over at Lucas, then back to me. "I'm gonna admit something. It's really fuckin' hard not to get ahead of myself with you, and I haven't felt anything remotely close to that since I met Luke."

"Oh," I mouthed, stunned. Was I breathing?

"Same here." Lucas rounded the bed and lay down on top of the covers. "We want you to—goodness, this bed is comfortable."

"I know." It was meant to sound smug; instead, I coughed because I hadn't, in fact, been breathing. "Shit. Smooth."

Colt chuckled and gathered my hand in his lap. "We wanna be honest with you, Kit. Just like we expect honesty from you."

Lucas cuddled closer, much to my joy, and kissed my cheek. "We're going to keep a lid on some of our...dreams, I should say —for a while, at least—but we want you to know we're excited to explore more with you. You're a wonderful boy."

I didn't know what to do with myself. Heat bled across my skin, and the sensations that surged up nearly bowled me over. So I turned to Lucas and tucked my head under his chin. I held him tightly, wishing he were under the duvet with me.

"I'm afraid all this is in my head," I croaked. Fuck. I cleared my throat and swallowed back the emotions. "Are you even real? Happiness is kind of foreign—sorry."

"Oh, sweetheart." Lucas wrapped his arm around me and pressed a kiss to the top of my head. "If you're half as happy to have met us as we are to have met you, we're the lucky ones."

He was wrong, of course.

7.

Fuzzy images of Lucas and Colt fucking me flooded my dreams with such vividness that I tried to reach for them. I squirmed and arched my back, feeling their hands and mouths on me. Fuck, I was hard again. I couldn't get enough.

Please. More.

Colt rolled me onto my stomach and covered me with his sexy body. His breath tickled my neck. His hand roamed my side, his cock was nestled between my butt cheeks, and Jesus fucking Christ, I startled at the distinct realization that it wasn't a dream at all.

"Easy, boy," he whispered.

I gasped and pushed my ass against him. Sleep clung to the edges of my senses, but I didn't pause to think about anything. I just knew what I had to have.

"I'm needy again," I groaned into the pillow.

Colt rumbled a low growl and bit into my neck. "You're testin' my self-restraint, Kit. You don't know how much I wanna hear you beg Daddy for cock."

"*Yes*...I want to, Colt. I want to so badly." I moaned mindlessly, only to be hushed.

"Don't wake up Luke yet. Goddammit—you tempt me too much."

I could've sworn Lucas was just—wait. I lifted my head from the pillow and blinked in the darkness. *Oh.* Right. Of course. That part had been the dream. Or, memories. They were memories from last night. They'd taken turns fucking me. A shiver rippled down my spine, and I swallowed dryly. They'd really taken me, both of them.

As if I needed another reminder, Colt chose that moment to swipe two lubed-up fingers between my ass cheeks and slide them inside. I sucked in a sharp breath and was momentarily overcome with the fiery soreness.

"Does it hurt?" He fingered me slowly, deeply, and placed kisses across my shoulder blades.

"Yeah," I mumbled weakly. "But I want it. It feels good too, Sir."

"That's a good boy. I like it when you hurt for me."

For Daddy.

He started pressing the blunt head of his cock into me, and I whimpered and did my best to relax. I felt strangely vulnerable, like my emotions weren't far away, and I tried to shove that aside. It wasn't the time. I could be a mushy idiot when Lucas and Colt had gone home.

I choked on a gasp as Colt pushed in all the way, and I pressed my face into the pillow again to muffle my sounds.

"It'll pass, baby boy," he whispered through clenched teeth. "Fuck, you feel so good." He stayed buried within me and lowered himself over me to kiss my neck. "I couldn't sleep without taking you again."

Oh my God.

He held me for the longest time, only moving to drop soft kisses along my shoulders, and that was all it took to seduce the pain into a dance with the growing pleasure.

"You're doing so well," he murmured. "You take me perfectly."

"*Hnngh*...more, please..."

He smiled against my neck, then sucked lightly on the flesh. "Christ...you set me on fire, boy. Beg me again."

"Fuck me," I breathed out. "Please, Sir, fuck me."

He hummed and did a slow roll of his hips, withdrawing a few inches while he slipped his hand between me and the mattress. Then he wrapped his fingers around my cock and gave it a downward stroke as he thrust deep inside me.

I moaned and pushed back.

"That's it," he said raggedly. "Wake up Lucas, sweetheart. Ask him if there's anythin' you can do for him."

"Yes, Sir."

Colt pulled me back to rest on all fours, and I took a shaky breath. At times, it felt like his cock was going to split me in half. But then...oh God, oh God, oh God, he shifted and caused the new angle to make me wanna scream in pleasure. My arms trembled, my legs shook, goose bumps rose all over. I couldn't find focus for crap. I swallowed around a strangled moan and managed to nudge Lucas carefully.

"Lucas, Sir," I whimpered.

"I think he'll be happy if you wake him up with a sweet kiss."

Yes, Sir.

I inched closer and winced when Colt's cock hit painfully inside me. Part of his fun, no doubt. He shifted with me until I was right there and could reach Lucas better. I wet my bottom lip and traced the contours of his beautiful face in the dark, then dipped down and kissed him softly on the lips.

"Sir," I whispered.

He made a sleepy humming sound and rolled onto his side, facing me.

"He's so handsome." I caressed his cheek and kissed him gently again. "Lucas."

"You both are." Colt gripped my hips and leaned over me to press a kiss to my spine. "You were so fuckin' sexy together last night when he took you."

Because I hurt like nothing else? Lucas went easier than Colt, but Lucas also had the girth to break a boy.

"You, Sir," I told Colt, "are a Sadist."

Colt let out a breathless chuckle and felt the need to give me a handful of sharp thrusts that hurt so badly, I whined out loud and fisted the sheets.

"Wanna rephrase that, Kit?" Colt asked.

I gritted my teeth against the pain, and I lost my brain in the fire. "Yes, Sir. You're a motherfucking Sadist—" *Shut up!* I froze in horror.

Colt grew still.

Lucas, of all people, let out a lazy chuckle. So, he wasn't asleep?

Before I could register what was happening, I was being thrown around. My ass fucking hurt, my stomach flipped, and I gasped. My back hit the sheets with a thuddy squeak from the mattress. Colt told Lucas to "get ready to fuck his little throat raw" and repositioned me so I was lying horizontally across the bed, my head and feet hanging off each side.

Lucas was already out of the bed and had disappeared out the door.

"I-I'm sorry," I stuttered. My heart slammed against my ribcage.

"For what?" Colt wrapped my legs around his middle and leaned over me.

I sucked in a breath, bracing myself for...anything. Pain. Punishment.

"I called you Sadist."

"Mmm, you did." He dragged his slicked-up cock around

my opening, then pushed in unhurriedly. It was at odds with his previous behavior. He was mad, wasn't he?

"Are-are you going to punish me?"

"Nah. Sadist is a fuckin' term of endearment."

"What!" I cried out. Pushing myself up to support my weight on my elbows, I glared at what little I saw of him. "Then why did you manhandle me like I was about to get it?"

I caught his smirk as he lowered himself over me and sank deeper into my ass.

"Because..." He kissed the corner of my mouth. "It makes me hard to fuck with your pretty little head."

"I..." I had nothing. *You're already hard,* part of me wanted to remind him. But I couldn't. He started fucking me again and kissing me and sucking on my skin and making those out-of-this-world sexy sounds... "Colt," I moaned and fell back.

"There he is," Colt breathed, picking up the pace. "My sweet, cock-hungry boy. You just wanna get fucked, don't you?"

"*Yes.*" The word left me in a drawn-out groan. The hurt simmered below the surface while waves of euphoria swept over me, and I began begging. I couldn't help it. This angle felt fucking amazing. He hit so deep with my legs wrapped around him.

He grabbed my jaw and kissed me hard, pushing his tongue into my mouth. "We're gonna own every inch of your perfect body." He slid his hand down to my chest and pinched my nipple hard.

I hissed and turned away from the kiss, letting the sting sear through me.

He kept pounding into me, and I lolled my head from side to side, unable to escape the sensation of drowning. I didn't know why I wanted to. The lust was everywhere and spurred me on, but it weighed me down too. I had to gasp for air.

He'd succeeded. My head was thoroughly fucked.

Colt cursed.

In the distance, as if everything took place underwater, I heard Lucas's low voice.

He appeared by my head and caressed my jaw with both hands.

I could see him clearer now. The light from the hallway... He must've left the door open.

He tapped my cheek. "Open up for me, little one."

I shuddered like a desperate slut who'd just found out he was about to get laid, and I parted my lips for his delicious cock. With my head tilted off the mattress, I waited for him to take the last step. He stroked his semi-hard cock and brushed the tip against my bottom lip.

The second I felt his thick cock sliding against my tongue, I moaned embarrassingly loudly and wrapped my lips around him.

It took me a second to realize Lucas had washed up earlier, and I was glad I didn't taste any remnants of lube.

"Prettiest spit roast I ever saw," Colt said, out of breath.

Feeling bolder for a second, I lifted my hand and flipped off Colt. And his gruff laugh made me smile around Lucas's cock.

"You really are a brat." Colt leaned over me and kissed the corner of my mouth. "Don't ever change that." He inched closer and licked the base of Lucas, and it was so fucking hot I could die. "Tell me you won't, Kit."

I swirled my tongue around Lucas and pulled away slowly. "I promise, Sir."

In response, he kissed me hard, wetly, around the head of Lucas's cock. I whimpered and threaded my fingers through his hair, needing him close. I needed them both right here, with me.

"Nooo," I complained when Colt sucked on Lucas. All of

him. "He told *me* to do it. Unfair." I pinched Colt's arm. "You have to share."

Colt hummed and released Lucas, only to capture my mouth in a hard, swift kiss. "You don't know how close I am to breakin' all the rules right now."

I poked his nose.

Lucas chuckled huskily. "Glad it's not just me."

"What're you talking about?" I asked and grabbed Lucas's cock. Then I sucked him into my mouth and hollowed out my cheeks, all while glancing at Colt curiously. For real, what rules?

"Jesus Christ, you're filthy," he whispered to me.

"And he doesn't even know it," Lucas murmured. "That's perfect, little one."

Okay, but they hadn't answered my question.

They had no plans to do so either, it turned out. Because Lucas pushed his cock deeper into my mouth, and Colt eased into the best fucking I'd had in my life. For being so big and rough, he had the ability to move with seductive grace. His hands on me, his big cock buried deep, his kisses, his sounds—everything. He controlled everything, including me.

Colt and Lucas found the best rhythm, and I was drowning again. Though, this time, everything became super-clear. We moved together, took what we ached for, and pleased one another. Colt ground his pelvis against my balls and stroked me firmly, swiping his thumb over my tip. Lucas's breathing turned uneven and shallow, and Colt and I weren't far behind.

For a long time, I was mesmerized by our noises. The labored breathing, the grunts, the moans, the slip and slide of our bodies, skin slapping—

"Mmhhh!" I groaned around Lucas's cock as Colt tightened his hold on me. Sweat trickled down my temples. The air became stuffy and smelled of mouthwatering sex. My orgasm came at me too fast. Oh God, oh God—I tried to warn them. I gripped Colt's arm, but he didn't stop.

A whimper slipped free, and I shivered and shivered and shivered.

"Time to come, baby." Colt swallowed hard and went in more forcefully.

The surging euphoria spiked, and I arched my back.

"Let us see you," Lucas grunted. "Come for us."

Mere seconds later, I lost my fight, and the orgasm crashed down on me. I screwed my eyes shut, moaned loudly, and Lucas leaned over me, taking over to stroke himself off. Hot ropes of come splashed against my stomach, and I vaguely registered that it wasn't just me. Another groan left me, and it set off Colt's groan. He rocked jerkily into my ass and buried himself to the hilt.

"Ohh," I whined, overcome with the sensations. "I can't—I can't." I grasped blindly at something that could steady me. A shoulder—it had to be Colt's. And Lucas's thigh. "Too much," I mewled. My body was hypersensitive, and I couldn't stop squirming.

"We've got you." Lucas's voice pulled me toward him, and I felt his hands on my chest, on my face, up and down my arms. "That was so fucking beautiful." He touched my spent cock next, sliding his fingers through the mess we'd made and rubbing it into my skin. "You make my mouth water."

I swallowed and made a *hnngh* sound.

Colt drew out his cock from my ass and collapsed next to me.

Lucas wasn't done, evidently. He reached over me, sucked my cock into his mouth, and cleaned me off.

I couldn't move an inch.

I couldn't think.

I was done.

"You have to tell me if I'm too clingy," I mumbled to Lucas.

The sunbed did fit two, so I had no valid excuse for being half draped over him.

"There's no such thing, I assure you." He hugged me to him, and I closed my eyes, too content and sleepy to overanalyze.

He and I were lounging together on the deck while Colt was doing laps in the pool. That man had so much energy. Not that I didn't enjoy watching him. He'd dived in twenty minutes after we'd had breakfast here outside, only smirking at Lucas's fatherly reminder to wait at least half an hour.

I nuzzled Lucas's neck, where he smelled delicious and all man. He and I had showered while Colt had prepared breakfast, and I even got to borrow Lucas's body wash.

Overnight, it seemed my life had exploded with color. The sky was bluer, the sunrays that bounced off the water ripples flashed brighter, the hedge was greener, and...and flavors! Breakfast had been delectable. Rosa's bagels, a big spread of toppings, and eggs that Colt had made. Even the OJ had tasted fruitier.

"Colt gets the nicest tan in the summer," Lucas murmured. "I turn into a lobster if I'm not careful."

"Same here," I giggled sleepily. I liked the shade, though. It was comfy and cozy here under the deck's canvas roof. "I have to be careful because of the tattoos too."

"We'll have to make sure you've got on plenty of sunscreen before you go into the pool." Lucas kissed the top of my head. "Mind if I ask a personal question?"

"Nuh-uh." I yawned and sat up to reach for my soda. The ice clinked against the glass, and I took a big gulp. I really, really loved Coca-Cola, but I rarely had it at home. My mom never liked soda. Then Lucas and Colt had brought a bottle, and I was too weak to resist.

"I told you I've had my eye on you for a while, yes?" Lucas welcomed me into his arms again and adjusted the thin blanket over me. I nodded in response to his question and watched Colt swim underwater. "So it was impossible not to notice that you seem to have a favorite outfit to wear—for every munch. And probably not just there...?"

Crap. Maybe I didn't want him to ask *that* question.

I wasn't sure he'd understand. Abel hadn't.

I sat up again and drew up my knees to my chest, and I had to decide if I was going to give him the short or the long answer.

In the end, I suppose I knew the correct answer. They'd asked for honesty, and if we were actually planning to explore some sort of relationship together—which I desperately wanted —they needed to know. Because more questions would arise eventually.

"My mom was very protective of me," I started by admitting. "She used to run all kinds of charities for children, and there was this one in particular. It focused on missions to bring children to safety from...I mean, anything that was dangerous. A broken home, war zones, trafficking..."

Lucas gathered my hand in his and squeezed it gently.

"She got all the ugly details that were kept from the public," I said. "And...over time, it affected her to the point where she tried to shield me from everything." I still remembered the day she told me a personal driver was going to take me to school. I was six or seven. Up until then, Mom or Dad would drive. Or a few parents had taken turns to pick up us kids. I scratched my ear and cleared my throat. "I've never been on public transit, for instance."

I could tell Lucas tried to hide a bit of his surprise.

Growing up, those changes had been mildly strange at best. Because I came from an affluent family, and many of my classmates had drivers or au pairs. Especially those who were old money. My mom came from wealth, but my dad had earned every dime of his own fortune. He'd worked in security and eventually branched out to build an empire of secrecy. Stealth technology, protection against cyber warfare... There was a real estate company in his name, as well as a travel organization for those who worked with or for him. And for clients with a single goal: discretion.

Long answer, it was. I told Lucas everything.

"So when Mom told me that she and Dad had hired Vincent, I guess I was a little uncomfortable...? But no more than that. And I liked him from the start. He'd joke around with me after school and take me to burger places." My smile faltered as the next memory hit me. "Until Mom found out and said our outings would have to stop. She said it wasn't safe."

"She was afraid something might happen to you."

I nodded. "I..." I swallowed the burst of unease and grief that struck me. "Before she died, I defended her. And I hate going against her now, but...I mean, in retrospect..." I huffed at my own inability to form a fucking sentence. "She became paranoid. She *was* paranoid, and it bled into other things—like what I ate, how I dressed." I coughed into my fist. "I think Dad didn't want to see what was happening—or what had happened." But there was one time. Mom was cleaning out my closet in a near-panicked state, and she was telling Dad it was stupid for me to wear nicer brands. Because I was essentially a walking target for muggers and murderers.

I stammered my way through the story of Mom taking it so far that she was yelling at my father. That if I wore an expensive-looking shirt, I would get kidnapped and end up on the evening news.

"I remember how terrified my dad looked." I shook my head. "He managed to calm her down with statistics of kidnappings, but I think it was partly so he could go on like nothing was wrong. She was the love of his life, and he was afraid to lose her —to lose our family."

"My God." Lucas brought my hand to his mouth and kissed my knuckles. "That couldn't have been easy for any of you."

Both Mom and Dad had been good at shielding me from the worst of it. Of course, I recalled some of the fights that had occurred at home. They were often on my mind, like a ghost that wouldn't be put to rest. But much of it, I'd learned after the funeral. I'd learned some of it from Richard and Linda's daughters, some of it from my grandmother on Mom's side. She passed away last year. My grandfather was still alive, but we didn't talk much. He was... Cantankerous would be an understatement. He and his housekeeper lived in Connecticut.

I scratched the side of my head and tried to circle back. "So, the outfit... I don't know if I'm trying to keep my parents alive or if I'm attempting to give my mom's spirit some peace, but I follow some of her rules. And I know it's silly—"

"It's not, sweetheart," Lucas murmured. "It's not silly at all. You lost your entire family, and you were so young. You still are. You hadn't learned how to manage on your own because no one had taught you. We do what we can. *You* do what you can."

Maybe. I wasn't sure.

More often than not, I felt incredibly dumb. I'd been eighteen when I lost my parents, and yes, I'd lived a sheltered life, but I couldn't do shit. Rosa had taught me how to boil freaking water. I couldn't drive. I couldn't pay bills. Vincent had taught me how to start the dishwasher. I mean, I had people for everything. Richard managed the money. So...for me to wear the same style of a Gap shirt because my mom preferred me not to be kidnapped...when, instead, she could've been the one to give me a SmarTrip Metro card...yeah, it felt silly.

Sometimes, I got angry.

Then I felt suffocated by guilt.

She'd done her best. My parents had loved me... They'd been there when I came out at thirteen. Mom had taken me to my first Pride parade. We'd been escorted by two security guys, but still. And Dad had personally dropped me off outside the movie theater for my first date, though not before giving me a very awkward version of the birds and the bees discussion. He'd picked us up too and witnessed my first kiss.

The words kept tumbling out of my mouth, and Lucas listened. At one point, I caught him gesturing to Colt. A subtle shake of his head, presumably telling Colt now wasn't a good time.

I forgot where I was, and I saw my parents before my eyes. I wanted to yell at them and hug them and say how much I missed them, and I wanted them to be *here*. A stupid drunk driver had taken their lives—and, sorry but...thankfully, also his own life. I balled my hands into fists and drew in a long breath, trying to calm down.

I wanted to yell at my mom for the stupidest things. For not letting me go out past dark when she'd had a "bad episode." For not allowing chips and soda in the house.

"I've never had Cheetos," I blurted out. "My mom's job broke her, and because of that, I've never tried Cheetos. Or Taco Bell. Funyuns—first time I tried those last night." Colt had brought them, or so I assumed, because he'd devoured half a bag. Lucas hadn't touched them. "They were gross, but now I know."

Lucas smiled sympathetically and offered a hand, silently asking if I wanted to get closer. I definitely did, and I was sick of talking. Sick of my issues. Sick of my weird ways of trying to keep my parents around.

"I agree with you." Lucas spoke in between kisses in my hair. "They are gross. So is Taco Bell, in my opinion, but Colt would have them on speed dial if the one near us delivered."

I chuckled tiredly and relaxed in his embrace.

"I'm going to tell you a short story," he said. "Second year of college—I was struggling to pick my major. My father had high hopes that I would one day take over the family business, but I already knew real estate wasn't going to be for me."

I scooted down to be able to look up at him better. "You picked marketing, right?"

He nodded. "It didn't stop my dad from wanting me involved in his company, and I tried it for a few years after I graduated. He created a position for me that wasn't entirely necessary for such a small agency. But in the end...I had to go my own way. And he was disappointed. He didn't say it outright, but I could tell." He touched my cheek. "You know what would've disappointed him even more, though?"

I shook my head.

"If I'd stayed with him and been miserable," he replied. "Considering how protective your parents were of you, I think it's safe to say they wanted what's best for you. They wanted you to be happy."

I chewed on my bottom lip and nodded hesitantly. "Are you saying I should do what I want?"

He smiled and released my lip from my teeth. "I'm saying that sometimes a parent's personal dream doesn't go hand in hand with what they ultimately want for their child. My father hoped I'd want to get into the family trade, but not as much as he wanted me to find my own way."

I hummed and rested my head on his chest, processing what he'd told me. I felt Lucas was right, but... "I don't know where to start," I confessed. "Somewhere along the road, I'm not sure whose fears I was following—my mom's or my own." In one way or another, I'd been hiding for four years. "I hate making decisions, so whenever I remembered my parents saying something, I just went with that."

That juice contains too many chemicals. I didn't drink it anymore. *You look wonderful in blue, honey.* The year after my parents died, I only wore blue. *Don't take that street; it's not safe.* I didn't even let Vincent drive there. *T-shirts aren't*—wait. No. That was me. I had stopped wearing tees of my own volition because they'd exposed too much of my skin. I'd forgotten. That one wasn't on Mom.

"You know who would be happy to help you?" Lucas murmured. "Colt and I."

I glanced up at him again and furrowed my brow. "Why? You'll get sick of my baggage in no time."

"Don't say that." He frowned. "The work would be your own. We would just give you a nudge here and there—and be there for you when you need it." He paused. "Some decisions, you have to make on your own. As boring as adulthood can be." He lightened the tension a bit and kissed me on my forehead. "And some, we can make for you."

Uncertainties came at me quickly. Moving forward with anything Lucas and Colt offered would mean I was shattering the carefully crafted life of monotony I'd assembled for myself. I hated it with every fiber of my being, yet it was safe and comfortable. I knew my place. At night, when the house was empty, I sat at my computer and talked to online friends. In the morning, I took an extra-long shower so that I knew Rosa would've arrived by the time I got downstairs. When the loneliness was particularly overpowering, I fell asleep with my headphones playing music my dad used to listen to.

I'd learned to cope.

God, what was wrong with me? They were literally offering for me to be part of something—which I'd fucking cried myself to sleep that I was missing—and I was hesitating?

Nausea and anxiousness swam higher up in my chest. It was time to take a leap. It was freaking terrifying, but it was time.

"I'll gladly accept any help," I croaked.

Lucas hugged me to him, a hard squeeze that put me back together as much as it threatened to tear me apart, and all I could do was hang on for dear life.

1.

"Time to wake up, sweetheart."

Nooo.

I hadn't truly been asleep. I'd been dozing on and off, which meant I'd constantly felt the comfort of Lucas next to me on the sunbed, the softness of the blanket, and the slight breeze that drifted under the roof every now and then. But I'd been out of it enough to miss the moment Lucas told Colt about my rambling. I hadn't wanted to do it all over again, so I'd asked Lucas to do it.

"I wanna nap more," I mumbled.

Lucas chuckled softly and brushed some hair away from my forehead. "Colt's about to fire up the grill and wonders where you keep the lighter fluid. He found the briquettes."

"Oh." I scowled sleepily and lifted my head, then waved in the general direction of the door leading inside. "There's a cupboard in the laundry room in the hallway—wait. I'm being lazy. I'll get it." I yawned and stumbled out of the sunbed.

They both looked sinfully sexy wearing only boxer briefs, and I could see what Lucas had said about Colt getting a nice tan. The waistband of his underwear rode an inch or two low today, revealing he'd already spent time in the sun this year.

He stood nearest the door and stopped me on my way inside.

He didn't say anything at first. He just wrapped his arms around me and hugged me hard.

I closed my eyes and let out a shaky breath.

"We're not goin' anywhere, all right?" He kissed my temple.

"Okay," I whispered. Beyond thankful for what they'd already done for me, I stood up on my toes and popped a kiss to his cheek, and then I headed indoors to get the lighter fluid.

I would have to show them how grateful I was.

On my way back to the terrace, I was just past the living room when I heard Colt outside.

"I'm this close to throwin' in the damn towel."

My steps faltered, and I entered the dining room at a slower pace.

"I know, baby, me too," Lucas sighed. "I don't know how many times I've stopped myself from just fucking announcing he belongs to us now."

Oh. My heart jumped up into my throat.

Colt chuckled.

"Everything about him calls out to me," Lucas said.

"I know," Colt replied quietly. "And Christ, seein' you with him, darlin'... I know you've been yourself with me, but there's somethin'."

"Because we can finally be Daddies."

Colt hummed. "That's it, isn't it? I feel it too. Problem is, I'm like a kid on Christmas. We haven't been able to live this way to the fullest yet, and now we get a taste of it... Whatever we've tried out with others doesn't fuckin' compare."

I pinched my lips, and my eyes welled up.

"I love you so much," Lucas said, and then I heard them kiss. "We went all in with each other after one weekend together, Captain. For chrissakes, you were literally deployed when we decided to go for it. If Kit feels the same, why wait? Why not establish something for the three of us?"

"Hey, you're the one who gets on my case when I break rules, not me. I told you from the beginning, I'd need two minutes alone with him to see if there's chemistry."

I grinned and wiped away silly tears. It was overwhelming. So overwhelming. My chest constricted, and I had butterflies in my stomach.

"Always my cocky fighter pilot." There was amusement in Lucas's voice. "So, you agree—you think we should talk to him?"

All of a sudden, my stomach did a crazy flip, and I stumbled forward, my toes stuck under the rug in the dining room.

"I think—"

"Shit," I yelped, just barely managing to steady myself with a hand on the table.

Colt cleared his throat. Then his head appeared in the doorway. And he raised a brow at me before sliding Lucas a smile. "I ain't sure we have to."

Oh my God, I was such an idiot. My face turned beet red as both Colt and Lucas eyed me from the doorway, one of them looking just a tad more amused than the other.

"Are you okay?" Lucas asked with a soft smirk.

"Yes, Sir," I coughed. Fuck, shit, fuck, I couldn't believe myself. I was so mortified that I couldn't look them in the eye. On the plus side, they couldn't see I'd gotten mushy. "I'm sorry."

"For what? Stumbling?" Colt's smirk was downright wolfish. He walked over to me to get the lighter fluid and to... fuck, grip my chin and force me to face him properly. I'd been perfectly happy keeping them in my periphery, thank you very much. I prayed my eyes weren't red. He lowered his head and nipped at my bottom lip. "Or are you apologizin' for eavesdroppin'?"

I screwed my eyes shut and let out a pitiful little groan. "The latter, maybe. I'm sorry, Sir."

He laughed under his breath and smacked a kiss to my forehead. "Too cute. I guess you're lucky it ain't against the rules to listen in on us—yet. Let's go." He took a step back and nodded toward the terrace. "I reckon it's time we all talk."

Gulp.

I was ridiculously nervous returning outside, because I wanted this more than...I didn't even know. My heart, body, and soul ached to belong to them. I couldn't fuck this up. I'd hate myself forever if I did.

While Colt got the grill started, Lucas gestured toward the sunbed. It was closer than the regular table and chairs, which were on the other side of the pool in a corner shaded by a big tree.

Lucas adjusted the backs of our seats so they were more upright.

I drew my blanket around me and crisscrossed my legs.

"Before we dive in, Kit," Lucas said, "if you don't mind, I'd like to hear your thoughts on the weekend."

My gaze flickered between him and the space between us. There was probably a whole foot, and I didn't like it. He'd want a response that went beyond, "It's been great!" And I didn't want it to turn into a performance review where everything was formal.

"Can we hold hands?" I asked hesitantly.

Lucas smiled and scooted closer, and he found my hand with his under my blanket. "Always."

I exhaled and squeezed his hand. "I like you guys lots. I even like myself better when you're here. There's so much I want to try out, and I think—I think, with you, I won't be too shy to ask for it. You've..." I thought back on how they communicated with me, how open they were. "You've put me at ease in a way I wasn't sure was possible."

It was Lucas's turn to squeeze my hand, and judging by the look in his eyes, he liked my answer.

"Way to break a Sadist's heart." Colt set the lighter fluid aside and walked over to us, taking a seat at the foot of the bed. "I haven't made you uncomfortable at all?"

I snickered nervously. "Not in the bad way," I amended. Because the truth of the matter was, I could tell Colt had the ability to push me very hard. It would be uncomfortable and painful to the extreme, but it would be the kind of suffering I'd wanted to explore forever.

"That's good. Only the good pain." Colt shelved the humor and put a hand on my knee. "So we know this is fast. And I think, to take the pressure off you, Kit—" he glanced at Lucas and received a nod in agreement "—what we'll do is just tell you that Luke and I are ready for more. You will wait until you're sure, until it feels natural, and then we'll set up boundaries for a Daddy/Little relationship. With titles."

With titles.

Perhaps I was high on giddiness that was overriding my nerves, but I suddenly felt mischievous. The way he'd phrased himself, the formality of it all, made me want to lighten the tension.

"Before I answer," I said, and I pushed away the blanket and got on all fours to crawl over to Colt, "can I ask you something?"

He furrowed his brow. "Of course."

"How many fighter pilots does it take to change a light-bulb?" I kissed his cheek and received a sharp, narrowed-eyed look from him. Behind me, Lucas spluttered a chuckle. I grinned and nuzzled Colt's jaw. "Just one. He holds the bulb, and the world revolves around him."

Colt had disbelief written all over him. "What the—"

"Also, who says I'm not ready now?" I giggled.

"You *shit.*" He grabbed me under my armpits and pushed me back, all while Lucas collapsed into a fit of laughter. My stomach did a somersault, and I joined in on the laughs as my back hit the cushions and Colt landed on top of me. "You thought that was funny, huh?" He planted wet kisses and playful bites all over my face.

"Very funny!" I squirmed to evade his tickles, and I tried fruitlessly to shove him away. Or, at least, end the assault. "Gah! If you don't stop, I'll tell more—*tickles!*—jokes!"

"Oh, look at that, Luke...the kid is threatenin' me." Colt dug his fingers into my sides mercilessly.

Tears sprang to my eyes, and I was completely breathless. "What's the difference b-between God and a fighter pilot? Fuck! Ahh! God doesn't think he's a pilot!"

"Oh Christ, I can't," Lucas wheezed out. "How come I've never heard these before, Colt?"

"Because you're laughin' so hard that you're cryin'!" Colt exclaimed, finally stopping the tickles. "You think I'd share this shit with someone I can't punish?"

I gasped and wiped my eyes.

"And *you*..." He returned his attention to me and dipped down, rubbing my nose with his. "You wiseass. You can go get a notepad and a pen for all the rules we're about to give you, and you can start callin' us Daddy, you delightful little slut boy."

I beamed and, admittedly, got a little horny. Okay—a lot.

"Yes, Daddy," I whispered.

His eyes darkened, and he clenched his jaw. The humor was long gone. "Jesus, that sounds good. Go before I take you."

Mondays still sucked, but not as much.

I was in the kitchen rubbing the sleep from my eyes when Rosa arrived, and she gave me a slow once-over before smirking and getting started on breakfast.

"You had a good weekend, *mijo*," she sang.

A yawn interrupted my grin. "Yeah. How was yours?"

"Same old. Good." She grabbed something from the freezer. "I'm surprised Vincent is not here yet."

I snickered and took a sip of my coffee, or sugared milk with a bit of coffee flavor, as Colt called it.

Vincent had been good, though. He'd texted me twice on Sunday, just to check in, that was all. And by the last text, Colt and Lucas had gone home.

They'd left around nine with the promise that we'd meet up tomorrow for dinner.

Returning my attention to the notepad in front of me, I couldn't help but smile at everything. Even the boring rules they'd set up for me were reminders that they wanted to be involved in my life. Like, clean my room before bedtime. Boring!

I checked the time and huffed to myself. It was still too early to call Abel on the West Coast.

He was going to be so freaking smug that I might as well get it over with.

My phone vibrated in the pocket of my pajama bottoms, so I retrieved it and saw I had a message from Lucas.

Good morning, sweetheart. I hope you slept well. Colt and I missed having you between us…but that's not why I'm texting. It turns out I have a work lunch in Georgetown today. Would you like to meet up quickly afterward for ice cream?

Yes! Maybe Mondays didn't have to suck anymore!

———

"Uhh…" I squinted up at Lucas, the sun directly behind him, and grinned sheepishly.

He was equally amused by the difference in our treats. He'd

gone with a dark chocolate gelato with crushed pistachios, and I'd ended up with a fucking rainbow of frozen yogurt. Strawberry-flavored, vanilla-flavored, chocolate-flavored, and then the toppings. Granola crumbs, Cap'n Crunch, gummy bears, chocolate chips, two types of sprinkles, and strawberry sauce.

"I couldn't decide on toppings," I admitted self-consciously. "I kinda like sprinkles a lot."

Hey, Lucas had encouraged me to "go nuts." Which was practically the only topping I hadn't put on here.

"I think it looks perfect." He touched my cheek, then gestured to a table in the sun. We were only five or six blocks away from my house, and I felt dumb for having had Vincent drop me off.

We took our seats, and I watched curiously as Lucas took a picture of our desserts.

"Are you sending it to Colt?" I guessed.

"Oh. No. I'm uploading it to Insta," he chuckled. "Our friends in the community will get a laugh thinking your ice cream is Colt's." He showed me the screen, where I read the caption to the photo. *Hot date.* Heat flooded my cheeks, and I struggled to contain my grin. I was the hot date! "You mentioned it's been hard finding friends at the munches, and I hope you won't get overwhelmed when everyone descends. Being as involved as Colt and I are, we don't have many vanilla friends left because of the time we spend with kinksters. And they know very well that we've never dated others like this. Not in a vanilla setting."

Nervous butterflies started flying in my stomach. It wasn't a bad thing, though.

"I haven't made enough of an effort," I replied. "I've been too shy. I mean, I've asked some people if they wanna do something sometime, but I haven't been bold enough with specifics."

"I understand." He nodded and pocketed his phone again,

then sat back and folded one leg over the other. He was so fucking handsome, it almost hurt to look at him. With the suit and the sleekness and the Ray-Bans. "Either way, we're both excited to show off our boy." I caught the wink behind his shades. "You have the cutest blush."

I shook my head and pressed my cheek to my shoulder, as if that would rub the blush off and onto my shirt. "I'm so *thrilled* that you want to point that out all the time."

He laughed and slipped the small spoon with gelato into his mouth.

I followed suit and shoveled a bigger spoonful into my mouth, chewing on the gummy bears and the granola soaked in frozen yogurt and strawberry. It was delicious.

"Speaking of," he said, "there's an event at the house in Mclean in a few weeks. Have you been there yet?"

I shook my head. "No, only to a few events here in the city." I'd been way too anxious to visit their kink haven. I'd seen the big, black-painted Victorian house in pictures online, but...it was half an hour outside of DC, and it'd just been too much. Especially if showing up alone. Too intimidating. "I noticed you guys don't host many parties here anymore."

"True. We can go all out at the house in a way we can't at a club," he said. "It was the reason River and Reese bought the property in the first place. We wanted to get away from the city."

I nodded in understanding and ate more froyo. "What's the theme for the next event?" I'd seen the community's schedule online, and there was always a theme.

"I'm glad you asked." Lucas's expression was almost...Colt-like. There was mirth and a threat; there was sadism. Fuck. "The Games are starting. It's...a new project. It'll be great fun."

"Fun for who?" I blurted out.

He found that funny. "Colt helped plan it, so take a guess."

I squeaked.

There was no end to his creativity, and I didn't have to know him well to know that. I'd read the stories online from other members. River and Reese were even worse.

"Ivy posted something once," I said. "She took so much pain from Colt and River." I shuddered. "Seriously, they'd caned her *fingers*. And! And...they had a giant beetle crawl over her while someone fucked her with a dildo."

Lucas grinned and nodded. "Clark—a play partner of hers. Yes, they can get quite rough."

Quite.

"Well, let me tell you, Daddy," I huffed, "I *never* want a bug on my body."

Lucas merely smiled at me, a soft smile, and he leaned over to kiss me. "It will never get old to hear you call me that."

Oh. Oh hell. I quickly glanced around us to make sure no one had heard me. Discretion in public was still a thing. Yesterday, after we'd established a tentative Daddy/Little relationship, it'd felt wonderful and freeing and so hot to call Colt and Lucas Daddy, but it'd been a conscious choice. This time was an accident. I hadn't thought about it.

"It's fine, sweetheart." He probably knew where my mind was at. "And I solemnly swear to protect you from bugs." He cupped the back of my neck, his hand cold from holding his ice cream, and rested our foreheads together. I exhaled in relief and relaxed. "I hope you'll attend with us, though...?"

"Of course. I want to be where you are."

"Me too." He kissed me again, and I tasted chocolate on the tip of his tongue. "I want everyone to know you belong to us."

I shivered. "Yes, please," I whispered. I wanted nothing more than that too.

I signed up for an Instagram account the following day.

Sending texts to Abel, Lucas, and Colt quickly gave me three followers.

Then I sat there at my desk and stared at my blank profile in my phone. Glancing up at my computer, I saw the almost six hundred followers I had on Twitter, and I was instantly struck by how much more important it was to have followers who were actual friends. Those three people cared about me. The six hundred followers on Twitter didn't know my name, had never seen me, and only tweeted a shout-out if I hadn't posted an "I hate Monday" meme in a month.

Lucas was the frequent poster on Insta. Meals, friends, and sights filled his grid. Colt's profile was emptier. There were fourteen photos in total, and nine of them were of fighter jets. It made me grin. The other five were of Lucas and... I leaned closer. Family, maybe. There was an older woman and a woman in her thirties.

A visit to Abel's profile made me snort. Okay, he was the prolific one. Thousands of pictures—selfies, hockey-related posts, family, more selfies, gym photos, and family and friends.

I didn't know what to take pictures of.

Squinting up at my shelves, I shrugged and snapped off a handful of photos of my most recent models. Colt might appreciate my model of the AC-130U, a gunship he had no doubt seen in real life. They were massive.

Okay, then. The gunship became my first official photo on Instagram, and because I couldn't help it, I had to add some facts about the aircraft. Lastly, I assumed hashtags were popular on this site too, so I used the same ones I would in my online forum.

It didn't take more than a couple minutes before Colt liked the picture. His comment followed shortly after, and I grinned at what he wrote. He'd also tagged Lucas to poke fun of him.

If it ain't the Spooky. ;) Nice work, my boy. I have a feeling I'm gonna enjoy your content more than @LuWeInDC's with all his food pics and motivational quotes. See you in a few hours, and don't forget to bring your homework.

I wasn't going to forget. I'd worked on it all morning.

9.

"You don't think it's messed up that two strangers are giving you homework?"

I frowned and met Vincent's gaze in the rearview mirror. Um, no, I didn't find it messed up, and they weren't strangers, damn it. "You've been testy today," I noted. And yesterday, he'd been mostly quiet. "Is something wrong?"

He shook his head and stopped at a red light. "Just making conversation."

I bit at a cuticle and looked out the window. I could tell he wasn't fond of my new relationship with Colt and Lucas, but I didn't know why. Yesterday, I'd answered a bunch of questions Vincent hadn't asked, mostly to ease his worries. I'd told him it was kink-focused—and that was partly for my own benefit. As a reminder. The last thing I needed was to get ahead of myself and fall in love. After all, Colt and Lucas hadn't made the slightest mention of this turning into something beyond Daddy/Little.

I'd also told Vincent I was being careful. I was exploring and testing my wings, something he should encourage. Unless he didn't believe I was able to fend for myself. Not an unfounded opinion, if that was the case. I wasn't sure I believed I could do that either.

I was trying, though.

My knee bounced as we got closer to the restaurant near Logan Circle. There was a rock of unease in my stomach, and I couldn't figure it out. I'd missed Colt and Lucas all day, and now I was about two minutes away from seeing them. It had to be something else.

We passed a restaurant with big windows, and the sight filled me with a fluttering sensation. The place was crowded, people at every table and at the bar, and I could see the laughter among friends and the intimacy shared between those on a date. How they leaned in close to each other, how they shared food from their plates, and the flirty grins. And I wasn't just looking in anymore. I wasn't the same outsider I'd been a week ago.

"Impossible for me to find parking here, buddy," Vincent said.

"That's fine," I answered quickly, ready to leave the car. Because I was down to seconds. Seconds until I would be in one of those restaurants on this street, seconds until I was one of the many who got to share laughs and jokes and intimacy. "And I think I mentioned this earlier, but Colt and Lucas are taking me home."

"Yup, you said that," he sighed. "Have a nice night, Kit."

Oh! I could see them. Colt and Lucas were standing outside the tapas restaurant we were going to. "Okay, thank you, you too." I opened the door and hurried out so Vincent didn't hold up traffic. "Bye!" I shut the door and walked between two parked cars, and then I hit the busy sidewalk.

DC in the summer was energetic. It didn't matter that it was a Tuesday. In this town, you met up with friends after work, and you had dinner and drinks and a good time.

For the first time in my life, I was becoming a part of the DC nightlife. The busy traffic, the lights, the clinking of glasses in outdoor seating areas, and all the voices flooded my senses and made me buzz. Darkness was falling, and yet, everything was shining.

Lucas was extremely handsome as always in a suit, sans jacket, and Colt dressed for the occasion—reluctantly, I bet. He didn't look tremendously comfortable in his button-down, but damn did he look hot in it. It was black and hugged his body, suntanned forearms exposed for ogling.

I clutched the cuffs of my own button-down, still too apprehensive to show my arms. I was so stupid.

Lucas spotted me first and nudged Colt, and I smiled widely and closed the distance between us.

"Hi." I came to a stop in front of them, a little unsure of how to greet them—oh, never mind. They knew. Colt yanked me in for a tight hug and a kiss to my forehead.

I melted a bit. The rock in my stomach shrank.

"I reckon it's safe to say I can't go two days without seein' you again," he told me, the city lights twinkling in his sea-green eyes. "I missed you."

"I missed you too." I grinned shyly and pressed a quick kiss to his neck, and right then and there, I almost died. His cologne hit my nostrils. Jesus Christ, he smelled amazing.

Lucas slipped his hand around mine, and I easily fell into his arms. He was the calm. He always radiated structure and safety.

"How's our boy?" he murmured.

"Better now." I smiled when he dipped down to kiss me, and I kissed him back and cupped the back of his neck. I wanted to sniff him too, but they had dinner on their minds. Colt took the lead while Lucas held on to my hand, and we stayed in the background.

"Table for three under West," Colt told the host.

It would be ten minutes, we were told. So the three of us

huddled near the exit with people coming, going, and waiting around us.

A red glow from the lights in the ceiling was cast over the restaurant, and everyone looked like they were having a good time. Envy didn't burn in my chest. I was just...happy. Happy to be out, happy to see people, happy to be with two wonderful men. A lot of men were here with other men, though that wasn't strange, given the neighborhood we were in.

After a minute or two, one of the small stools along the half wall in the entrance became available, and Colt took a seat and patted his thigh for me.

"I didn't get to go out for ice cream with y'all yesterday," he said. "Get over here."

I snickered and sat down on his lap, and he snaked his arms around my middle.

"Let that be a lesson," I told him over my shoulder. "You should have meetings in Georgetown."

Lucas's eyes shone with approval. "Excellent response."

"All right, all right, let's not gang up on the poor Texan," Colt said. "Give me your arms. There's no reason for you to hide your sexy tats."

I swallowed hard as a rush of insecurities smacked me in the face, though I didn't say anything. I let him fold up the sleeves of my shirt and expose my arms.

When it was done, Lucas leaned down, cupped my cheeks, and kissed me softly. "Be proud of everything you've survived, Kit."

I exhaled shakily and made a conscious effort not to look around me. I didn't want to see if anyone was staring, if anyone could see right through me. Because one, it was all in my head. And two, no one else should matter.

I had to get a grip already.

Colt scratched my neck gently, probably feeling the tension

in me. "Tell me why it's bad to have scars, baby. You've seen mine."

I had. I'd seen them, felt them. All across his left hip.

"Will you tell me how you got them sometime?" I asked, turning on his lap so I was sideways across his thighs.

He nodded once. "Sure."

I put one arm around his shoulders and played absently with his ear as I thought about my response. "I think...for me, they show too much. I don't know. I look broken. I don't care about the scars on their own—it's what they reveal. There are some things I don't want people to know without my consent. There's no choice for me. I don't get to decide when I'm okay with telling that story. My ugly skin does it for me."

"Hey." Colt gripped my chin, and I caught Lucas's frown in the corner of my eye. I barely reacted. It was tiring talking about my scars...and whatever. Just whatever. I wanted to forget and move on, though that was another thing the scars prevented me from doing. Always that fucking reminder.

"I think we should change the topic now," I said stiffly.

Colt didn't release my chin. "And I think you do as we say, Kit. Don't test me on this. I don't care where we are, you hear? You won't talk about yourself like that."

I flushed with embarrassment and swallowed audibly. The severity was all in his stare. He didn't get worked up for no reason in these situations. He'd just shown he had no problem taking things a step further if he felt the need.

"I get it." This was still a sore topic for me, and it prevented me from using my manners. If he wanted a sweeter or more respectful reply, he'd have to wait.

He finally let go of my chin. "You're angry with me."

"No, I'm annoyed, and I don't want to talk about this here." I tensed up further and made a move to get off his lap.

He didn't allow that, and he only tightened an arm around

me. His stare was so frustratingly unnerving. "I think I'm gonna have to push you until you quit holdin' back so much."

"Oh, here we go," Lucas muttered.

I scowled. "I'm not holding back. I just told you I'm annoyed."

The bastard smiled. "Annoyed won't break down any walls, baby. But we'll save that for another day."

Fucking great.

We were shown to a table somewhere in the middle of the restaurant, and the menu was a good place to hide while I regained my composure. I ordered a Coca-Cola with lots of ice, my favorite, but took more time to decide on my meal.

I didn't know if I was angry with myself or with Colt, perhaps a little bit of both; either way, it was messing with my appetite.

Tapas, tapas, tapas... I scanned the menu. Two pages of options. I was fucking up this relationship already, wasn't I? I didn't know how to stop it. I was sensitive about my issues and didn't know how to hide them. Chorizo, sure, I'd go with that. Lucas recommended I pick four items to get a full meal. I nodded in thanks and never looked away from the binder. Was Colt staring at me? The tension was back. Or maybe it hadn't left. God, I was uncomfortable. The olives and artichokes were probably good...

Ugh.

Our drinks arrived, and I thanked the lady for my Coke and placed it right in front of me so I could take sips while settling on what to eat. Mashed potatoes with garlic butter and herbs sounded nice, though I'd been to Spain and never, ever found that on a menu at a tapas bar.

I chewed on my straw in between slow pulls and figured the stuffed peppers would make a decent addition.

"Have you decided, dear?" Lucas asked. "We could always get a platter, otherwise."

I angled myself closer to him and showed the items on the menu. "Is that one good?" I pointed to the chorizo.

"It's one of Colt's favorites," he replied.

Blah. Colt, Colt, Colt.

The server came back, and I ordered four dishes when it was my turn, but I skipped the chorizo and went with the spicy sliders.

"So, they want me at Langley at the end of October," Colt said.

"Oh?" Lucas gave him all his attention.

I did too, but I didn't want it to show. I was still in a mood.

"It's just a training mission," Colt went on like it was no big deal. "They want me as one of the aggressors."

Oh my God. I pinned my stare to a spot on the table and struggled to keep it there. Fuck, was he doing this on purpose? He knew I would have questions! Aggressor meant he'd be the enemy; he'd be the one the other pilots tried to chase down! Oh my God. That was so cool. Back in the day, we actually had trained Aggressor squadrons. Their job was to make our pilots sharper.

"Your favorite," Lucas said, amused. "You're still undefeated, aren't you?"

"I mean...pretty much." Colt leaned back in his seat and took a swig of his beer. I kept him in my periphery. "If you've singlehandedly taken care of four Flankers, you can't let a bunch of cadets outta Laughlin beat you."

My gaze shot up. "You did *not*."

Colt tilted his head at me, a lazy smirk playing on his lips. "I didn't what?"

"You didn't singlehandedly take care of four Flankers in an F-16," I stated confidently. Christ, I had limits, and even a pilot couldn't spew out whatever the hell he wanted.

"Were you there?" He raised a brow.

I faltered, struck by a moment of uncertainty, but then...no. I wasn't particularly fond of Russian aircraft—perhaps it was the stubborn patriot in me—but I'd be an idiot if I didn't acknowledge that plane's superiority over our F-16.

"Our F-16 fleet doesn't even have AESA installed," I said, referring to a certain radar that some newer multirole fighter jets had. "You can't compare..." I trailed off when I realized what Colt was doing.

His grin confirmed it. He'd just said all that to get me to talk.

Bastard!

I gnashed my teeth and tightened my hold on the napkin in my lap.

Colt leaned forward and rested his forearms on the table. "It was two MiGs."

Jesus, that was impressive. And somewhat believable. "I'm still mad at you."

"Yeah? I guess you won't be interested in visiting me on base, then."

A whimper bubbled up, and it took all my strength to push it down again. Fuck! If my napkin hadn't been made of linen, I would've torn it to shreds by now.

"Oh, take pity on the poor boy," Lucas said. "No more torture. Tell him the MiG story instead."

I chewed on my bottom lip and glanced hesitantly at Colt. I would like to hear the story very much.

Colt smiled and scratched his scruffy chin on his shoulder. "If you want the story, all you gotta do is ask."

I let out a breath. He'd already got me talking, damn Sadist, so I supposed I could swallow some pride and keep going. "How did you take care of two MiGs on your own?"

"Oh, funny story." He grinned. "So, we're providing air support for a ship off the coast of Iraq when I see two bogeys comin' in fast on my radar." That was how quickly he sucked me into the story. "It's not my first rodeo with one, so I ain't pissin' my pants. But when you haven't encountered a MiG before...I mean, it's got a notorious reputation. And next to my Viper, it's big in size too."

I nodded along, understanding. "You had a wingman, right?"

"Right, and it was his first tour. His first encounter."

I winced in sympathy, fully aware that I would be his worst wingman too, and took a gulp of my soda.

"He panics when we don't get our orders right away," Colt continued. "I figure, it's up to me. I decide to lure them off by flying like I'm just outta flight trainin'. I make myself an easy target and get the bandits away from Brian, but most importantly, away from the ship."

My heart started hammering. How many nights had I spent reading these stories from pilots? They were my crack.

"Now, the pros." Colt ticked them off on his fingers. "I'm better at high-speed, I have greater visibility, and while the MiG is feeding two thirsty engines, I'm only feeding one, and we carry about the same amount of fuel. Lastly, I'm an aggressive pilot." He paused. "Given that they were hostile, I knew what I thought was the smartest move. And as soon as I received the go, I gained altitude, did a maneuver, and flew past right between them. Then when I came back and they were trying to reposition to follow, I locked on target and launched a missile."

"Holy shit," I whispered with my straw in my mouth. "Then what happened?"

"So, one pilot punched out—and one to go." He was

enjoying how enthralled I was. "The other pilot was more experienced. He wouldn't take my bait to go faster, because he knew he had the advantage in low-speed. Technically, he had more options to take me down than I had to take him down. But... well, I'm me."

Lucas smiled and shook his head.

"I dragged him farther out to sea," Colt said. "Remember what I said about the fuel?" I nodded. He lifted a shoulder. "He refused to let me get behind him—I admit, he was good. But sooner or later, he was going to run out of fuel, and he'd do it much faster than me. And that became his downfall. Had he not pissed me off royally—and had I not been given the order—maybe I would've let him go when he had to turn back to where he came from."

"But you didn't," I said quietly. "You shot him down."

He inclined his head. "The MiG's restin' at the bottom of the sea, and the pilot got a nice swim with his friend while waiting for rescue."

I had to see Colt fly. I had to. He was... I mean, Jesus! I had to see him.

"That's amazing," I said, clearing my throat. "I can't...just wow."

"Wow was not what I said when I had to hear about this on the news," Lucas drawled. "Thank God it was your last deployment."

Colt reached across the table and put his hand on Lucas's.

"How many deployments has he been on while you've been together?" I asked Lucas.

"Three," he answered. "The first one was right after we met —also the longest one. The other two were four-month-long stints, one in Afghanistan and then his last one in Iraq."

Colt picked up Lucas's hand and kissed his knuckles.

"These days, we go to war together, and our enemy consists of two nieces. We each have one, and they have us wrapped."

I smiled.

Lucas chuckled softly. "Very true."

I didn't know why they didn't have mashed potatoes with garlic at tapas bars in Spain. This shit was fucking amazing.

"Don't eat too fast, sweetheart," Lucas cautioned. "You'll get a stomachache."

"But this is so good," I mumbled around a mouthful. It was practically swimming in butter.

Colt handed me another napkin when I got some butter on my chin. "You know what would slow you down a bit? If you took us through your homework."

Crap. "Okay." I wiped my mouth and dug out the folded piece of paper from my pocket. On Sunday, they'd told me to come up with three things to complete before next weekend. Three things that would begin the process of breaking some patterns that didn't make me happy. Or held me back in one way or another. "One, I'm gonna retire ten white shirts and replace them with other clothes. T-shirts, long-sleeved tees, etcetera."

Lucas's eyes flashed with a bit of mirth. "Ten? You're allowed to keep a few, you know."

"I have thirty-one," I replied frankly.

Colt coughed on whatever he was chewing, and he reached for his beer.

Lucas grinned faintly and gave my leg a squeeze under the table. "Why don't you go on to the next item on your list?"

All righty. "Number two," I said, reading off the note, "I am going to take over laundry duty at home."

"That's a bold one, dear," Lucas chuckled. "I don't let Colt do ours. He's ruined too many of my shirts."

"I fold fitted sheets like a fuckin' king," Colt retorted. "That's enough."

Lucas didn't argue with that.

His hand traveled farther up my leg as I read number three.

"I'm going to increase my activity in our online community again."

Lucas was quick to respond. "I think that's an excellent goal. Clearly, you read what's on there, but you haven't left a mark in years."

True. My profile was a ghost town. Something I scanned through every once in a while to see how confident I used to be. Okay, not confident, but nothing like I was now. I used to have a backbone and a voice I wasn't too shy to use.

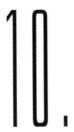

10.

I had a stomachache.

I should not have ordered a second serving of the mashed potatoes.

Lucas had warned me, but...

"Does anything catch your interest?" he asked me.

I was pretending to read the dessert menu.

"I, um...I'm not sure..." I shifted carefully in my seat and withheld a wince. It felt like someone was stabbing me in the stomach. "I suppose I am kind of full."

Lucas took on an expression of concern. "Is everything all right? You look a bit pale."

I took a short breath and nodded once. "Yes, Sir. I'm just full."

Full of five tapas dishes and three big glasses of Coke. Heavens, this was agony.

Colt leaned forward in his seat, and he was watching me pensively. "Remember we talked about honesty, Kit?"

Fuck.

I swallowed hard and dropped my gaze, and the increasing pain was ripping my composure away from me. It hurt so much that a cold sweat broke out across my forehead.

"I didn't mean to ruin the date," I mumbled, putting down

the menu. "I'm sorry." Why did I have to ruin everything? I'd already crossed a line earlier when I got grouchy with Colt. *Ouch.* I flinched at a particularly sharp stab, and I discreetly wrapped my arms around my middle.

"Sweetheart, you're in pain." Lucas leaned over and felt my forehead. "Why didn't you say something?" He turned to Colt. "Can you take care of the check? I'll bring Kit outside for some fresh air."

Colt nodded and looked out over the restaurant, presumably to flag down our server, and Lucas got out of his seat.

"We can address the nonsense about you supposedly ruining our date later," Lucas said, extending a hand. "Come here."

I was too weak to argue. I let him guide me through the restaurant, but holding his hand stopped being enough. By the time we reached the sidewalk, I was clutching his arm and had my eyes screwed shut.

"My stomach hurts, Daddy," I whimpered.

"I know, little one. I know." He found us a somewhat secluded spot next to the building and carefully hugged me to him. "Our hotel is not far from here. You know what I suggest?"

I sniffled and shook my head.

"A long night of cuddles and watching movies in bed. How does that sound?"

Tears spilled over as the last of my self-control disappeared from me. "I-I want that," I cried. "But I didn't bring a toothbrush."

He chuckled softly and pressed his lips to my hair. "I think we can work something out."

I sniffled again and wiped at my eyes. "I'm sorry I didn't listen to you earlier."

"It's okay, dear. I fear you're paying for it now." He slipped a hand between us and unbuttoned the top button of my pants.

And that small thing brought me so much relief. "I've discovered you eat with your eyes more than usual. Do you never go out to restaurants?"

I half shrugged and shook my head. He'd probably noticed that when we went out for ice cream too. The way I picked too many toppings, how I ate—I ate fast when it was really good—and that I didn't quite know when to stop.

I'd gotten a brain freeze four times.

I decided it was best to go with a joke at my own expense. "I guess I'm too excited to finally have a life."

Lucas didn't laugh. He caressed my stomach under my shirt and hummed against the top of my head.

They said it was only a five-minute walk to their hotel, but it was excruciating nonetheless. I had to walk so slowly, and the pain kept growing, that I contemplated calling Vincent.

Colt glanced back at me at one point and furrowed his brow. "You're hidin' again. Why do you feel the need to keep your wits about yourself?"

I don't want to be a burden.

"I'm not a child," I mumbled.

He snorted and turned to stand in front of me. "That's the beauty of being kinky adults, baby boy. We can pretend to be whatever the fuck we want. Come here." He picked me up right then and there, his hands under my armpits, like I weighed nothing. I squeaked and clung to him, wrapping my legs around his middle, and then he literally carried me like one would carry a toddler. I sat on his hip.

"People can see us," I hissed.

"I don't fuckin' care," he whispered back. "Let us take care of you. It ain't like we're tearin' up your ass in the street."

I turned a wide-eyed look to Lucas.

He offered a slight shrug. "He has a point, Kit. You're in pain. You don't have to force yourself to handle it on your own."

I huffed, only to be interrupted by a crippling amount of pain, and then I put my tail between my legs and buried my face against Colt's neck.

"I like this." Colt smacked a *mwah* kiss to the side of my head and placed one hand right on my ass. "I haven't been your size since I was eleven. You're what, five-six?"

"Five-seven, I'll have you know," I grumbled uncomfortably. He made me flush, and more than that, he was pushing hard at my mind-set. He made me feel smaller, and it wasn't bad... It was just different. So different.

"Five-seven and a hundred pounds soaking wet," he chuckled. "But hey, we can't all be six-five behemoths like me."

I was way more than a hundred pounds—close to 150, actually—and as soon as my stomach wasn't dying, I would show him.

"Six-four, you bullshitter," Lucas said with a snort.

"Dammit. I forgot you knew," Colt said. "Six-five just sounds so good."

"I think you won the genetic lottery enough, baby."

Did Colt ever break a sweat? All the way to the hotel, he carried me that way with only one hand under my ass to keep me in place.

I kept my face hidden as we crossed the hotel lobby toward the elevators. It was a little embarrassing, to be honest. Yet, I was feeling too clingy to let go.

The clinginess stayed with me throughout most of the night. In a hotel room mostly made up of one huge bed and four big pieces of luggage, Colt and Lucas told me there was no space for pride. One second, I could be snuggled up in between them, only for one of them to wait outside the bathroom when I was being tortured from within the next. They wouldn't freaking budge.

"We'll take all your moods, sweetheart," Lucas said one time when I was complaining.

"You can bitch all you want. I ain't leavin'," Colt said another.

Around four in the morning, I had no energy left. The pain had thankfully dissipated, but my body was sore and I felt weak as hell.

Not to mention guilty. Lucas had told me he was staying home from work tomorrow—or technically today—and I knew it was because he'd barely slept. He'd stayed up and rubbed my stomach and cuddled and watched three movies with me.

Colt had gotten a couple more hours, though not nearly enough.

Because of me.

I left the night-light on as I climbed into bed a last time. Hopefully.

"I'm glad you're feeling better." Lucas gathered me in his arms and hiked my leg over his hip. "I might kidnap you and keep you with me all day tomorrow."

I smiled sleepily, but I was still troubled. "Are you sure I'm not being too much?"

"You couldn't possibly." He cupped my cheek and pressed a kiss to my forehead. "Colt and I have dreamed of having someone to take care of, Kit. Then you come along, and you're so much better than the dream. I don't think you fully grasp how happy you make us. Especially when you let down your guard and let us take over." I searched his eyes. How could a man be so kind? What had I done to deserve this? "We notice how you try to stay in control," he murmured. "Our relationship is very new, so it's completely understandable. But know that what we ultimately aim for is you surrendering that composure and leaving things to us. That's how we want you. That's how we want to make you happy. So you can be the little boy you identify with whenever you feel like it. We'll be there for you."

My vision became blurry as I let his words settle. The concept of letting go was foreign to me these days, and evidently, I clung to that composure harder than I'd thought.

In my head, the way I reasoned, it was because I didn't want to be a chore. I didn't want to add a burden to their already stressful lives. Lucas ran a marketing firm and had four employees, and Colt was in the middle of starting his own security business. Plus, they had friends and family, and I came into the picture...

They've been looking for you.

I bit my lip and met Lucas's gaze again. "Letting go these past four years hasn't been an option. Every day, I think about how easy it would be to give up. No one would miss me anyway. Because that's the thing. Letting go even for a second would break me. There's no pause button. There's play, and there's stop. If I don't keep moving—if I don't..." I let out a ragged breath, my chest tightening. "I can't allow myself to break, Lucas."

"You speak in present tense. Letting go doesn't have that meaning with us, sweetheart. We *want* you to break. We want you to let go. That's when you can get to know the little boy trapped inside of you. And he can push play, stop, and pause whenever he wants to, because he'll know we're here for him." He brushed his thumb over my cheek when I sniffled. It felt like my heart was going to explode. My breathing turned shallow, and I couldn't hold back the tears. For the second time tonight. "We have all the patience, Kit. Don't force anything. We'll earn your trust in time. And while we wait, we will soak up every glimpse we get of that giggly little darling we met last Saturday."

I let out a small laugh and wiped away my stupid tears. "That's still me, Daddy."

"I know, and you're fucking wonderful." He smiled and kissed my nose. "You'll see. Daddy's always right, and you're stuck with two of us. Good luck with that."

I grinned and chuckled and cried and cuddled up against him, the utter mess that I was.

"I heard what you said to Kit earlier."

Colt's quiet words roused me from sleep, and I lifted my heavy head off the pillow and blinked drowsily. The room was still pretty dark, and I couldn't see anyone. Then I realized they were in the tiny hallway, which was out of my view.

I must've missed something. I heard Lucas chuckle softly, and I heard them kissing.

"I'm serious," Colt murmured. "Eight years together, and I find new ways to fall in love with you every day. I love seeing you as a Daddy."

I was filled with the warm fuzzies, and my head landed on the pillow again.

I'd heard Lucas sigh before, but this one, the one he let out now, was all adoration and affection.

"Ditto, baby." There was more kissing. "It's like coming home, isn't it?"

"Yeah."

"Okay, you go to work. See if you can get off early. If I'm still with Kit, we'll ask him about Norfolk."

"Mmm, make sure you're with him, then. See you later."

Norfolk? Oh, yesss! His parents lived there, and it was close to where Langley Air Force Base was! I definitely wanted to visit Colt when he flew an F-16!

The next time I woke up, I was in Lucas's arms, and he was kissing my shoulder.

I yawned and snuggled closer, hoping to find him hard. I—Jesus, I wasn't disappointed. I hummed and wrapped my fingers around his cock as much as I could. He was all warm and smooth and perfect.

"As tempting as you are right now, we should get some breakfast in you." He gripped my chin and planted a firm kiss on my lips. "We will revisit me using your cute little body for my pleasure after we've eaten."

I whined. "But I want you *now*..."

"Patience, young boy." He pecked my nose before slipping out of bed, leaving me all lonely and horny. He stepped into a pair of dress pants and reached for an undershirt. "We don't say no to free breakfast, which they stop serving in twenty minutes."

I sulked. "I'm not hungry." Okay, that was a lie. I was just hungrier for my Daddy. A Daddy who looked good enough to eat while he shrugged on a shirt and buttoned it up. It was his fingers. His long piano fingers. They did it.

"I don't believe you. Come on, up you go."

Fiiine.

I was not at all happy about the idea of putting on my clothes from last night, so when Lucas offered me a pair of his basketball shorts and a T-shirt, I didn't think twice. Within a couple of minutes, we left their hotel room and took the elevator down to the ground floor.

I yawned and struggled to keep my eyes open.

"May I take a bath after breakfast?" I wondered. "Your

bathtub is so deep." I loved deep tubs. I used to have one, but my mom thought it was unsafe.

"Of course." He squeezed my hand. "Anything to keep you here longer."

I smiled bashfully and hugged his arm. "I don't have plans."

"Even better." He winked at me, then opened the door to the breakfast area.

There were fewer people than I expected. Stragglers, I supposed, at this hour. The hotel had a business feel, and I guessed most businessmen who were in town for work ate early if they ate here at all.

"Oh! They have a waffle station." I pointed.

"Mmhmm." He rumbled a chuckle and pressed a kiss to my temple. "I think you'll have some yogurt and toast before you dive into the waffles. The whole-grain toast."

Whoa. I looked up at him in disbelief. "That's the brown toast."

"I know. Can you imagine?" He widened his eyes at the mock horror he felt the need to subject me to. "People actually eat that. *I* eat that."

"I've eaten it all my life," I exclaimed, following him reluctantly to the toasters. "I thought the point was for me to try things I actually like now."

"Absolutely, dear, in moderation." He lifted a brow to put emphasis on that last horrible word. "A healthy breakfast is a good start to your day."

It was also boring, but whatever.

We sat down with our gross whole-grain toast, yogurt, and some fruit Lucas had selected.

"I can't believe I forgot my coffee," he muttered, and he made a move to stand up.

I rose instead. "I'll get it. How do you like it?"

He smiled. "Thank you. Just some Splenda will be great."

"Yes, Sir." I made my way over to the coffee machine and watched in envy while some guy in a suit made himself two waffles. *Hmpf.* I poured myself a glass of juice, not in the mood for coffee, and returned to our table when I had everything.

Lucas had grabbed a copy of the *Washington Post* and put on a pair of reading glasses.

Holy fuck, did he look sexy in those glasses.

"I didn't know you wore glasses."

He glanced up from the front page, and he nodded in thanks for the coffee. "I didn't always. Then I woke up one morning and found myself squinting when I read the paper. I'd also gained four pounds, so Colt told me to quit putting regular sugar in my coffee." He smirked ruefully. "That's what turning thirty-five did to me."

I snickered and bit into my toast. *Oh, yuck.*

11.

I loved, loved, loved this bathtub. The water came up almost to my shoulders! And Lucas had one of those suction stands for his iPad so I could watch a movie in the water. It was the *best*. I'd put on one of my favorite comedies, *Anchorman*.

My laughter echoed as I watched the scene where Will Ferrell screamed inside a phone booth.

Lucas appeared in the doorway with an amused expression. "It's lovely hearing your laugh, little one. Are you enjoying your bath?"

I nodded a lot. "So much. And look." I gathered some bubbles and put them on my face like a beard.

Lucas grinned and came into the bathroom, and he sat down on the edge of the tub. "You are too cute for words. Can I see your fingers?"

I showed them to him. "Only a little pruny."

"Only a little," he agreed. He folded up the sleeves of his shirt. "Hand me that shampoo bottle, will you?"

"Yes, Sir." I scrunched my nose as he poured shampoo in his palm. "I don't have to get out yet, do I?"

"No, not yet. I'm just done doing the work I can from here, and I want to take care of my boy."

Oh. I guess he could do that. I grinned goofily. "If I get you wet, you'll have to join me. Then we could take care of each other."

He laughed quietly and started massaging the shampoo into my hair, and it felt...so...fucking...good. I moaned and closed my eyes.

"Please, Daddy? We can wash each other."

He hummed. "You'd like that?"

"Yes."

"Let me do this first. I love touching you."

He was making that abundantly clear. He took his time massaging my scalp, and when he decided my hair was done, he dipped his hands into the water and slid them up between my legs.

"Daddy has to get the suds off his hands," he murmured huskily.

I swallowed hard, a ball of lust dropping heavily into my stomach, and I opened my eyes. He ordered me to lean back and pull my knees up a bit. Jesus Christ. I shivered when his long fingers brushed over my balls.

"Nope. Stand up for me instead," he said and cleared his throat. "I need to see you."

I faltered and grabbed my cock under the surface. "But I'm getting hard, Daddy."

"That's perfectly fine, dear. It happens."

While I obeyed, he quickly dried his hands and removed the iPad. Then I just stood there, rivulets of water washing away most of the bubbles.

For a moment, he merely watched me. Hands in the pockets of his pants. I could see a bulge forming, and I wanted it. He made me even harder, and he didn't do anything!

"Do you want to know one of the reasons Colt and I want you to surrender everything to us?"

I nodded hesitantly.

He took a step closer and reached for the body wash. "Because you forget your insecurities," he murmured. "You did it at breakfast. You wore a tee that displayed all these cool tattoos, and I'm not sure you gave that a single thought."

Holy crap, I hadn't.

I exhaled shakily at the revelation, and Lucas began soaping me up in unhurried strokes. Up and down my ink-covered chest, over my shoulders, down my arms... And no more words were said for a long time. He rubbed my cock firmly, burying it under a thick layer of suds. My breathing became ragged. He was fucking milking me, and it was driving me insane. I couldn't stop the whimper.

When he wanted me to turn around, he twirled a finger. I complied instantly, and he guided one of my hands to the wall. I took the hint and placed the other one there too, and then he drew two fingers along my spine. More pressure as he got lower, silently telling me to arch for him.

I swallowed dryly. He turned me on beyond words.

"Such a smooth, soft, perfect little boy." He ran a hand over one of my butt cheeks. Next, one finger slipped between and circled my hole. "Do you like it when Daddy washes you?"

I nodded quickly. "Yes, Daddy. I like it lots."

"Mmm..." He pushed the tip of his finger inside, and my knees nearly buckled. "Colt would've loved to see this."

I couldn't dig my fingers into the tiles, no matter how hard I tried. And the thought of Colt watching us... Maybe he'd stand in the doorway first. Maybe stroke his big cock while Lucas played with me. Oh *God*...

The iPad.

I gulped at the idea. Could I be that gutsy?

Lucas fingered me deeper. He rubbed me all over, then settled for finger-fucking me and stroking my cock at the same time. I was losing my goddamn mind. I just needed. I needed, needed, needed.

"We can film ourselves," I gasped.

Lucas slowed down.

All I heard was our heavy breathing.

Then, Lucas stepped over to the double sink and washed the body wash off his hands. He was going to do it, I could tell. I couldn't believe this was happening, and I couldn't wait. I wanted it. I was so far gone. Crazed with lust.

He set up the iPad so it would capture everything that happened in the bathtub. It was propped between the two sinks. Lucas checked the screen once more before joining me, and he commanded me in a quiet voice to turn on the shower head.

Was the camera on? It was, wasn't it?

After grabbing the shower head from me, Lucas ran the hot water over my ass first. His free hand never left my body. He spread my cheeks and aimed the streams of water right over my opening, and I let out a breathless groan. My head fell forward. My heart thundered. My cock was rock solid.

"Please, Daddy," I begged. I arched more for him, wanting his thick cock to just take me. Take me hard. Fucking do it. He was making desperate.

"I love it when you're so greedy." He rubbed a finger along the crease, then spread the cheeks farther apart. So the camera could catch it, I realized. "I'm not sure you're ready for Daddy's cock, though."

"I am, I promise," I whimpered.

For several seconds, he literally fucked me with the water stream. It was on the sharpest setting, and I felt the water entering me. Hot water, so hot, so good.

"Soon." He switched the setting and ran the shower head farther up. "What an exquisite boy we have. Turn around for us, Kit."

Us.

I turned around on shaky legs and no longer cared in what state they saw me. Let them see how needy I was. Let them see it all.

Lucas lifted the shower head and murmured, "Close your eyes." And we waited for the shampoo to disappear down the drain. All the suds. "Hold this while I go get something."

Finally. He was getting the lube, I hoped. In the meantime, I showered off the remnants of the shampoo, and I...I may have touched myself a little. I couldn't help it. My hand was glued to my cock, and I rubbed it fast until I heard Daddy coming back.

He set down the lube on the edge of the tub.

I'd gotten him wet. His light-blue shirt showed where the shower had sprayed him. I was ready to jump him. Instead, I had to pretend I was patient. I waited. And I waited. He was in charge of the shower head again, and *he* had patience. Too much of it.

Once he lowered the stream, I pushed back my hair and glanced into the camera. Hell, I didn't know who was the most sadistic of the two at this point.

Lucas made me lift my arms so he could get my armpits too, his hand always following. Washing and touching every inch of me. He pinched my nipples, and I went for my cock. I *had* to do something.

"So desperate," he muttered. He flicked the top of my hand, and it actually stung. I yelped and pulled it away to cradle it to my chest.

"Meanie," I complained.

"You ask for permission to touch yourself when we play. Are we clear?"

Crap. "Yes, Daddy," I answered sullenly.

"Good." He cupped his hand over the head of my cock and twisted it on the downstroke, and that was the end of me. I quit.

I gave up. I had no self-control left, so I leaned forward and kissed him. "*Umph.*"

Scratch that, I threw myself at him.

I got him wet. The shower head landed in the tub like a wild snake, and I didn't give a shit.

Neither did he, though. Daddy surrendered as well, and he groaned lustfully into our messy, hungry kiss. We were making out like animals, and while he groped my butt, I started unbuttoning his shirt. He pushed two fingers inside me, which he shouldn't have done. I think I stopped being human. I fisted his shirt and pulled him into the tub with me.

"Look at the mess we're making, boy." He pressed me up against the wall and kissed me hard, all while pushing his shirt off of his shoulders. "Do you need my cock that badly?"

I couldn't speak. I nodded furiously and sank to my knees in the water. Once there, I got to work on his pants.

"Can I taste you in my mouth, Daddy? Please?"

He groaned and scrubbed at his face. "Since you asked so nicely."

Excitement tore through me, and I didn't even bother pushing his pants down past his hips.

He managed to shut off the shower.

I sucked him into my mouth. I coated him with my tongue, and I looked up at him. And I felt my eyes light up as a spurt of pre-come hit the roof of my mouth. Then I sucked harder, wanting more of his come.

"Jesus Christ," he whispered hoarsely. "That's a good boy. You know how to make Daddy happy."

If only he didn't make me stop so soon... It felt like just a few seconds had passed when he ordered me to stop and to pull down his pants.

"I want you to ride me." He hauled me to my feet as soon as his pants were pooling in the water, and then he took my place.

He eased down into the water and extended a hand for me. "Get the lube too."

I grabbed it for him, and he told me to move closer to his face. Oh God, so close. My cock was right there, but all he did was kiss my thigh. He was more focused on slicking up his fingers.

"Please, Daddy?" I asked, hopeful.

"What do you want? Ask me." He slipped one finger inside me.

I flushed bright red. "You know," I whispered.

Lucas's eyes flashed with predatory decadence. "There he is. That sweet little angel of ours. Ask Daddy for what you want."

I mewled at the pleasure of his fingers. Two now, with a third pushing right at the opening. "Like I did with you..."

"Mmm, what did you do?"

I gasped as he forced in a third finger all the way. "Oh God —I sucked on your cock, Daddy," I moaned. "Can you do that to me also?"

"Close enough." He dropped an openmouthed kiss at the base of my cock and licked the entire length. "Is this what you want?"

I held my breath and nodded quickly.

The sensations washing over me when he slowly took me into his mouth were almost too much to handle. So wet, so warm, so perfectly tight. I slid my fingers into his hair and thrust cautiously. It earned me a hum of approval, and it didn't take long before we found the most seductive rhythm. I fucked his mouth, he fingered my ass, I rolled my hips, he took me even deeper. All of me. And swirled his tongue around me. I choked on a breath and thought for a second I was going to come.

Perhaps he noticed it too, and that was why he eased out.

"You're ready, little boy." He licked around my head and stroked my thighs soothingly. "Daddy's cock is waiting for you."

He helped me down so I could straddle his lap.

"Look at me."

I looked at him. I sucked in a breath and held his gaze as he positioned himself at my hole and pushed slightly. The sting flared and morphed into a fire the more he pushed. Inch by inch, slowly filling me with his thick cock.

A gulp became a low sob when I'd taken all of him.

"Shh, baby, I've got you," he murmured. "We'll take our time, yeah? I know it hurts."

"You're so big, Daddy," I whimpered.

He hugged me to him, pressed light kisses to my skin, and massaged my softening cock. It was the greatest conflict my brain had known, being torn between pain and pleasure like this.

It did something to me.

"That's it," he whispered comfortingly. "That's my good boy. Keep relaxing for me."

I took a breath and let it out slowly, getting adjusted to his size. I felt oddly shy and vulnerable, but at the same time, needier than ever. And not afraid to latch on to him like a Band-Aid.

"Fuck," he said, letting out a heavy breath. "Look at your beautiful cock, darling."

I unburied myself from the crook of his neck and looked down between us. "I'm getting hard again, Daddy. That means I like it when you're in my bottom, right?"

"That's exactly what it means." He smiled and kissed me softly. "You're a smart boy, aren't you?"

I blushed and shrugged, and I looked down again. He stroked me from base to tip and swiped his thumb over the slit, and it made me shudder.

I wanted more.

Taking it oh, so carefully, I shifted back a few inches and drew in a sharp breath. *Oh, fucking hell.* Both pain and pleasure exploded inside me, and I pushed forward again. Then again and again and again. It hurt so goddamn much, yet I couldn't stop chasing the intense rush of euphoria.

"Perfect," Daddy muttered breathlessly. "Just like that. Fuck—you feel so good."

"Daddy, I can't stop," I gasped, going faster and faster. "*Owww.*"

"Don't stop. I'm getting close."

Despite the burning hurt, I rode my Daddy's cock for all I was worth, scratching an itch that demanded more and more. With my hands behind me, planted firmly on his thighs, I slid back and forward as quickly as I could and let my head fall back.

Daddy cursed through a moan, one of his hands roaming my chest while the other stroked me off.

"Come, darling. Let me see you come all over us."

I cried out, unable to hold back, and felt the orgasm roll in heavily. It swept me away in crushing waves, and it made Daddy come too. He grunted and pushed me down on him as he let go. Oh God. I felt him inside me, impossibly thick and pulsing, filling my little hole with his release.

Holy smokes, I was going to need a nap.

No, no, why did he roll me over? I'd finally found a position that didn't kill me.

"Oww, Daddy..." I hugged my pillow tighter, burying my face in it.

"I'm sorry, baby, but I gotta make sure I didn't tear anythin'."

Colt pulled down my bottoms and carefully spread my butt cheeks. "Hmm. Definitely red, but I don't think you'll be out of commission very long." He brushed a finger over my sensitive butt, and I tried not to squirm. "Gimme that lotion on the night-stand, will ya, darlin'?"

I assumed Lucas handed him the lotion.

"This will make you feel better, I promise," Colt murmured.

I lay absolutely still as he opened the bottle.

There was nothing positive to say about this type of physical pain, but even so...how he'd made me feel earlier when he came back from work... I had no words. Lucas and I had sent him that very lengthy video of our playtime in the bath, and Colt had come home on a mission. He'd barely spoken a word. He'd grabbed me, manhandled me into position, on the damn floor, and taken me right there in the hallway. My left cheek had rug burns.

"Your cheek is gonna be the color of your safeword by the time I'm done with you, boy."

He hadn't been lying.

I'd never felt so utterly helpless, objectified, little, and desired. My Daddy'd had to have me, so he'd taken me. Simple as that.

I owned that part of him. The part that couldn't control his need for me.

It just happened to come with a price. Immense pain in my butt!

"Guh!" I stiffened as icy cold liquid was spread across my opening.

Colt chuckled quietly. "Relax. It's a cooling gel."

"Yeah, but a heads-up would've been nice," I groaned.

"Where's the fun in that?"

Sadist.

I grumbled into the pillow. Now that I knew what was

happening, I could melt into the mattress and admit that it did feel good. In slow, gentle motions, Colt smeared the cold gel around my entrance. Then he wriggled his pinky inside to get some cream there too. Or, at least, I hoped that was why he did it.

"There. All done. We'll leave the shorts down, though. You have the cutest little ass." Colt landed next to me, and I lifted my head from the pillow to see him placing a hand behind his head. He was enjoying himself, that was for sure. "What a day. I got to see the hottest video ever created, Luke took a bath with his clothes on, and Kit got ass-fucked twice and left a come stain on the floor in the hallway."

I blushed furiously and shot him a weak scowl.

He grinned and touched my cheek. "Adorable."

I huffed.

On the other side of me, Lucas gave up on reading his book and scooted closer to me. The Sadist antidote that he was, he drew his fingers over my back, raising goose bumps in his wake. I purred in pleasure and rested my unscathed cheek on the pillow.

"Lift up a bit, dear." Lucas tried to slip his hand underneath me, so I rose up cautiously. He just wanted to touch my cock, and I liked having it snuggled in his hand. "There is a way to make this day even better."

"Oh?" I yawned.

"Mm." Colt seemed to know what Lucas was talking about. "Kit, you know my folks live in Norfolk, yeah?"

I nodded sleepily. Were they going to ask me to come visit when Colt was down there this fall? It was possible he'd stay with his parents when he had super-cool work stuff to do at Langley.

"Perhaps we should start at the beginning?" Lucas suggested. Maybe he received the go-ahead from Colt, 'cause he went on. "When we were making plans for our renovations, Colt's parents offered us to stay at their place because they won't be there. They're going on a six-week-long cruise around South America." He received a hum from me as he scratched my neck. "But since Norfolk is four hours away, it would mean six weeks off work. So Colt and I ultimately decided to stay in the city."

"Then we met you," Colt murmured.

I cracked one eye open and looked at him quizzically.

He rolled onto his side and kissed my shoulder. "We appreciate you findin' us a temporary place here, but the day we met up at your house, I had a feelin' that Luke and I would want to steal you away pretty fast. Get some time just the three of us to establish a relationship that works for us."

They wanted to go away with me? Holy crap! I couldn't believe my luck. This wasn't happening. It couldn't be. It was unbelievable.

"With some infrequent commuting, we'd like to make it work," Lucas said. "And we haven't taken a proper vacation in over two years..."

I pushed away my pillow so I could face them better. "We'd go to Norfolk soon, in that case?" They weren't talking about this fall at all.

Lucas nodded. "Colt's starting to go stir-crazy in this hotel room."

Fuck. I bit my bottom lip, thinking about Abel. "My friend from Washington comes to visit in a couple weeks. He's bringing his Daddy. They'll be here for like a week."

"Oh." Colt's forehead creased, and he smiled faintly. "We can save Norfolk for another time. Tell us about your friend."

But...but we could still get time together, right? "Why can't you stay at my house? It's not like I don't have space, and I really, really, really, *really* want to be closer to you."

They both hesitated.

I had to plead my case. "Please? We can have sleepovers in my room every night! And sit by the pool and barbecue and cuddle and be together. My TV is better than the one you have here too, and you wouldn't go stir-crazy over there. There are three guest rooms." If we included my parents' bedroom. "Please, please, please, please? Plus, I have my dermatology treatments on Mondays that I shouldn't miss, which..." I made a face. "I haven't taken care of myself the way I should this week. I've missed some mornings."

Lucas was displeased about that last bit. "I wish I'd known, sweetheart. That goes into the daily schedule right away." He glanced over at Colt, sort of in question. "It would be nice to stay together to learn one another's routines better."

Colt dipped his chin. "We'll have to work out a plan, though." He slid his gaze to me, and I could tell he was serious about what he was going to say. "We want you to be comfortable, Kit, but we don't want to tip the scale too much. If we stay at your place, it's your turf. It's the place where you've built up all your walls."

"Valid point," Lucas said with a kiss to my shoulder blade. "And you being who you are, sweetheart—you're more likely to try to be the perfect host instead of our Little whose sole responsibility is to turn to us before anything else."

I could see how that might pose a slight problem, maybe.

"So, what I think we're gonna do," Colt continued, "is that we pretend your house is one of those temporary places on the listings you gave us. While we stay with you, Luke and I will cover everything—don't interrupt."

"But—*gah.*" I so wanted to argue.

"See my point?" He raised a brow. "You need to hand over control to us."

"You can have it anyway!" I couldn't believe we were actually discussing them paying for stuff. It wasn't my decades of hard work that had given me that house. I didn't even have a job —or an education, for that matter.

"It's ingrained in you, baby." He pushed some hair away from my forehead. "You gotta lose the sense of what's yours so you can get into the mind-set of asking your Daddies for permission. That's the deal."

"Hmpf." I wasn't super-happy about this, even though I did see their point. It was just... They'd already done so much for me. On the other hand... "If I agree, you can move in, like, right now? Today? And we can maybe celebrate with pizza?"

Colt rumbled a warm chuckle and leaned in for a kiss. "Correct."

Okay, I agreed.

12.

"**D**addy, look at me now." I reached the very corner of the backyard and took a couple big breaths.

Lucas glanced up from the book he was reading on the sunbed and cocked his head at me. "What are you doing in the bushes?"

"I'm gonna run," I said frankly. And since my backyard wasn't huge, I had to be almost in the hedge in order to gain proper speed for my cool jump into the pool. "Where's Colt? He should see this too."

There was no time for Lucas to respond. An upbeat rock-country song started pouring out from inside the house, and Colt stepped out shortly after.

"Daddy, you gotta see this," I said.

He tightened the drawstrings of his boardshorts and eyed the short distance between me and the pool. "You gonna jump?"

"Yeah."

He squinted out at the end of the backyard, then back to me. "You're gonna trip on the deck. Better you take one of the corners out there."

I glanced down at where the deck started. Maybe he was right. I'd done this a million times before, but before the deck was built. Okay, fine. So I jogged across the yard until I reached the end. The sun shone brightly, and the grass under my feet felt nice. There was no grass around the pool; Dad had had it removed to lay stone. But I liked this little patch in the back. Grass was summer beneath your feet.

"Be careful, sweetheart," Lucas cautioned.

"Yeah, but look," I responded and shifted my foot back. More deep breaths. I was going to impress! After crouching a bit, I sped forward and darted as fast as I could for the pool. Then I shouted, "Geronimo!" and jumped high, doing a wicked cool flip that made my stomach do a somersault before I landed in the water.

Woot! Fucking crushed it!

I resurfaced with a triumphant fist toward the sky and found a grinning Colt right on the edge of the pool. "That's a solid eight, baby."

Lucas looked he'd just survived a roller coaster ride. "Sweet Jesus, you almost gave me a heart attack."

I snickered. An eight, though? I swam over to the edge and squinted up at Colt. "How do I nail a ten?"

"Oh God," Lucas muttered. "So wide open."

Colt laughed at him and turned to me. "You'd have to fuck me to do that."

Wha...? *Oh.* A giggle burst through my lips, and I understood now why Lucas had said wide open.

Colt took a step off the edge, and I turned my head for the splash. When he broke through the surface, all tanned and wet and running a hand over his head, I could only agree with him being a ten. A smoking-hot Daddy ten.

"The use of Geronimo took two points," he said. "Old Army war cries don't belong in this family."

Family. He said family. A warm, fluttering sensation made its way through my chest.

I bit my lip and failed to hide a smirk. "The Air Force was born from the Army, though."

He narrowed his eyes and closed the distance between us. "We don't talk about that, you little trivia barn."

I laughed, and he gathered my legs around his hips. "What if I put it this way," I proposed. "Out of the Army ashes rose a big, strong phoenix, and we named it the Air Force."

He chuckled and planted a kiss on me. "Much better."

I hummed and kissed him deeper, snaking the tip of my tongue around his.

He liked that.

"Do you bottom, by the way?" I asked curiously. I couldn't take my hands off him. Running my fingers up and down his chest, feeling his chest hair, was becoming a favorite of mine.

"Reluctantly." He nipped at my jaw. "Luke's my one and only, but I kinda had to give him my ass on a platter every once in a while so his Top could come out and play too."

"That's very kind of you," I chuckled.

"The shit we do for love, eh?" He looked over at Lucas, then back at me with a crooked grin. "Whenever he came home with a bottle of Jameson, I knew what he needed."

That image was so funny to me, I couldn't help but crack up.

Colt responded by dunking me under the water.

While I coughed and spluttered through the giggles, he hugged me closer and blew raspberries on my face.

I locked my arms around his neck and licked his cheek.

He grinned and shook his head.

"I've never topped," I admitted.

That was a surprise to him. "Ever? I'll be damned."

I shrugged. "Can't say I'm super curious about it."

"Hmm. But a little?"

Well... There was no forgetting the time Colt told me Lucas

would want me to take him sometimes... Since then, the fantasy had visited me quite a bit.

I was sure my blush gave me away.

Hunger darkened his eyes. "I'll tell Luke to make sure I'm there to watch the first time he wants our little boy to fuck him."

Hnngh. Lust coursed through me, and I ducked my head to his neck. "I'm getting horny just thinking about it, Daddy. Will you help me if I need it?"

"Of course, baby." He kissed my shoulder. "Do you want somethin' now before I start dinner?"

I nodded a lot. "I think that's best. I want you in my mouth. It's been way too long, if you think about it."

He chuckled huskily and moved us toward the ladder. "Trust, Daddy thinks about that a whole lot."

Me too!

Could one fall in love with a moment? If so, I was in love.

We hadn't lost our swimwear, but we'd moved our little party to the kitchen where Colt was cooking, and Lucas and I sat at the kitchen island with our laptops. At first, it'd only been Lucas with his laptop, and it'd looked so adult and sexy that I'd fetched my laptop too. I wanted to be like my Daddy and do important stuff.

He was going through emails, it appeared, and he was wearing his hot glasses.

I was shopping for T-shirts online.

"How do I skip this depressin' fuckin' song?" Colt asked.

"This is country, love," Lucas drawled.

"No, it's a depressing country song," Colt argued.

I snickered. "Alexa, skip."

Alexa changed to the next song.

"Goddamn smart homes," Colt muttered. "Never thought I'd live to see the day we had gadgets—with *names*—that we talked to. In my opinion, the only place we want advanced technology is in the military."

That sounded mildly terrifying.

"He wouldn't let me install an Alexa at home," Lucas told me. "That was two years ago. Maybe he's warmed up to—"

"No, I haven't," Colt said.

"We'll discuss it," Lucas replied. "It's a convenient way to keep reminders."

"That's the only reason Rosa agreed to one," I said. "Vincent wanted it for my appointments." These days, though, I was sure Rosa used the device the most. Vincent had helped her program a Spanish-language radio station she liked, and she'd listen to it while cleaning and cooking.

Colt turned away from the stove to face us, and he furrowed his brow. "I forgot about them. Is it gonna be an issue with Luke and me here?"

I tilted my head. "Why would it be an issue?"

I'd already told Rosa that Colt and Lucas would spend the summer here. I'd called her from the hotel lobby while the guys packed their stuff. She was happy for me. She'd told me she'd been praying for me.

Colt cleared his throat. "Well, I cook. Lucas has a dozen dishes I approve of, but cookin' is my thing. My mother would also tan my fuckin' hide if I didn't clean up my own mess."

"She actually would," Lucas chuckled fondly.

I didn't see the problem. "So, she'll have less to do." I shrugged and scratched my elbow. "Her position is secure, and she knows it. She probably changed my diaper more than my mom did when I was little, and because I'm still somewhat of a useless—"

"Watch it!" Colt snapped.

"Kit," Lucas chastised.

It was followed by matching angry stares from two Daddy Doms.

Shit.

"Heh." I chuckled uncomfortably and backtracked. "I just m-mean, I never learned. I got comfortable. And I wanted her company. She worked for my parents, but for me, she's family. But either way, if she doesn't have anything to cook or anything to clean, she'll survey the place and go home. That's her job, to make sure things are running smoothly for me." I shifted in my seat. "Securing her future with me and after she's retired was one of the first things I did after Mom and Dad died because everyone else left. Except for Rosa and Vincent."

Lucas covered my hand with his and gave it a squeeze.

Colt rubbed the back of his neck. "Exactly how many people did your folks have on staff?"

"Five," I answered. "Mom had a PA who used to stay in the studio in the basement most of the time. Vincent, Rosa, Dad's security guy—Brent, he was a funny dude." Given the sensitive information my father dealt with and had access to, he'd always had Brent nearby. "Oh, and Tina. She ran errands for the family. She and Brent are married."

Vincent once asked my father why Brent was assigned to Dad, since it was Vincent who was one day going to get a position at the company. In another department, where Vincent could go farther. And my dad had said, "There's no greater test than taking care of my son. I'm trusting you with the best thing I ever helped create."

Vincent told me that story after their funeral.

Colt let out a low whistle. "Talk about a life I've never lived."

I didn't know how to respond to that, so I went in another direction. "Aren't you starting a security business? My dad only hired those he deemed necessary." My mother had been another matter.

"Not on a government level." Colt turned down the heat on the stove and moved to the counter across from Lucas and me.

"My dad's company is private."

"Sure, that's who the government employs." Colt smirked. "It's only in the private sector that secrets can be kept."

That was true, I supposed.

"Okay, so that's Rosa." Lucas stroked his thumb over my knuckles as he held my hand. "Will we be stepping on any toes where Vincent is concerned?"

"I don't see how we won't," Colt stated, a crease forming in his forehead. "I'm just thinking out loud here, but Kit, your ultimate goals are to one, fend for yourself better, and two, leave control and guidance to Luke and me." He straightened and patted his— "It's in my jeans," he said to himself. "Never mind. Luke and I have already bought you a SmarTrip card. We thought we'd try it out together this weekend."

Oh wow. Me, taking the Metro? Butterflies filled my stomach. I'd be just like any other person.

"I want to do that," I said with a bashful grin. "It's weird I'm excited about it, isn't it?"

"Absolutely," Colt said. "The Metro sucks. There's never any place to sit, and if there is, you gotta give it up to a pregnant lady."

Lucas chuckled. "It's not weird at all, dear." He raised a brow at Colt next. "Your mother would tan your hide for that comment too."

"I know, I already feel bad." Colt winced and rubbed his chest. "Either way, you see where you're headed, baby. I don't know where that leaves Vincent." He wasn't the only one who didn't know. I frowned. "Does he do anything other than drive you around?"

I half shrugged, then nodded. "He does stuff. He has a sense for knowing when I'm down. Sometimes, he'll show up out of the blue and pretend his TV is broken." I didn't think a TV could break twenty times a year. "He's sort of the handyman, and he makes sure the gardening service comes to take care of the backyard. And the pool cleaning service, etcetera, etcetera."

Vincent also had job security with us, but whereas Rosa's security was in the family, Vincent had a place in the company. Richard would help Vincent find something more fitting to his capabilities.

We weren't there, though, were we? Colt and Lucas were only here temporarily. But...as Colt had said, I had my goals. Sooner rather than later, I didn't *want* to rely on Vincent. Because once I was able to handle those things on my own, having Vincent here would just be a luxury. A comfort. A crutch.

"I'll talk to him," I said.

For some reason, I felt uneasy about it, even though I knew it was time.

---

ur bored a lot lately. i dig it.

I snorted at Abel's text and responded.

Lately? I've lived in boredom.

He didn't agree, evidently.

not like this. u would fill your hours with stuff. your outings and hobbies, but since meeting daddy pilot and daddy suit, none of that is enough anymore.

He had a point, I had to admit. It was why I found myself wandering my house aimlessly after Colt and Lucas had left for work. Rosa was downstairs preparing some snacks to put in the freezer, and Vincent wasn't due for another hour or so. I had an appointment with Linda, Richard's wife, at noon.

Abel sent another text.

almost done @ gym. calling u in 2 mins

Cool. I kept my phone in my hand and wandered down to the living room where the empty spot above the couch caught my eye. The faint outline of our family portrait didn't stab me with as much pain as it just...bugged me.

This was my home, yet it was put together piece by piece by my parents. The house had turned into a museum. A shrine, almost. And I was tired. I was frustrated and tired and restless.

Colt had called my living room New England. Everything was white, so white, and had dark blue accents.

What if I wanted gray? Or green? Or fucking neon pink?

I didn't want neon pink.

My phone rang, and Abel's goofy smirk lit up my screen.

"Hey, hot stuff," I said, staring at that damn wall.

"Hey, yourself," he chuckled. "Have I mentioned I like the new you?"

He had. When we talked the other day, he'd said I was more "chill."

What he didn't know was that it was the old me.

I went with it, though. "The new me is thinking I might want to repaint my living room," I said.

In fact, what kept me from redoing *everything*? I'd watched enough home-makeover shows to know it didn't have to take that long, nor did it have to be very complicated. It wasn't like I needed to renovate. Kitchen, bathrooms, and laundry stuff was all state-of-the-art. But walls? New furniture? Freaking knick-knacks? I could do that, couldn't I? Not that I would hold the paintbrush personally, or assemble the furni— Actually, why not? There were instructions, right?

"Mad and I had a blast decorating our condo," Abel said. "I say go for it. It's about time you move out of your parents' place and into your own house."

He was so right.

I'd never understood why some people who ran charity organizations had to have massive offices in the most expensive part of a city. I liked Linda very much, but I had to side with my dad here. He used to joke that the rent on this place for one month would provide for a whole village in Africa for a year.

Right now, she was going through checks for a fundraiser. When they were short, they had a list of people to call, and I was on it.

In the corner of the office was a rollup banner for the cause they were raising the money for this time. It was about putting more girls in developing countries through school.

I sat in one of the chairs on the other side of Linda's desk, and I tried not to scratch my elbow. Fuck. I'd forgotten to use the lotions again, despite Lucas's reminder this morning.

"There. Sorry you had to wait, sweetie." Linda put the stacks of checks into the top drawer of her desk and faced me with a smile. "How are you doing these days? We always miss you at holidays, you know."

I nodded. "I'm doing better, actually. I'm meeting more people."

"That makes me very happy to hear." She looked it too. "So. Do you want the spiel, or would you like Richard and me to handle this like before?"

"You can handle it," I replied. I'd had Richard put most of the family money aside for charities they were passionate about.

Thanks to Dad, there would always be an influx I hadn't earned whatsoever. "I have a question, though."

"Of course." Linda waited patiently.

I cleared my throat and felt a bit nervous. This would be new to me. "I, um...I was wondering how I might go about finding a job. Like a volunteer thing."

Her brows knitted together. "Is something wrong, honey? You know you don't have to work, right?"

"Yes." I shifted in my seat. "I want to, though. I want to learn something."

"Oh. Well." She raised her brows, then let out a little laugh. "I wish my daughters would want that too." Her gaze softened. "I will be happy to help you, Kit. In fact, we're starting a new project in August, and I think I know just the position for you. Something you can ease into."

I let out a breath in relief. "Thank you, Linda. I appreciate it."

"You're in a good mood today." Vincent pulled away from the curb.

"I am." I smiled and hummed along to a tune in my head. Damn country song! Taking out my phone, I chose the perfect "Lucas way" to announce something. I took a silly selfie with a thumbs-up and went to Instagram. I uploaded the photo with a black-and-white filter and wrote a caption about me getting a job today. "Life is good," I said, grinning. To all of my seven followers. Aside from Colt, Lucas, and Abel, one of Richard and Linda's daughters had followed me, as had Vincent. I didn't know the other two.

Colt and Lucas clearly got notifications whenever I posted

something, because just like the other three photos I'd uploaded, they liked and commented very quickly.

Lucas's response made me blush and feel all warm.

Guess who's spilling all the details at dinner when his Daddies come home more than a little curious, not to mention proud? You! Congratulations, darling boy.

I giggled under my breath at Colt's comment.

What the hell? You were crawling a second ago, and now you're getting a job? They grow up too fast. (This is where you pick up the phone and call your favorite Daddy.)

I replied to him.

You want me to call Lucas? ;) (I'm out with V. We'll talk later. Kisses!)

"Yeah..." I sighed and pocketed my phone. "Things are finally happening."

Vincent snorted. "I noticed."

Did he have to ruin it? "I know you don't like Colt and Lucas, but—"

"I don't know them." He shrugged.

"You know *me*," I said, irritated. "You could try to trust me. You could be happy for me."

"I'm fuckin' thrilled." He was lying, and he didn't even try to hide it. "I'm also fully aware of how this is gonna go. You've got your guys now, so it's only a matter of time before I'm out."

I clenched my jaw and looked out the window. I was angry and—fuck, I felt guilty. I hated it. He was right, wasn't he? This whole thing hurt.

He stopped at a red light. "Do you have more errands, or am I taking you home?"

"We have errands, and I want us to have a nice time," I said sharply. "Okay? I'll need you a lot. I don't know anything about redecorating, so I thought we could look around while Colt and Lucas are at work. Will that freaking work for you?"

He stared at me bewilderedly in the rearview.

"Well?" I asked impatiently. "No, I can't promise I'll need you to drive me as much while they're staying with me, but for goodness' sake, I'm trying here. I don't want to feel bad for spending time with them. It's not permanent. I just..." I let out a big breath. "I just want to be happy, Vincent. Please help me out."

Vincent refocused on the road as he started driving again, and I heard him sigh. "Fine. I get it. It's ridiculous that you believe this is temporary, but I'll help you."

"Thank you so much," I replied, my voice heavy with sarcasm.

I couldn't see his face, only his eyes, and they crinkled with mirth.

I glared. He thought this was funny now? Asshole.

He cleared his throat. "Would ice cream put you in a better mood again?"

"Yeah, I fucking think so," I snapped. "Go to the place with the good sprinkles."

"You got it, boss," he chuckled. "Where are we off to after that?"

Good question. I didn't know the name of it—or where it was. And I was still too annoyed to show my lack of knowledge, so I huffed and hoped for the best.

"To the wall paint store."

He coughed. "Ah, that place. Gotcha."

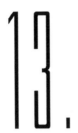

13.

That was the color! I crawled over to the green samples and snatched them up, and then I sat back on my heels as I flipped through the booklet of green tones. I had the exact shade in my head; it had to be in here.

"He said what?" I scrunched my nose and cocked my head, listening to the lyrics of the song pouring out. "Ohh…" So Jack, the singer's friend, wasn't a person. Boy, country music sure loved its alcohol. There was a drink for everything. No, legitimately, that was a song title. I shook my head and dragged a finger along five shades of green. We were getting warmer. Next page, maybe. "Bingo!" There it was. A light, warm shade of khaki green. "Hello, my next wall color."

After crawling back to the spot by the TV where I'd dumped all the swaths of fabric samples, I grabbed the one with the dark red I'd found and held it up against the green. Just perfect. Rosa was a genius. She'd told me about the place that had created the cover for our couch and suggested, because I actually did love the couch, that I didn't buy a new one. I could just order a new cover. And it was going to be dark, dark red.

I was bobbing my head to the beat of a song when I heard keys wiggling in the front door.

"Alexa, stop the music," I said.

I leaned back as much as I could to see who it was, and then I grinned. Good lord, Colt was hotter than hell today too. I'd never seen him in a polo shirt. I kind of wanted to be the collar so I could sniff his neck all day.

"Hi, Daddy! Come look!" I held up the samples next to each other. "Don't they look great together?"

Colt left a couple binders of...something...on the hallway table and entered the living room with his brows high up. "Hey, baby. Is Home Depot turnin' this place into a showroom?" He was staring at the hundreds of samples that littered the floor. "Or is that where you got a job?"

I laughed. "No, that's not starting until August, and it's with Linda's charity organization. I don't know what I'll be doing yet."

"I'm sure you'll ace it."

I stared up at him expectantly, and he smiled and dipped down and kissed me.

"Sight for sore eyes." He touched my cheek and straightened. "So, what exactly is the plan here?"

"I'm gonna redo *everything*." I scrambled to my feet and held up the green. "That's gonna be the color here, I think. If you and Lucas like it. And the couch is gonna be dark red, and then I was thinking, um..." I scanned the floor for the strip of wood I'd found perfect. *There!* I picked it up and read the label on the back. "Walnut. Furniture in walnut. What do you think? I want your approval."

I want you to want to be here forever with me.

"Huh." A slow smile took over, and he gave my neck a squeeze. "I like it. Right up my alley."

Awesome! I tapped my cheek. "What is up Lucas's alley?"

Colt shot me an amused look. And he waited. Well, so did I. I was curious.

"Do you really not see it?" he chuckled.

My forehead creased. "I mean, I know he likes both black and white."

Colt coughed into his fist, and he seemed to be trying not to laugh. Except he was definitely laughing.

"*What?*" I asked. What was I missing?

He cracked up and squeezed me to him. "You're killin' me, kid. He'll like this just fine. It's pretty close to the theme he picked for our bedroom at home."

Color me pleased as punch!

I wormed my way out of Colt's hold and piled the living room samples on the coffee table so I didn't lose them. I figured the dining room should have the same theme since the rooms adjoined. There was just a waist-high wall separating the two areas.

"So, how's laundry going?" Colt wondered. "I figure that's why you're runnin' around in nothin' but underwear." He checked out my butt, and I had to say I thought it was cute in my Ironman briefs.

"This project got in the way," I said and picked up a catalogue. "I'll get to it later. I'm thinking Monday after my dermatology appointment."

"Really." Colt peered toward the doorway and rubbed his jaw. Then he walked out, presumably heading for the kitchen.

I flipped through the catalogue, searching for inspiration. Glancing up the stairs, I wondered how far the khaki green would go. I didn't want green everywhere. Maybe blue in the hallway up on the second floor? Or something more neutral? So many options.

I scratched my stomach and stopped at a spread where everything was decorated in navy and gray. Hmm. Possibly for one of the guest rooms...

Colt returned to the living room and surveyed my floor of chaos.

"Oh! What do you think about this, Daddy?" I showed him a spread in the catalogue that Lucas might love. It was a bedroom design of white-painted brick, a low bed with black details, black hardwood floors, and a New York photograph on the wall. It was so different from what I had now. This was... grown-up. Stylish.

We didn't have exposed brick in this house, but I'd seen a type of paneling in one of the stores Vincent and I had been to today. You could fake it.

Colt hummed as he eyed the catalogue pictures. "Looks good."

I scratched my chest. "And maybe a cool chair and some plants and more pictures on the walls?"

He nodded and eyed the floor again, as if he were looking for something, and he appeared to find it. Another booklet of color samples.

"What do you think of this one?" He showed me a lighter shade of burgundy.

I liked it, but he didn't strike me as a burgundy type of guy. "It's nice," I said, scratching my arm. "For the bedroom or one of the guest rooms, maybe?"

"No, for your ass."

What? I looked at him quizzically.

He closed the booklet and tossed it onto the couch, then faced me fully with his arms folded over his chest.

Uh-oh.

"Did you go through your skin treatment routine this mornin'?"

Fuck, shit. My expression gave me away, I was sure of it. Because I felt like a deer caught in the headlights.

He shook his head. "Figured that was why you were scratchin' yourself like a crackhead jonesing for his next fix."

I flinched.

"Luke left a note on the counter in the kitchen," he pointed out. "You saw it, didn't you?"

I nodded and stared at my feet. "I'm sorry. I'll do it tonight, I promise."

"Tonight...?" He let out a chuckle. "All right, follow me. We've been goin' easy on you, but you need discipline."

That didn't sound pleasant at all!

I set down the catalogue on the table and reluctantly followed Colt into the kitchen. He'd stopped near the stools. It was where Lucas had left the note on the island. It was still there.

"Look at me, boy."

I dragged my gaze upward.

His stare was so stern. "First of all, I'm crazy proud of you for making changes in your life. People and change don't always mix well, and we're often afraid to do things that frighten us." He paused. "But we can't allow you to forget everything else. Your recovery ain't for kicks. You've got doctors tellin' you to do certain things, and then you fuckin' do them."

"Yes, Daddy," I whispered.

He nodded. "Good. Now, take off my belt and push down your briefs."

Oh my God. I felt my face go pale, and my fingers started shaking as I closed the distance and unbuckled his belt. It was weathered black leather, soft to the first touch, but... I swallowed hard. Nothing about this would be soft. He was going to strike me. Discipline me.

With the belt in one hand, I used my other to push down my bottoms.

I'd never stood naked in the kitchen before.

Colt took the belt from me and tapped the note on the counter. "Rosa's been here today, hasn't she?"

I nodded, confused. "Yes, Sir."

"I figured. See how everythin' is spotless? It means she's also seen the note, but she didn't put it on the fridge with all the other notes you've got there. She wiped down the counter and purposely put the note back. Maybe because she fucking knows how important it is for you to follow your doctor's orders."

I bit down on my lip to keep it from trembling.

"How many times today have you walked past this?" he asked. "Is it hard to see? Does the neon yellow fade against the marble?"

Oh, he was going to make me cry. I sniffled and wrung my hands awkwardly. "I'm sorry, Daddy. It won't happen again."

"No, it won't—and you know why? Because Luke and I will make sure of it," he said, folding the belt in his hand. "Put your hands on the counter and push out that ass."

Oh shit. Shit, shit, shit. He moved the stools aside so I could take that space, and I gripped the edge of the counter. Arms straight, elbows locked into place, and I was bent over enough that he would have all the access to my butt he wanted.

"Read the note for me, Kit."

I didn't want to, I didn't want to!

I blinked back the emotions that were already threatening to spill over. "Good morning, sweet boy. Just reminding you to put on your lotion. Please do this right after breakfast if you haven't done it already. See you tonight. Kisses, Lucas."

I tensed up as Colt ran his belt over my butt.

"Please do this right after breakfast," Colt quoted. "Where in this note did you decide that maybe Luke meant it was okay for you to do it tonight?"

I hung my head in shame and screwed my eyes shut. "I disobeyed," I whispered.

"Yes, you did."

A second later, a loud *thwack* flew through the air, and it felt like the skin of my butt cracked open. I swallowed the scream, a whimper slipping out instead.

"Read the note again."

"G-Good morning, sweet boy. Just reminding you to p-put on your lotion. Please do this right after breakfast if you haven't done it already. See you to—gah!"

He struck me a second time.

"Again, Kit."

"Ow," I whimpered. "Good morning, s-sweet boy. J-Just reminding you to put on your lotion. Please do this right after breakfast if— Ow, Daddy!"

"That sentence—the one you just read. Do that one again."

I drew in a ragged breath and tried to push down the fiery pain that was spreading. "Pl-Please do this right after breakfast."

"After" *thwack* "fuckin'" *thwack* "breakfast."

The pain tore a sob from me, then another and another. It hurt so badly. I didn't know how much more I could take. What if he hit a more sensitive spot—no, wait. He wouldn't. Even in my wretched state, I could tell he was being mindful of where he beat me.

Colt was far from done. He had me read from the note over and over, and he struck me with the belt across my butt, down on my thighs, and up on my butt again. Tears were streaming down my face, and I was shaking like a leaf.

"Luke and I both love it when you're bratty and mischievous," Colt told me. "But when we tell you to do somethin', it ain't a suggestion. Those are orders, and we don't tolerate disobedience."

"I'm s-sorry, Daddy," I sobbed.

Thwack, thwack, thwack.

My hoarse scream pierced the air.

One more. A forceful strike. Then he stopped the beating, and the belt landed on the counter with a clank from the buckle.

But before relief could set in, he was kneading the flesh of my butt—hard. Spreading the cheeks, squeezing, digging his fingers in.

"Why do you think Lucas told you to put on the lotion?" he asked. His voice came from somewhere else; he was lower, down on the floor. He'd taken a knee.

I choked and wiped my cheek on my shoulder. "Because he c-cares." And I was so stupid! My torso was itchy and sweaty, and it felt like I had bugs crawling under my skin.

"That's right." Daddy leaned closer. I felt his warm breaths hitting my ouchy places, and then he used his tongue. Softly and wetly, he swiped the tip of his tongue over my opening.

I let out a whimper. He fucked with my head. Those sensations had no place in this moment. There was only pain and suffering, and now... I didn't know what was happening.

"It ain't nice to defy someone when they're lookin' out for you, is it?"

I shook my head, a rush of grief washing over me. "I'm so, so sorry. I got excited about r-r-redecorating."

"I know, baby. And there's no reason you can't do both." He grabbed two fistfuls of my ass, squeezed so fucking hard, and pushed his tongue inside me.

"Ahh!" I couldn't take it anymore. The hurt was too overpowering. "Daddy, p-please s-stop!"

At the same time, a thick fog of mindfucky dizziness and need rolled in. It short-circuited my brain.

Daddy alternated between tongue-fucking me and torturing me. At one point, he dragged his scruffy chin across my butt cheeks, and my knees buckled. He had to hold me up. I could barely breathe. Gasps and sobs racked my body.

"Do you get it now, Kit? Playtime comes after you've done your chores. Dessert comes after you've eaten all your vegetables."

I was out of air, and speaking was officially impossible. I managed a nod while I choked; that was it.

Maybe it was good enough. Daddy rose to his feet and picked me up.

I kind of checked out. I existed in flashes of brutal pain and glimpses of what was happening around me. Daddy's low murmurs, the couch was there, Daddy left, but then he was back. It hurt, it hurt, it hurt, and I was so sorry.

Something wet and cold touched my buttocks. I gasped and groaned and cried. Daddy cradled me to him—on the couch, I was pretty sure—and held what I assumed was a cold towel on my butt.

"Let it all out, baby." He rocked me slowly, and he pressed light kisses to my damp forehead. "Daddy's here, okay? I've got you."

He couldn't leave. I couldn't let him. I cuddled as close as I possibly could, and I kept apologizing as my cries died down.

"Shh, all's forgiven, little one," he murmured. "That's the beauty of punishments, innit? Soon as it's over, it's over."

"Promise?" I croaked. My heart rate was finally slowing down. I could breathe again, even though every intake of air sounded hitched and hiccuppy.

"I promise." He brushed his knuckles over my cheek and wiped away some tears. "Do you think you can stand?"

"Already?" I whined.

He flashed a small smile. "Only for a few minutes. I thought we'd take a quick shower together, and then I can put the lotion on you."

I sniffled and let my eyes flutter closed. "I wanna nap, please..."

"Oh, there will be a nap. Naps and cuddles are mandatory after punishments. But after the shower. Then I won't have to worry about you scratching your skin off."

Ugh, fine.

He cared about me. I wasn't going to argue. He and Lucas made me so happy.

"I have the best Daddies," I whispered instead. "Even when you're a pain in my butt."

Daddy chuckled warmly and kissed the top of my head. "And we have the best little boy. Especially when we're a pain in your butt."

I giggled.

I, Kit Daniel Damien, had just used my very own SmarTrip card.

Booyah!

I was so nervous, and probably squeezing Lucas's hand too hard, but I was excited. There were people literally everywhere. It was DC on an early Sunday afternoon in the middle of summer. Tourist alert!

We were supposed to go earlier. Then I fucked up doing laundry, and Lucas had to help me bleach sheets. I had not seen that my dark-blue Superman briefs had been in there.

"Can we get ice cream later?" I asked. Ice cream was a must for where we were going.

Colt, who was walking two steps ahead, looked back at us over his shoulder. "I'm gonna take a goddamn bath in ice cream after this hot hell."

I grinned and crossed my eyes at him.

He did the same, making me snicker.

"Watch your step, dear." Lucas cautioned me as we reached the platform and I almost tripped over a child. Oops.

"Pretty drawings." The little girl pointed to my arm and tugged on her mother's hand. "Look, Mommy."

I mustered an awkward smile, still not used to the attention, still not used to people seeing tattoos and not scars.

Lucas kissed the top of my head, then nodded at the dark tunnel at the end. "Train's coming in."

This was it. We were going to take the Metro to visit the Lincoln Memorial, and we were departing from one of the stations that was closest...and going to the other station that was closest. Lucas was sure Foggy Bottom—*giggle*—was closest, and Colt was certain that the Smithsonian was our best option. But since there would be no going on the Metro at all if we went with Lucas's route, the Smithsonian won. We'd just end up at the same place from another direction.

My heart pitter-pattered as the train slowed to a squeaky and screechy stop, and then everybody was moving. People poured out of the train, and the air became stuffier. I kept my hand firmly in Lucas's and vowed to apologize later if I broke any bones.

"We're not going to miss it, are we?" I asked worriedly.

"No, it's almost our turn. See?" Lucas pointed at something.

He was forgetting that he was almost a head taller than me.

I did see when Colt was the next person to board the train, however, and I dragged Lucas along half a second later. Phew. We made it. It was so crowded in here, but we were on the train now. It wouldn't depart without us.

I stood right at the doors, and they freaking shook when the train rolled away from the platform. *Jesus Christ.* I sandwiched myself between Colt and Lucas.

I had to settle for holding on to them. There was no handrail in sight, except for above me, and that only looked easy for Colt. I did appreciate how his biceps bulged when the train jostled.

"Is it everything you thought it would be?" Lucas asked, amused.

"A tad sweatier than in my imagination." I grinned impishly.

He chuckled and freed his mangled hand to wrap an arm around me instead. Wait, nope. He was just going to grope me a bit. I flushed and looked around to make sure no one could see, and Lucas ghosted a hand over my crotch.

"It's still there, I swear," I joked.

"I have to make sure." But if he kept fondling me, I was going to get hard.

Oh God. It was happening.

He stroked me along the zipper of my chinos and slid two fingers under my balls.

When the train slowed down for the next stop, I panicked and pressed myself up against him. No one could see!

"Daddy," I complained under my breath.

"Hush, boy." He didn't stop. If anything, he rubbed me harder, more seductively. And Colt didn't make things easier. When people were getting off the train, he shuffled closer and pressed his chest to my back. There was a bulge in his jeans, and I wanted it inside me.

A bead of sweat trickled down my temple, and I wiped my upper lip.

"When we get home," Lucas murmured in my ear, "I'm going to need you. It's been so long since Daddy got to taste his little boy's come."

"Oh God," I exhaled.

This was quickly turning into the train ride from hell. Now I was horny, and I couldn't do anything about it. Just my luck.

Why were we not at home right now? Oh right, I'd wanted to try the Metro, and I'd thought it was a brilliant idea to introduce Colt and Lucas to my old tradition of people watching at the Lincoln Memorial.

"Wait! I want a picture." Lucas retrieved his phone from the back pocket of his jeans and studiously ignored Colt's ribbing about being an Instagram slut. "I'm not going to apologize for finding Kit's ice cream choices fucking adorable."

What was weird about my ice cream? It was a regular vanilla soft serve. Okay, it had rainbow sprinkles on, but that was just pretty *and* yummy.

"At least it's not boring like yours." They didn't have sprinkles on theirs. "They're just so...vanilla."

Colt chuckled. "Yeah, that sums me up pretty well. I'm vanilla."

His ice cream sure was.

The three of us held our cones together, and Lucas took his picture. Then, while he was browsing for the appropriate filter, we sat down on the nearest empty bench we could find.

I was snug as a bug in the middle and had Colt's arm draped behind me.

"I want a picture of the three of us too," Lucas said. "Your arms are longer, love." He reached over me and handed the phone to Colt. "It's time to collect memories."

I smiled, and the three of us huddled together so Colt could take the picture of us from slightly above. My first picture ever of this nature. Not counting senior prom in high school when I'd gone with my best friend at the time. We'd struck funny poses for the photographer, and Mom had sighed in that "I love you, but you are a goofball" kind of way.

Afterward, Lucas stared at his phone with a fond grin. "We look good together."

"Of course we do. We're us." Colt slid down his shades from the top of his head and tasted his ice cream. "This is a good spot to come people watch."

"Mmhmm." I licked at my ice cream and looked out over the Reflecting Pool and everyone walking alongside it to and from the Lincoln Memorial. How many times had I come here with Vincent?

I wondered what he was doing today. He'd so rarely had weekends off like this when it was only me.

"Are you excited about your friend visiting?" Lucas asked.

I nodded lots. "Super-excited. Can we make more plans? Abel asked what I wanted to do, and I want us all to be together every minute of the day. That's what I've decided, in fact."

"Oh, have you?" Lucas laughed softly. "We'll certainly do our best. He and his Daddy will be here a week, right?"

"Yes, Sir," I replied. "Is it possible for them to attend the event with us in Mclean?"

It was members only, so I had doubts.

"I'll talk to River and Reese, definitely," Lucas said. "We've made exceptions before. We just have to be able to vouch for the visitors."

"I gotta take y'all to a proper steakhouse too," Colt said. "With some good ol' Texas barbecue."

"There's one near us," I exclaimed. "I've never tried it, but it's very popular judging by the reviews online."

"I know. They do all right, but it ain't Texan." Colt scratched my head lightly. "I'll get you out on the dance floor with me, too."

"I'm not a good dancer," I warned.

He turned his smirk on me. "If I can teach Lucas some moves, I can teach anyone."

"I wasn't that bad," Lucas defended.

"No, you were much, much worse, darlin'," Colt drawled.

I gigglesnorted.

14.

As the days went by, I fell in love with more moments than I could count.

I fell in love with our mornings, whether we ate in a rush before they were off to work, or they skipped work and breakfast by the pool morphed into brunch and lunch. If Colt made breakfast, Rosa insisted on making snacks. The two formed a strange connection based on cooking and one-upping each other. And if Rosa reached her limit with Colt's "my way or the highway," she switched on mother mode, at which point Colt's Southern manners made him heel and be respectful.

I fell in love with the evenings we went out together and tried new restaurants. I discovered quirks and routines of Colt and Lucas that they'd cultivated in the eight years they'd been together. If anything was served with black olives, Colt handed his over to Lucas. In turn, Lucas gave up his coleslaw and pickles. He shuddered in distaste when Colt made yummy noises. And there was more. The little things. Colt would reach for the salt, and Lucas would remind him that too much sodium was bad. Sometimes, Colt said something along the lines of, "I can't enjoy anythin'!" Sometimes, Colt got even with a made-up "I read that kale causes cancer, so you enjoy your fuckin' cancer salad" that made Lucas turn to Google.

I fell in love with the tiny moments that never ended up in photo albums. Like the time I stumbled out of the bathroom and Colt caught me as he smirked and went, "Was it gravity or your shadow this time?" Or the time Colt was making meatballs in marinara sauce and Lucas stole one when Colt ran out to buy more butter. When he returned, Lucas managed to convince Colt he must've miscalculated the meatballs. Because Lucas would *never* steal food like that. The mere idea was *preposterous*. Or...the time Lucas came home from work and tossed me a bag of Cheetos and I went to heaven. He and I shared the bag before Colt got home, at which point we pretended to be monsters and attacked Colt with our Cheeto-dusted fingers in the hallway.

As Colt threw his once-white tee into the hamper, he told Lucas, "Probably a lot of sodium in that, but that's none of my business."

I...I was just falling in love.

Fuck.

"Why is it important that I choose?" Lucas asked curiously.

"Because it is!" I held up the two different plates.

We weren't repainting anything in the kitchen, so I'd thought we could pick out new plates and silverware.

"Daddy's in charge, *remember*?" I didn't want to admit I was redecorating the house with the hope that they'd like it so much, they'd stay. If I had more time, maybe I could trick them into falling in love with me.

So...blue plates or these white ones with black paint splashes?

Lucas cleared his throat and decided to humor me, and he shifted his gaze to the plates on the shelves. There were two aisles in the store with nothing but china. I wasn't leaving without a new set.

"What do you think about these?" He showed me a multi-colored side plate, its design reminding me of Mexico. Rustic reds and faded blues in a bunch of circles. "What you could do is put together your own set. For example, a colorful side plate on a white regular plate." He showed me by putting the smaller dish on a plain white one. "Then perhaps a blue or red bowl that matches the patterns here."

I liked it. Question was, did Lucas? "Would you call that your style?" I prodded.

"I would, I think. For this, yes."

"Then we're getting that." Jeesh, it shouldn't be this difficult. Just move in with me and love me already. "Help me pick out wineglasses, please."

"Sweetheart, why is this—"

"You ask too many questions," I huffed.

He lifted a brow in warning. "Manners, Kit."

Crap. I slumped my shoulders. "I'm sorry. This is just important to me, and I value your opinion. Can we please go look at wineglasses now?"

"Sure." He sounded anything but. "You don't drink wine, though."

You and Colt do.

One Saturday, after Colt had casually put the suggestion on the table, we started painting the living room. *Ourselves.* Without professional painters nearby.

It was nuts, but Colt claimed he'd done it countless times before.

We had the paint. The furniture had been pushed into the

dining room. The floor was covered in plastic, and Lucas had applied tape around outlets and such. I never would've thought of that. Lastly, we had two hot Doms wearing only jeans. I could work with this.

"Wait!" I panicked a bit as Colt ran his rolling thing through the paint thing, and I swallowed nervously. "Are we all in agreement that we want this color?"

I had to make sure.

Colt and Lucas exchanged a frown of confusion.

"We've told you we like the color," Lucas replied slowly. "Are you sure nothing is wrong? You've seemed more uncomfortable the past few days."

Uncomfortable? Me? Never. It was only my middle name.

"It's just a big change," I lied outright. I had no excuse. "I would feel better if you helped me with this decision. I want you to want the color."

Colt shifted his weight from one foot to the other and tilted his head. He was studying me, and I didn't like it. Where Lucas prodded gently and waited for me to be ready to be honest, even when he knew something was up, Colt struck like a rattlesnake. No, wait. Like a viper. He didn't wait around. He pushed.

I stuck my tongue out at him and forced a smirk into place.

He narrowed his eyes.

Energy crackled between us, and it was heady. It was...it was something. It was a battle. Like chess or...something else. I couldn't put a finger on it, but I loved the challenge and the strategy. His move, my move, his move.

After a moment, he straightened and glanced up at the wall, then down at the paint he'd placed on a stool. "I would've chosen this color," he said with a nod.

That was his move? He wasn't going to push?

Sweet. I must be getting better.

"Yes, it's a lovely color," Lucas agreed. "It will look great, Kit."

Colt handed over the paint roller to Lucas. "Y'all can start. I gotta call River about something."

Lucas cocked a brow. "Care to share?"

"Just...something about the event. I wanna make some changes."

That was sudden. Though, he did play an integral part in the planning, and he was probably thinking about The Games a lot as the event got closer. Lucas had said they'd put hundreds of hours into the preparations.

"It's okay, Daddy," I said to Lucas. "We can start, and then he can fix our mistakes."

Lucas chuckled.

Colt smirked. "Kid ain't wrong."

Much of the frustration and the growing unease left me momentarily a couple hours later when we ended up having a good time.

Colt was in a great mood, and it showed that he loved to do things himself. He was a fixer.

Lucas was good with a smaller paintbrush, so he followed Colt and painted the spots the roller was too big for, like right by the baseboards and up by the crown molding.

I was the DJ, the snack-getter, and Colt's personal ladder-holder. Keeping the ladder steady also gave me the best view of his ass in those jeans.

The only downside was standing in the splash zone. I had dots of paint all over my tee, face, and arms, and Colt thought it was too funny.

"Darlin', we gotta take Kit fishin' sometime," he said,

bobbing his head to the beat of the song. To no one's surprise, it was country, and it was about huntin' and fishin'.

Lucas scratched his neck and squinted. "I really feel that's more of a *you* thing."

"I agree," I said with a straight face. "Daddy, you can go fishing alone."

Lucas laughed. "Kit and I are city boys."

"For life," I replied with a grin.

Colt shook his head at us. "Y'all don't know the peace of gettin' up at four and lookin' out over the lake and the mornin' mist."

"And you don't know what peace is," Lucas muttered under his breath.

I snickered.

Wanting to mess with our country boy, I changed the music and immediately earned myself a groan from Lucas, who apparently knew the song.

"This is even worse than country, sweetheart," he said, appalled.

"What the fresh hell is this rapin' my ears?" Colt exclaimed.

I pretended to love it and got into the beat, making sure I shook the ladder a bit too. And then...oh, I had to do it. Abel and I had goofed off to this song...how many times? I'd almost forgotten. I had to do the dance.

I raised the volume and started shaking my butt as I waited for the chorus. "Don't you love it?" I yelled over the music. "Embrace the Gangnam Style, Texas kiddo!" I took a few steps back and bobbed my head, and when the chorus began, I jumped into the silly dance Abel and I had practiced until we were pros.

When I saw the guys' reactions, I remembered how much I used to love being a clown. Colt was standing on the ladder, and he was watching me with amusement dancing in his eyes, and

Lucas was retrieving his phone, his shoulders shaking with laughter.

I yanked off my tee and twirled it in the air as I did the dance again.

Lucas was either taking a hundred pictures, or he was filming me. Regardless, I felt it was vital that I gave it my all. Close to cracking the hell up at myself, I took goofball to the extreme and exaggerated every move. I spun around and moved my hips to the beat.

"If you're good boys, I'll teach you The Floss later," I hollered.

The song ended with an explosion, and I turned around again and bowed for my audience, completely out of breath.

"Shit, I'm out of shape," I panted.

"That was..." Lucas was speechless, not to mention teary-eyed from laughing. "Well, I'll say it," he said and pocketed his phone. "You're the best goofball in the world."

I grinned widely and bowed again.

"I wanna see much more of this side of you." Colt shook his head and smiled. "Come here and give me a kiss."

I could do that.

When I was in high school, a friend of mine had a dog. More specifically, a border collie. A furry black-and-white darling that was the happiest and most relaxed when the entire family was gathered in one room, be it the living room in the evening when they watched TV, or the dining room at breakfast or dinner.

My friend's father explained that she, the dog, was a natural herder. That was why sometimes she'd give us a headbutt on the leg—which was her way of saying, "Hey, why don't you join the others in the living room so I can watch you all?"

The week leading up to Abel's arrival, I was that dog. I was the happiest and most relaxed when Colt, Lucas, and I were gathered in our new living room. It felt like our space. We'd built it together. The faded khaki-green walls were ours. Lucas and I had wrestled the new cover over the couch, making it *our* couch. Colt and Lucas had moved the new furniture into place —our furniture. I had sat on Colt's shoulders to hang our new curtains. While Colt had assembled the bookshelf, I'd gone online to buy books upon books, searching for titles I thought they would like. I'd filled the shelves while they were at work, and Lucas had found his spot in the living room that very night. He'd gone through the shelf, found the first book he wanted to read, and made the new comfy chair his chair. In our living room.

A new, large canvas hung above the couch, a black-and-white picture of the Lincoln Memorial, but it was the smaller pictures that mattered. Lucas had helped me edit a bunch of photos he'd taken of us, and we'd ordered prints together that I'd put into frames. There were two in the entertainment center. One of Colt when he threw a smile over his shoulder as he made dinner one night. One of Lucas and me on the sunbed in the backyard.

My favorite picture sat on the small table next to Lucas's chair. It was the three of us having ice cream.

The living room was home. We'd breathed life into the space together, and we had to spend our time there.

Lucas was watching the news one evening, and I sat restlessly on the couch waiting for Colt to be done in the kitchen. He should be here too. We could eat here, in my opinion.

"I'll go see if Colt needs any help," I said and left the couch.

"Hmm...? Okay, sweetheart." Lucas looked away from the news and gave me a smile. "Could you bring me back a glass of wine? There's a bottle in the door of the fridge."

"Yes, Sir." I ran out and skidded into the kitchen on my socks, and I found Colt at the stove. He'd taken something out of the oven and was drizzling melted butter over whatever it was. I snuck closer. Some kind of fish. Yum. It smelled amazing. "Hi, Daddy, can I help?"

"You can sit here and give me somethin' pretty to look at." He sent me a quick wink and finished pouring butter over the vegetables around the fish.

"Easy peasy." I grinned and opened the cupboard where Rosa had placed our new wineglasses. "I'm just gonna bring a glass of wine to Daddy. Do you want one also?"

"Yeah, I'll have a glass. Thanks."

I poured two glasses and excused myself a second to give one to Lucas. Then I was back in the kitchen, and I hopped up on the counter next to the stove while Colt checked one of the pots. I'd requested mashed potatoes.

Colt took a sip of his wine and came to stand between my parted knees. "I love this new look. We should make it a rule for you to wear nothin' but bottoms."

I blushed and glanced down at my body. Having discovered they preferred to see me in briefs instead of boxers, I'd purchased a bunch of new underwear. Some cool ones with colorful patterns or graphics, some plain ones in different colors. Today's pair was solid black, but they were so soft and fit so snugly. I loved them.

"I never walked around like this before," I admitted.

Colt smiled softly and set down his wine. He knew it was he and Lucas who had made me comfortable enough.

He planted his hands on the counter and leaned in, kissing me slowly instead of saying anything. I slipped my hands up his chest, feeling the muscles underneath his tee, and locked my arms around his neck.

I think I'm in love with you.

Was I crazy? Was it even possible? It'd only been a month, yet my feelings for Colt and Lucas terrified me.

"Wine kisses are the only wine I drink." I sucked on his bottom lip and earned myself a chuckle, and then he deepened the kiss. One of his hands went up and down my thigh in sensual strokes, and the other came up to my neck. He was such an amazing kisser.

Colt hummed and pulled me closer to him. "Do you hear the song?"

Song? No. I was lost in Colt. But if I concentrated... Yes, I heard it, and I knew exactly which one it was. Country music produced some sweet romantic songs too, ones where they didn't even mention alcohol or heartbreak.

This particular song, I'd heard before. Lucas played it in the car sometimes, and he'd told me of the significance. "If we have a song, it's this one," he'd said. "It captures Colt and me, and it did that years before it was even released."

"It's your song." I broke the kiss and breathed heavily, dropping my forehead to Colt's shoulder.

The man sang of love that went beyond the grave, that when the good Lord called him home, he'd take that love with him.

"Luke told you?" Colt was surprised.

I nodded, unsure of how to feel. It wasn't envy, far from it. Just...a desperate need to share that with them. My chest hurt. My *heart* hurt. Underneath my hand, Colt's own heart beat rapidly.

"Kit," he murmured. I swallowed hard, and he lifted my chin and kissed me again. And then he smiled, and I wanted to slap him. I didn't know why. All I knew was that I felt so damn exposed. "My beautiful boy." He kissed me hard and cupped my jaw, then rested our foreheads together. "You should enjoy what's happening, baby. I know it's scary, but we're not going anywhere."

I knitted my brows and searched his eyes. Was he... I mean, what exactly was he saying?

He smiled and smoothed down the crease between my eyebrows. "You'll get it soon. I promise. In the meantime, don't be afraid. Trust us."

"Okay," I whispered. He'd left me confused as hell, but I did trust him. Both of them. If they told me not to be afraid, I was going to try to relax. "I trust you."

"Good." He gave me one more kiss. "How about we eat in the living room?"

My eyes lit up as relief pummeled me, and I caught the glint of amusement and happiness in his expression.

Did he understand?

"Yes, please," I answered. "I promise I won't spill."

He chuckled.

He was a little less amused a couple days later when we over-slept and got on the road late to pick up Abel and Madigan at the airport.

"Daddy, can you drive faster?" I asked.

"You want me to ram the car in front of us?" Colt shot me a sleepy, annoyed look in the rearview. "I didn't think so."

"Hmpf." I fell back against my seat and folded my arms over my chest. Abel and Madigan had landed, and I bet they were hungry for breakfast. Lucas was back home right now preparing eggs and muffins and bacon and pancakes for us. Or as Colt had called it, about half of the things Lucas aced in the kitchen.

"Don't give me attitude, Kit," Daddy warned.

Crap. I chewed on my lip and wrung my hands. "I'm sorry."

"Hmpf." He sounded like me there.

Perhaps it was my good mood because I was seeing my friend in a few minutes, but something made me want to...poke.

He may be tired, but he hadn't been too tired to give me a big spiel earlier about "kids riding in the back." To be honest, he was just overprotective of his car. Lucas had explained that Colt had hated their old one, which Lucas had already had when they met. So when it was time to buy a new one, all Lucas had asked was that Colt didn't pick a truck. In a very wry tone, Lucas had told me, "Of course he went out and found the biggest gas-guzzling SUV we could afford."

Lucas let me ride in the front when he drove, though.

"Daddy, I feel like being bratty," I informed Colt politely. It was his cue to either leave the door open or shut it down.

"I dare you," he yawned. "If you think I'm a Sadist already, try raisin' hell before I've had my coffee."

I covered my mouth with my hand and giggled.

He must've heard me anyway, because he shot me a wink in the rearview. Then he promptly yawned again.

Finally, we reached the airport, and I scrambled to unbuckle my seat belt.

"Be careful and don't run," Daddy said. "Text me when y'all are ready. And you be polite to Abel's Daddy, you hear?"

"Yes, Sir!" I opened the door with a grunt and jumped out. He was going to "circle" so we didn't have to find parking. "Oh, and Daddy?" I poked my head in, and he looked back at me. "I shouldn't have been on your case about driving faster. It's not your fault country boys from Texas don't know how to drive properly in the city. Okay, thanks, bye!" I shut the door on his stunned expression and laughed all the way inside the airport.

That was going to come back and bite me *so* hard.

But not right now.

National was a small airport right across the river, and I didn't have a long walk to where the arrivals poured out. I sat down on a bench between the exit doors and the first luggage carousel.

I yawned and pulled up the hood of my new shirt. I'd ordered it online, a matching set of sweats and hoodie, and they had the Air Force emblem printed on them. Colt had given me the biggest nod of approval.

A rush of people emerged from the exit, and I stood up to see if Abel was— He was! I saw him!

"Abel!" I hollered.

He spotted me and grinned sleepily.

I'd forgotten he was quite a bit taller than me. Even taller still was the man right behind Abel, carrying two duffel bags. I'd seen pictures of Madigan on Abel's Instagram, and he was heavily inked too. He was a tattoo artist.

Unable to stand still anymore, I jogged the last distance, and Abel did the same. Then we threw our arms around each other, and I smiled so hard. He was here!

"It's so good to see you, babe." He smacked a loud kiss to my cheek. "Even if you're hiding."

I laughed. "I promise, no hiding. We overslept and just threw on whatever we could find."

"Good." He smirked and glanced back at his fiancé. He was a total hottie, obviously. Rugged and much older. Not unlike Colt. They were sort of close in age, if I wasn't mistaken. Madigan was a little younger. "Okay, so this is Madigan. Mad, meet Kit. He's not as innocent as he looks. He's got more ink than you do, and he dragged me along to my first munch."

"And you dragged me along to my first play party, so I think you've got me beat," I retorted. Extending my hand to Madigan, I took a much more polite route. "Nice to finally meet you, Sir. Abel's told me many things about you."

"Probably all true." He smirked faintly and shook my hand. "Good to meet you too, little one."

Yup, Daddy Dom.

Abel nudged me. "Where are your two?"

"Oh shit, I was gonna text him." I brought out my phone. "Colt's outside. Lucas is making us breakfast to have on the porch." I sent the text and glanced at their luggage. "Are we waiting for more?"

"Nah, we pack light," Abel replied.

Madigan lifted a pierced brow at Abel. "Is that short for 'Daddy, we don't have to bring more because we can shop till we drop in DC'?"

I pressed my lips together to hide a grin.

Abel stared at him. "Maybe."

I snorted and linked my arm with Abel's. "Okay, come on. Vacation starts now!"

"Fucking finally," he groaned, letting me drag him toward the exit. "This season's been brutal."

"At least you made the play-offs this year," I offered. "No matter what, you're always my NHL star."

He batted his lashes.

Daddy drove up right as we exited the airport, and I released Abel to open up the back of the SUV.

"May I take your luggage, Sir?"

Madigan gave me a little smile before turning to Abel. "See how well-mannered he is?" Then he sent me a wink and took care of their bags himself.

Abel stuck his tongue out behind Madigan's back.

I snickered under my breath.

I opened the door to the passenger's side for Madigan, then, lastly, the door for Abel and me.

"Daddy, this is Abel and Madigan," I said. "Abel and Madigan, this is Colt the Sadist."

"You don't even *know*, boy," he told me. "That stunt you

pulled earlier..." He shook his head, amused. "Pleasure to meet you, kid." He nodded at Abel.

"The pleasure is mine, Sir." Abel buckled in.

Madigan climbed into the passenger seat and shook hands with Colt. "So yours is more polite to other Tops too?"

"Yeah, don't let the brat fool you," Colt replied wryly. "Truth be told, Luke and I are relieved he's finally relaxin' enough to be a brat with us, but the balance...?" He whistled. "The balance, I gotta beat into him at times."

Feeling cockier with Abel next to me, I said, "I think I'm a fucking angel."

Madigan let out a laugh. "Oh boy."

"Duuude." Abel held up his fist, and I bumped it. Adrenaline coursed through me.

Colt pulled away from the curb. "You'll get your beatin', Kit. No need to beg."

"I didn't," I argued.

"I think you did," Daddy replied. "I heard it. You...?" He looked to Madigan.

"Loud and clear," Madigan said. "Same language Abel speaks. You become fluent after about a minute."

Abel and I went blah-blah-blah with our hands and rolled our eyes.

15.

"I like cuddling with you like this, Daddy," I whispered.

Lucas smiled affectionately and caressed my cheek. "I like cuddling with you like this, too."

Hiding under a soft blanket on our sunbed, we'd found the perfect spot for a post-breakfast nap. And no one could see us. We were invisible to the whole world. If we couldn't see them, they couldn't see us. That was the rule.

Abel was taking a nap in their guest room. Colt and Madigan were bonding over ridiculously strong coffee on the other side of the pool. And I was just staring at my Lucas.

"I love your eyes." I drew a finger over his cheek, captivated and enveloped in his warmth. "And the gray in your scruff."

The corners of his eyes crinkled with his chuckle.

He wouldn't understand. The feelings that were flowing through me were overwhelming. Never had I experienced something like this. I wanted to keep it forever.

I didn't care what anybody said. It was fast, but I felt it.

"I want to serve you better," I admitted.

Curiosity filled his gaze. "What do you mean?"

I shrugged lightly. "Do more stuff for you. Like submissives. Not just be a Little who depends on you. I want you to be able to count on me too."

He understood. I could tell. His eyes were expressive, and he never concealed anything. Perhaps that was one of the reasons it was so easy to trust him, because I did. With everything I was.

I trusted Colt as well. I couldn't not. I was drawn to them like a moth to two different kinds of flames. With Colt, there was a thrill. A challenge and that energy. I craved it, and I wanted to explore it further. It felt like...like, like we could go far together? I wanted him to push me. I wanted him to toy with me. He'd shown me he would be there through it all.

"Our kinks will always evolve," Lucas murmured. "As long as you don't want to serve us for the wrong reasons, we're happy to try new things."

"What would be the wrong reasons?"

"Hmm. For instance, if you felt the need. If you felt like a burden. Something you—" he poked my nose "—have a history of."

I grinned sheepishly and rubbed my nose. "It's not that. I just want to make you as happy as you make me."

"Sweet boy." He rested our foreheads together and adjusted the blanket over us. "You make us incredibly happy. Out-of-this-*world* happy." He kissed my smile. "That said, structure suits you. You thrive when you feel safe, and you feel safe when there are rules." He was definitely correct. "We can add more chores for you if you'd like."

I nodded and snuggled lower so I could tuck my head under his chin. "Yes, please."

"Then consider it done." He gave me a squeeze. "I do love watching you grow, Kit. We're very proud of you for the changes you're already making."

The warm fuzzies were back, and I could only hug him super-duper hard because I'd lost my words.

I'm just pointing out that I haven't worked a shift in over a week. Is this how it's gonna be now?

I pocketed my phone before Abel could see and made sure there wasn't a trace of anxiousness on my face. We were getting ready in my bathroom upstairs, and tonight was about having fun.

Tomorrow, I would do better. I would find a balance so I could keep everyone in my life. It was my fault. I was letting Vincent down because I was spending so much time with Colt and Lucas. Guilt seeped into my veins, heavy as lead, and I had to force a smile when Abel asked if he could wear those jeans.

"Of course. You always look good," I said.

I was wearing jeans too, and the material was going to take some getting used to. I was glad Lucas had helped me pick out a very soft pair because I would've fucked it up.

Abel put some product in his hair, giving it a messy bed head look, but all I saw was Vincent. He did that all the time. He even carried a small jar of some hair product in his leather jacket.

He was so New Jersey.

Abel eyed me in the mirror, and I composed my face. He quirked a brow. "You don't look like you're excited about an evening at a steakhouse."

"I will be." I smiled.

He rolled his eyes. "Honey, I've been there. Just stop. Whatever you're hiding, let your Daddies handle it—trust me on this."

"But I'm fi—"

"Bitch, I dare you to lie to me."

I shut my mouth.

He washed his hands and tilted his head at me. "Tell me. I'm your friend, remember?"

"I..." I hauled in a breath when my phone vibrated again. For one second, I closed my eyes and prayed it wasn't Vincent. "It's something," I whispered and pulled out my phone. Fuck, it was from him. "I don't know what to do about Vincent."

I read his message.

Ten years, I've been by your side. Now, nothing? No...'cause you've got your new boyfriends, and they take care of everything. Fucking great. Thanks, Kit.

My eyes welled up with burning tears, and I bit down on my lip.

"Aw, hell no." Abel grabbed the phone from me. "The fuck is his problem?"

I sniffled. "A few days after Colt and Lucas moved in, they picked up their car in Alexandria because my garage was empty. And..." Oh God, I felt so bad. "Thing is, I'd told Vincent right before that I had so many plans. That Vincent and I were going to drive around and check things out for the redecorating. But then Colt and Lucas wanted to come with me, and I thought...I thought...I don't know what I thought."

"It doesn't matter. I understand." He frowned at my phone and gave it back to me. "Why doesn't Vincent get it? I mean, you're in love and want to spend time with your men. He should understand that."

Maybe.

Abel shook his head. "No, no, wait. I remember you telling me that you'd been honest with him. You'd said you couldn't guarantee that you'd need him as much when Colt and Lucas lived here. What happened with that?"

"I-I don't know?" Either way, I felt like I was losing. I couldn't please everyone. "Fuck, what should I do? I don't want to spend less time with Colt and Lucas, but Vincent *has* been with me for over a decade."

He chewed on his lip, thinking hard. But then he shook his head again. "I'm not even gonna try. This is why you're supposed to tell your Doms. You have to. They will help you. In fact—" He stalked out of the bathroom, and I wondered what the hell he was up to. He stopped at the railing. "We have an emergency up here!" he yelled.

"Abel!" I whisper-shouted.

He wasn't done. "This requires one fighter pilot and one dude who looks hot in Hugo Boss!"

I let out a weird sound and looked at him strangely. "How can you identify suit brands like that?"

"Because *that's* what we should focus on here," he drawled.

I rolled my eyes and stalked into the bathroom again where I slumped down on the closed toilet lid.

Colt was the first one I heard coming up the stairs. "For the record, I could be both those guys, but you don't call me dude, subbie."

"Shit," Abel said sheepishly. "I clearly meant Sir."

"Clearly," Colt chuckled. "What's the emergency?"

"In there."

I groaned internally and buried my face in my hands.

Lucas wasn't far behind, and then I had my Daddies squatting down in front of me where I sat, and I was sort of embarrassed.

"I'm sorry. I should be able to handle this myself," I mumbled.

"Probably not," Colt replied. "What's up?"

"Talk to us, sweetheart." Lucas gave my knee a gentle squeeze.

Thinking about Vincent's last text, the guilt and hurt made

a swift return, and I lost my words. My throat felt thick, and I struggled to keep from getting weepy again.

"It's—it's Vincent." I pulled out my phone and showed them the texts. "I have to make things right with him." What an idiot I was. Of course, I couldn't hold back the tears. It was me. I didn't have my shit together. I sniffled and wiped my eyes with the back of my hand as they read the texts.

Lucas stood up abruptly, and I frowned up at him. His expression caught me off guard; he was freaking fuming.

"Daddy, I'll fix this," I rushed to say.

"Not you, dear. I'm not mad at you." He pinched the bridge of his nose. "Colt, tell me I shouldn't call that son of a bitch right fucking now. He has *no* goddamn right to push that guilt on to Kit."

"Gimme a minute. Can't be diplomatic yet." Colt stood up too, and he rolled his shoulders and took a deep breath. "Okay. Let's be smart."

"You're the one with the service gun, not me," Lucas replied flatly.

My eyes widened. What was happening here?!

Colt snorted and stared up at the ceiling, his hands on his hips. "We're protective because of who we are and because it's our boy, so we wanna beat Vinnie up, but—"

"Yes, let's go."

"Daddy, no!" Panic filled me, and I bolted after Lucas and grabbed on to his arm. "You c-can't!"

"Kit's got a point," Colt told Lucas. "It wouldn't be right."

"But it would feel good." Lucas pulled me to him and hugged me protectively, and I sniffled and wrapped my arms around his middle. "I'm sorry he hurt you, little one. Colt and I will take care of this. You have my word."

I shivered and hugged him harder. Some tension faded from

my head, preventing a headache I hadn't noticed was creeping in.

"You know what I think?" Colt said. "I think they both see each other as family, but the work shit is blurrin' the lines. They need to sit down and talk shit out, and they need to be friends or somethin'. Vincent shouldn't work here anymore. He should be at the company if that's what he wants, but he's done drivin' Kit places. Kit doesn't need it anymore."

I mulled over the words, a couple of things standing out. Firstly, I did want to be friends with Vincent. The thought of seeing him just because we wanted to see each other was very appealing. Secondly, Daddy was right. I didn't need a driver.

I hadn't considered—

"I also think they've been too blind to see this option," Colt added, basically finishing my thought.

He was right again. I hadn't thought of it that way.

Wiping my cheeks once more, I squirmed free from the hug and got my phone back from Lucas. Then I sent a message to Vincent.

Can we meet next week when Abel and Madigan have gone home? I think there is a solution for us.

"What did you text, dear?" Lucas wondered.

"What Colt said," I answered quietly. "I believe he's right. Vincent and I would be better off as friends. It's what I want. Not this—what it's turning into. It's toxic, and we both get hurt."

Colt slipped his hand back to my neck and kissed my temple. "It'll work out, baby. You care about each other too much to walk away." He paused. "Not that it wouldn't have been entertainin' to watch Lucas go full-on fisticuffs with one of the guys from *Jersey Shore*."

I spluttered a giggle and quickly covered my mouth with my hand.

Trust Colt to hunt down the one Texas barbecue place in the entire DC area that had as many longhorns on the walls as Pride flags. The steakhouse was packed with cowboy stuff and guests, and it was run by two women from Lubbock. Booths lined the walls, and tables were scattered across the floor, except for one end that had a small stage and a dance floor.

I liked it here. Real candles flickered on the tables, with most of the light coming from the big bar and kitchen.

"All right, I've opened a tab for us." Colt slid into our booth and put a hand on my thigh. "It's two days late, but here's to an official welcome to DC, Madigan and Abel."

Lucas lifted his beer bottle. "We're very happy to have you here, and I'm glad I got to meet you two."

Madigan smiled and tipped his bottle too. "Likewise, man. To new friendships and to nervous Littles."

"Whoa," I protested.

"We're not nervous." Abel scowled.

"Maybe not now," Colt agreed. "We haven't started exchangin' ideas yet."

Abel stared at him flatly. "Do you, like all smart people, find it cute when a Little sticks out their tongue at you?"

I snickered into my Coca-Cola.

"As a smart person," Colt said, "I gotta point out that you're askin' the wrong question. You should be askin' me if I can find somethin' cute as fuck but still carry out a punishment."

Abel bit his lip and flicked a glance at Madigan.

Madigan smirked. "I'd let him do it too, so it's up to you, trouble."

Colt draped his arm around my shoulders and leaned in. "Just so you know, that applies to you too. If you're a brat to

Madigan, we've given him permission to either spank you or use his belt on you."

"What the fuck?" I widened my eyes. "How could— Actually, I can see you abandoning me to the hands of the devil, but *you...*" I turned to Lucas. "*Et tu, Brute?*"

Three Daddy Doms found me very funny.

Bastards!

I huffed and slumped back in my seat and folded my arms over my chest.

Abel was about as amused as me, and we demonstrated our objection to this nonsense until the server arrived with our starters. The table quickly filled up with mozzarella sticks, onion rings, buffalo wings, dipping sauces, and fried pickles.

Abel was munching on a mozzarella stick when he picked up the drink menu. "Daddy, can I get a colorful drink?"

Madigan leaned closer to read the little menu. "After dinner, all right? You don't have enough food in your stomach yet."

"Yesss, I'm getting the blue one," Abel said happily. "Maybe it will turn my tongue blue."

"There's a drink that does that?" I asked, immediately interested. "Is it very strong?"

I didn't like beer, wine, or bourbon, which were the kinds of alcohol we had at home. Colt and Lucas both enjoyed a glass of wine with dinner or at the end of the night. Unless we were by the pool; Colt wanted a few beers then.

I hadn't had alcohol since high school, except for the time I reluctantly went out to brunch with Richard and his family. I'd had mimosas to survive the meal.

"You can have a couple drinks too, sweetheart. If you want." Lucas wiped some buffalo sauce off my fingers. "Colt might take advantage of you on the dance floor, though."

"Might?" Colt shot Lucas an amused look before he peered

down at me with a smirk. "You can count on it. I'm curious to see you tipsy."

That should happen fairly quickly. "I might get giggly." I dragged a piece of fried pickle through the dipping sauce, my mouth watering.

"Let's get you liquored up, then." Daddy leaned in quickly, and he—and he stole my snack! He ate it right out of my hand!

"That was mine, Daddy!"

He laughed, chewing on what was *mine*.

I was so mad!

"Look at him." Colt chuckled and hugged me to him. "You know you're doin' somethin' right when your Little's biggest problem is a missin' snack."

I snarled in defeat.

"Stop being so smug," I said, moving closer to Lucas. "I cry more these days. Congrats."

Abel let out a loud laugh. "Oh my God, me too. It took me forever to figure out why."

"It would've taken you two seconds if you'd asked me sooner than you did," Madigan drawled.

I cocked my head and grabbed a new piece of fried pickle, which I kept far away from Colt, the thief. "Well...what's the reason? I'm a bajillion times happier, but I cry at *nothing*."

Lucas smiled and kissed the side of my head. "It's because you regress. Your emotions are closer to the surface."

"Oh." I scrunched my nose, eyeing Colt as he took an onion ring. "I guess that makes sense." Reaching out super-fast, I stole the onion ring from him and threw it into my mouth. "In your *fasshe*."

He rumbled a laugh. "That washn't English, shweetheart."

Gah, I wanted to smack him sometimes—often. "You're mean." I lifted Lucas's arm so I could sneak under it, and I leaned back against his side. "I hope nothing happens to your food when you go do your honky-tonk dance later."

Colt merely grinned. "Keep at it. You know I'll just fuck you up later."

"Lucas will protect me." I hugged Lucas's arm to my chest and stuck out my tongue.

Lucas cleared his throat. "Easy now, little one. You choose to be a brat. Then you can take the consequences too."

"That's not fair!" I pushed away his arm and looked back at him. "Colt stole my food first!"

"Okay, that's enough with the tantrum, Kit." Colt squeezed my kneecap hard under the table, and I stifled a yelp. He was giving me one of those warning looks. "If you want, we can go home right fuckin' now. Your call."

I had the biggest urge to whine, but I knew the jig would be up if I pushed him now. He wasn't the type of man who made empty threats.

"Can you be nice?" Lucas asked.

"Yes..." I straightened in my seat and kept my hands in my lap. They were both meanies, simple as that. I'd just keep my eye-rolls and remarks to myself. I could do that. "I forgot that life's not fair when you're with Sadists. It won't happen again."

That was right; I called Lucas a Sadist too.

Lucas frowned at me.

Colt had this pensive expression, and he faced Lucas. "I had a feelin' we were headed this way. I reckon we've got ourselves an involuntary masochist on our hands, darlin'. It may not be what he wants, but I think he needs it."

"Welcome to my world," Abel said with a small smile.

I didn't know what the hell they were talking about. "We've already explored pain. I like some of it. This isn't news."

"Do you get aggravated easily?" Abel asked. "Restless?

Unsure of how to put feelings into words? Do you lash out and have a short fuse when you're frustrated?"

I blinked.

"Oh Christ. How did I not see this sooner?" Lucas said in wonder.

"What?" I asked irritably. "Are you gonna fill me in?"

Madigan chuckled and kissed Abel's temple. "You have some explaining to do for Kit."

Preferably right fucking now. Yes, I could admit what Abel said rang bells. But I didn't *need* pain. I accepted punishments when I'd been bad, and I felt better afterward. That was it. I didn't want pain for kicks, unless it was just sensual pain. I did enjoy rough play and spankings and such. That was different.

"I know you're confused, boy," Colt said. "But you'll see on Saturday."

My brow furrowed. "At the event?"

He inclined his head. "You and I are participating in the first game."

"You signed up?" Lucas asked, shocked. "*Colt.* You *know* what kind of game it is. How on earth did you think that was a good idea?"

I watched them like a tennis match, and I could feel the tension increasing in my brain.

"Trust me," was all Colt said.

"Meanwhile, we subs still don't know shit," I said. I'd logged on every day to see if there was any new info about Saturday. Instead, last time, I was met by a stupid note that said everything the Tops needed to know had been forwarded to them. "Fuck what we think, right?"

Abel winced. "Kit..."

Colt was leaving the booth, and I quirked a brow at him, wondering what he was up to. Our entrees would be here soon.

But he didn't have to answer. He simply grabbed my arm and yanked me out of the booth.

"Hey!"

"Quiet," he gritted out. To the others, he said, "Kit and I are gonna get some fresh air. We'll be right back."

Mortification nearly crippled me, and my heart started pounding. Some guests were watching us; one was even smirking. Shithead. Anger spiked quickly.

"It hurts," I hissed. "Let go of my arm."

"Watch your fuckin' mouth, boy."

Colt ushered me outside the restaurant and didn't stop until we were between two buildings across the street. A rush of adrenaline coursed through me, and it felt like it was trying to battle the fear that gripped me too.

"You're not bein' a brat in there. You know that, right?" He let go of me and put himself between me and the mouth of the alley. "You're plain disrespectful."

I snapped my mouth shut and folded my arms over my chest as I broke eye contact.

What was wrong with me? I knew I'd been beyond rude in there. And it wasn't the first time I had acted out. I'd let my frustrations set the tone for days now, and it happened more frequently. I was impolite and discourteous to Lucas for no reason, and I came at Colt as if he were a console with nothing but buttons for me to push.

"I don't know why I'm doing it." I swallowed hard and stared at my feet. "I know I've crossed the line." Saying that dealt a crushing blow to my heart, and emotions threatened to spill over.

I crossed the line.

Oh God. This was how they would get tired of me. This was how I'd become too much for them.

"Well...that depends on what line you're referrin' to, Kit."

I frowned up at him, even though it meant he could see I was getting teary-eyed. "There's only one line."

"That ain't true." He took a step closer. "Take safewords, for instance. Calling red doesn't mean the relationship is over. Just the playtime. Same with this line. You've been bad tonight, and Lucas and I will punish you for it. But remember last time? When you've taken the punishment, it's all good again."

"Until I fuck up too often, and you get sick of it."

He narrowed his eyes at me, and I broke away again. I couldn't face him. The tension was drilling into my head. It hurt. It hurt...and I didn't know how to stop it.

When he took another step toward me, I took one backward. Because if he touched me now, or got too close, I would explode. Strung tight and not knowing why, I did all I could to hold myself together.

"Don't work against me, Kit," he warned. "You don't wanna do that. You don't want this to turn into a self-fulfilling prophecy. Lucas and I haven't given the slightest indication that we're gonna leave, so don't shove us out the fuckin' door." It took him three steps to cage me in and push my pulse through the roof. "Look at me."

"I don't want to," I croaked.

"Yes, you do. You're just afraid. Fucking look at me."

I clenched my jaw and blinked hard, feeling two tears rolling down my cheeks, and then I looked up.

"I belong in there." He tapped my temple. "That's where I wanna be, as your Daddy and as your Owner."

Holy fuck, he was breaking me. I shook my head. "You take too much." I sniffled. "I'm already yours, goddammit. Where does that leave me? Huh? I will have *no* control."

"Correct," he was quick to say. "You won't be in control whatsoever. But as to where that leaves you...? It leaves you with me and Luke. We hold the leash that you allow us to put on you, and if you stopped wanting that..." He sighed and placed his palms along the sides of my face. "It's you, Kit. You're the one we've been waiting for. You're the one I lost hope of finding, but Lucas believed. And he found you. And..." He shook his head and licked his lips and looked away for a second. "The only way to get rid of us is to push us away."

I closed my eyes, overcome with fear and paralyzing sadness. I didn't want to push them away. I wanted the opposite. I wanted to never be left alone again. I wanted Colt and Lucas more than I'd ever wanted anything.

Colt rested his forehead to mine. "You want to surrender to us. I can see it."

I sniffled. "Being defenseless scares the hell out of me."

"You're not defenseless," he murmured, easing back a few inches. "You have the power to bring Luke and me to our knees."

My breath stuttered, and I felt the crease appear in my forehead. "I do?"

"Does that come as a surprise?" He smiled the smallest of smiles and cupped my cheek. "We want the good and the bad with you, the ugly and the beautiful. The tantrums, the giggle fits, seeing you spill dipping sauce on your shirt—"

I glanced down quickly, and Colt hooked his finger under my nose.

"Made you look."

I looked up sharply. Gah!

He smiled. "We adore you, Kit."

Hope expanded in my chest, but the vise grip of fear was constantly there to remind me not to get ahead of myself.

I whimpered and wiped at my cheeks. "What can I say when sorry isn't enough?"

His gaze turned softer. "Why wouldn't it be enough, baby?"

"Because I never wanted to hurt you like this, and it's what

I've done," I cried. "I'm crazy scared of overstepping. I d-don't have you like you two have each other, and it already makes me upset a lot. After a month. Think of what I'll do in three months. I'll be your nightmare."

"Or you'll still be our dream." He brushed the pads of his thumbs under my eyes. "Sweet boy. What part of 'it's you we've been waiting for' don't you get? Fuck three months. In ten *years*, I hope we're still findin' new ways to fall in love with each—"

I squeaked.

Amusement danced in his eyes.

Did he just...?

"It took me a while to figure out why you were so insistent on Luke and me deciding how you should redecorate your house," he admitted. "But when it dawned on me, no one was happier than me."

Maybe it was too dark in the alley for him to see my blush. Maybe not. I didn't give a damn. My heart hammered in my rib cage, and for once, it wasn't an unpleasant feeling.

"We're falling in love?" I whispered.

He nodded slowly and ghosted his lips over mine. "We're definitely fallin' in love. Wouldn't you agree?"

"Yeah," I exhaled. I was brimming with hope. The vise around my chest loosened. "I want the opposite of pushing you away."

"Good," he whispered back, and he kissed me once. "Who am I, Kit?"

I shivered and closed my eyes and drew a deep breath. "You're my Daddy."

"That's right. And Daddy will make you surrender. On Saturday, in fact. I'm gonna hunt you down and steal the last bit of control that you're clinging to."

I cracked one eye open. "You're gonna what?"

He grinned. "You need an outlet. What Abel was talking

about—he was right on the money. You get frustrated easily, and that's when you act out. So I'm gonna show you how we can get rid of those frustrations."

Funny how quickly I got nervous. "The hunting part is figuratively speaking, right?"

"Not even close." He trailed a finger along my jaw, his gaze following the movement. "You're gonna be able to fight back. It's gonna be you and me in the middle of the woods. I'll find you..."

I sucked in a breath.

"I'm telling you this now so you can prepare yourself," he murmured. "You often feel weak. You talk down to yourself. You lift others to the skies and bury yourself six feet under, and that's gonna change. You'll fight me with everything you have, Kit. Promise me."

"I-I promise, but—"

"Nope. Leave it there. You wanna tell me some bullshit about you not being a fighter, and I don't wanna hear it. You're stronger than you think, and you'll show me—but most importantly, yourself—this weekend. Okay?"

"Okay." I stowed away my questions for later. I didn't need to know the details right this second.

"Okay," he echoed. "You ready to go back in?"

I nodded. "Yes, Sir. I'll apologize to the others."

"That's a good instinct, but it can wait. I'm gonna put you on speech restrictions while we eat. You need to let your mind power down some."

How could he know such things? *I* didn't even know, and it was my mind.

"I'm not allowed to talk at all?" I asked hesitantly.

"Not a word, but I'll give you a quick moment to let Luke know we're good."

I nodded again. Maybe I did need this. I trusted Colt. "I will obey."

"That's my boy." He pressed a kiss to my forehead, and then he linked our fingers together as we left the alley.

I wiped at my cheeks to make sure I'd removed as many traces as I could of my crying fest, and I stayed close to Colt. He seemed to sense I needed the comfort, so he draped an arm around my shoulders and told me to shut everyone out. Only he and Lucas existed. I didn't need to pay attention to anyone else.

I took his advice to heart and drew in another deep breath.

I didn't see the other guests at the steakhouse. I shoved the cheerful din out of my brain and followed Daddy to our booth.

Lucas's eyes were on me as we took our seats, and I found his hand under the table.

"Is everything okay?"

I nodded and leaned close, and he took the hint to lean down a bit so I could whisper in his ear. "Colt explained I didn't have to be scared, because we're falling in love."

Lucas quickly inched away a few inches and searched my eyes, uncertainty mingling with affection. Then he smiled softly and touched my cheek. Maybe he'd found what he was looking for in my gaze. "We definitely are, sweetheart." The look in his eyes brought forth my blush again, because I felt it. I felt how much he cared for me.

I grinned shyly, and he kissed my nose.

Colt told the others I was on speech restrictions for a bit, and that was that. He'd been right again. I had no questions from Abel about what'd happened, because my Daddy had ruled out the option of asking. All I had to do was focus on myself and the two men next to me.

The tension faded, and I could relax. I could sink into my favorite mind-set and just be.

16.

"I feel bad for him, Daddy." I bit nervously at my thumbnail.

Colt shrugged and had a faint smirk playing on his lips. "He made his doghouse, and now he gets to sleep in it."

Abel was a brat to the extreme yesterday when we spent the day sightseeing, and Madigan had decided on a "good" punishment by breakfast this morning. So that was why we were currently at PetSmart. Daddy and I stayed at the end of the aisle with collars, while Madigan stood where Abel was fighting tears and struggling to pick a collar.

He didn't want a damn collar from PetSmart.

I couldn't blame him. I'd be embarrassed.

Studded leather collars made for kinksters were one thing. Being forced to wear one made for actual dogs was a whole other dog park of humiliation, unless you were into that kink. And he wasn't.

"He said he was sorry," I mumbled and slipped my hand into Daddy's.

"Mm. He also called Madigan a boring son of a bitch for not letting him go up in the Washington Monument five minutes before they were closing."

I made a face. Okay, so it hadn't been Abel's brightest moment.

Looking over my shoulder, I tried to see where Lucas was. He'd gotten a phone call as we'd entered the big store, and that was a while ago. Hopefully, we would be done here soon so we could go home and pack.

We were heading down to the house in Mclean early. The event was tomorrow, but Reese had called Lucas last night and suggested a barbecue tonight. Given that our night at the steakhouse hadn't gone super-well because of me, everyone agreed it would be nice to have a do-over.

"Can we get ice cream before we get back to the house?" I asked.

Daddy sent me a sideways grin. "You're more interested in the sprinkles."

Yeah, but the place we went to yesterday before Abel's mood soured had the biggest selection, and I'd never been there before! I'd picked eight kinds. Only, we'd just had lunch before, so I'd basically licked off the sprinkles and then handed over the cone to Colt.

"I like the ice cream too," I offered.

He laughed under his breath. "Fine. You've been a good boy the past two days, so we can get ice cream."

I slapped my hands to my cheeks and pretended to be shocked. "Oh my gosh, are you saying good behavior gets rewarded?"

His beautiful eyes lit up before the first laugh slipped out. "Imagine that." He yanked me to him and ruffled my hair, and I giggled and pinched his side. "Watch those little fingers. You wouldn't wanna lose 'em."

I yelped and quickly tucked away my hands.

He chuckled. "Come on, I think I know where we can find Lucas."

"Where?" I followed him toward the back of the store.

"If they have puppies here today, that's where."

"Puppies!" My heart filled with excitement. "I've always wanted one." But my mother hadn't liked the idea. She'd said you could never tell if one was hostile.

"Luke too," Colt said, peering down another aisle. Not there, apparently. "It hasn't been in the cards for us yet. We work too much."

But, oh! "Daddy, I—"

"Would walk the dog all the time. That what you were gonna say?" He put an arm around my shoulders and found my hopeful expression amusing for some reason. "I'm not saying no. Just not now."

I fist-pumped the air.

"My goof." He smacked a kiss to the top of my head. "Ah—there he is."

Oh my God, oh my God, oh my God. I took off in a run, toward the corner where a dog adoption agency had set up a small playground for six or seven tiny puppies. Lucas was there already, and he was holding one of them!

"Slow down, baby," Colt called.

Shit. Right. I didn't want to scare the puppies.

I slowed down shortly before I reached Lucas, and that was when he tilted his head and spotted me. He smiled and looked back at the puppy, who was playing with Lucas's fingers.

"It's so cute," I whispered. I touched the light-brown fur gently, and it was so, so soft I could cry.

"Isn't she?" Lucas spread the fingers of his hand and lowered it over the puppy's head, and she pawed at his fingers when he pretended to grab at her nose. "This one's a firecracker."

"Aww..." I was melting.

Colt reached us and slipped his arms around us, and he rested his chin on Lucas's shoulder. "Am I gonna have to be the bad guy here?"

Lucas and I nodded.

Colt puffed out his cheeks with a breath and let it out slowly. "You know, this is one of those things you get for Christmas or somethin'. The timing ain't right, darlin'. Our condo's still being renovated, and Kit's got us movin' to Georgetown."

"I'm glad you agree." I grinned up at him.

There'd been a sense of freedom in us admitting to one another that we were falling in love. I was able to trust that this wasn't temporary or all about kink, at the same time as I could now relax and enjoy the moment. All cards were on the table, including my desire for all of us to live together. More correctly, I wanted us to turn my parents' house into our house. We had the living room set already...

"She's just so precious," Lucas murmured. "I bet she'd love Georgetown as much as we do, Colt."

I hugged Lucas's arm super hard. They left me these little hints that they weren't saying no to *anything*. They had to be responsible adults with patience and all that nonsense, but I wasn't alone in my wishes. It meant the whole world to me.

"Y'all are hopeless." Colt stifled a chuckle and shook his head. "We gotta go. Kit, you wanted ice cream before we pack, and then we're hittin' the road."

I felt like I should've been better prepared for this. I'd seen the house in Mclean online. I'd seen a bunch of pictures. I'd taken the virtual tour of it! And yet...when we reached the end of the private road and the trees parted, I felt genuinely intimidated.

The large Victorian house was painted black, with white shutters, and there was a circular drive with a ghoulish fountain in the middle.

The place sat atop a hill, and I couldn't see anything behind the house from here. What I could see was a well taken care of front yard, no fence, a big porch, and a separate garage that had space for probably a dozen cars.

Unbuckling my belt, I scooted forward in my seat and snuck my arm forward to Lucas in the passenger's seat.

He gathered my hand and kissed the top of it, then held it close to his chest.

Abel was feeling anxious about tomorrow, so he'd asked Madigan to sit in the back with us, meaning both my Daddies were in the front and wouldn't protect me from this mansion of pain.

Colt rounded the driveway and drove to the garage where he pulled in next to an old classic. I didn't know the make, only that my dad'd had one of those at our summer residence.

"I guess River ain't here yet," Colt noted, killing the engine.

"No, he's running late," Lucas replied. I withdrew my hand and opened the door to get out. "August wanted to talk to him about Shay."

"I definitely want in on the decision-makin' on that kid," Colt told him. I stepped out of the car and wondered if something was wrong with Shay. "I don't want him banned."

Wait, what? Shay was still new in the community. Had he even attended a single event? I didn't know where else he'd be able to break the rules. And to be banned...? He must've done something bad.

"I don't either." Lucas slid on his shades and stretched his legs. "We'll talk things over with the brothers." He extended a hand to me. "Let's grab our bags later, Colt. I want to show Kit our place."

I quirked a brow as I grabbed his hand. The way he'd said "our place" made it sound like they had more than a room they favored.

"Nah, it's fine. Y'all go ahead—I'll bring the bags," Colt replied.

Madigan and Abel were speaking to each other in hushed voices, so I didn't want to interrupt. Instead, I went with Lucas.

Even through the soles of my Chucks, I felt how hot the pavement was. Lucas pointed out the seating area on the porch and told me he and Colt had spent many evenings there with their closest friends. And I smiled when he said he couldn't wait to make me part of the group.

Rather than walking up the path leading to the house, we hit the lawn and walked alongside the place. *Yikes.* I looked up at the house, all three stories, its presence extra ominous when I was so up close. How many had screamed in there? How many had cried out their orgasms? How many had Colt and Lucas— oh no, not going there.

"What was that cringe for?" Lucas asked.

I huffed out a breath and shook my head. "Jealousy. I was thinking about how many Littles you and Daddy have played with here."

He chuckled softly and squeezed my hand. "Fewer than you think, and precisely zero if we count subs we felt this kind of connection with—or anything remotely close to it."

As answers went, that one was really good.

"Damn. It's hot today, isn't it?" Lucas released my hand briefly to fold up the sleeves of his button-down. "I think I'll need a dip in the pool once we're settled in."

"Oh, I didn't know there's a—*whoa*..." I came to an abrupt stop as we reached the far corner of the house. "This place is huge, Daddy." I just gawked.

The massive wooden deck put mine at home to shame. There were two seating areas, each table seating ten, and two Jacuzzis. A barbecue area I just *knew* Colt had had something to do with. And maybe ten or so feet away from the deck, a big pool overlooked the football field-sized lawn. Beyond that was a forest. Oh, fun—right before the forest began, in a corner I'd almost missed, was an agility course for dogs.

There was more. Trees lined the property, and—

"The third guest house is ours," he said.

I was getting to that. Six A-frame cabins sat along the west side, and I guessed they were for those we called founding members. Possibly.

"Tomorrow, this place will be packed." Daddy liked that; I could tell. He studied the grounds with a note of pride, and I grabbed his hand again. *My* Daddy was one of the founders. Two of the founders, even. They'd been here from the start, working hard, putting in money and time to build this community for us. "I tried to secure one of the guest rooms on the third floor for Madigan and Abel, but they were booked already," he said. "They'll be fine with us, though. Come on, I'll show you."

I followed him at a quicker pace to the third guesthouse. The roof extended outward, giving the elevated porch cover from rain and such. There was a small couch and a chair and a fire pit, and I loved it already. I wanted to sit here at night with my Daddies, maybe have ice cream with sprinkles, and just be together.

I skipped up onto the porch as Daddy dug out his keys.

"Can we live here forever instead?" I suggested.

Lucas threw me a smirk over his shoulder, then opened the door. "It might be a little too small for that. But I do hope we'll visit often."

I wouldn't necessarily call it small. More...compact. Compact and very cozy. A wood stove whispered promises of winter nights where we could cuddle on one of the two couches. The downstairs was open, a combination of living room area and kitchenette, and, as Daddy explained, a bedroom upstairs.

"Colt hates the bathroom because he always knocks his

head on the doorframe." Daddy crossed the room and opened a door under the steep staircase. Ah, that was where the bathroom was hiding. Well, toilet and sink. I assumed we'd go into the big house if we needed to shower.

"I love it." I looked around me and couldn't help but grin. It was the closest I'd come to being in a log cabin. It had that feel, complete with a soft-looking fur rug under the coffee table, the fresh smells of the forest, and the dark, rich colors. I saw Colt in my head; I bet he loved it here too. There was no TV. A bookcase, flannel blankets, and, and, and the little things. The kitchenette in the corner—there was a shelf for a few plates, and mugs hung on hooks underneath it. It was the little things, right? Always the little things.

Last stop was the bedroom upstairs, and I vaguely registered a closet at one end before my gaze landed on the king-size bed. Mattress, I should say. There was no bed frame, just this thick mattress that reached above knee-level, and countless pillows.

Had they fucked anyone here?

Daddy joined me by my side when he'd adjusted the AC. My chest felt tight, and I cursed myself for having been too scared to seek out people before. Had Colt and Lucas not pursued me, I would've missed out on all this. I never would've felt the happiness they made me feel every day now.

"I think we need new bed linen here," I said stiffly and turned to Daddy. Something had taken over. Something possessed me to take ownership, and I couldn't stop it. I didn't want to. I started unbuttoning Daddy's shirt without having a real plan. I only knew I wanted to see my territory and mark it.

I ignored the mirth in his eyes.

"Whatever you're thinking now is a figment of your imagination, little one."

Pffft. Yeah, right. I pushed off his button-down and lifted his undershirt.

He took over and pulled the shirt over his head.

Fuck yes. I closed the distance and slid my hands up his chest, my mouth following. I had to taste him, breathe him in, be close to him. Take him...

"The others will be here any minute," he murmured. I didn't care. I kissed his neck, as far as I could reach, and I had him. He was caving to me. Daddy shivered and slipped a hand between us to palm my cock, and he rubbed it lovingly through my pants. "My irresistible little darling."

"I want you, Daddy. Please?"

"Soon." He dipped down and kissed me deeply. "Give Daddy a taste of your sweet cock, and then we'll join the others. Colt will have our swimwear."

I groaned, half in complaint and half in lust. Then I unbuttoned my shorts as Daddy fell to his knees, and he pushed them down along with my briefs.

"There's my boy." He wrapped his fingers around me and sucked me into his mouth, and I dropped my head back. He loved to suck on soft cock as much as I did, only we never stayed soft very long. But there was something about it. The way my Daddies felt in my mouth, smooth and thick and soft, before they hardened between my lips. It was the best.

Daddy hummed around my length when I heard Colt outside. The door opened downstairs, and he wasn't alone. Madigan and Abel had arrived too.

"Colt," I moaned. "Um, we need some help. Can—fuck..." I thrust into Lucas's mouth, and he grabbed two fistfuls of my bottom to hold me in place. "Oh God. Can you bring our stuff, please?"

I heard Colt and Madigan laugh.

"I'll go see what my sluts are up to. Y'all get comfortable," Colt said.

"No!" I whisper-shouted as Daddy stopped sucking on me. I'd just gotten hard, damn it! "Please, Daddy?"

He chuckled huskily and tucked me into my briefs again, though he didn't stop touching me, nor did he get up off the floor.

Colt reached the landing, and before I could look at him over my shoulder, his arms snaked around my middle, and he kissed my neck. "Why am I not surprised to find you like this?" I felt his smile against my skin, and then I smiled too. Colt cupped Lucas's cheek, and Lucas turned his head to kiss the inside of Colt's hand. It was a beautiful sight. "If I weren't in a desperate need to cool off in the pool, I'd suggest we stay right here."

"The pool isn't going anywhere." I pouted back at Colt.

He gave me a quick kiss. "You'll get yours, greedy boy."

***

"River and Reese seem like...interesting people." Abel smiled uncomfortably.

"If by interesting you mean terrifying, then I agree." Let's just say I was staying in this end of the pool now.

Shortly after we had changed and gotten comfortable at the pool, Reese had stepped out onto the patio to greet us. He'd been in the office working on some things, he'd said. He'd only worn a pair of threadbare jeans and bed head. In the sun, his hair was copper. His eyes were sea green, lighter than Colt's, and his torso was covered with scars and ink. He was Lucas's height, so I guessed around six-one, six-two, but the look in his eyes might as well make him ten feet tall. Either way, I didn't want to meet him in a dark alley. He'd been polite and smirky when Lucas introduced us, though there was something about him that screamed *keep your distance*.

The kicker? There were two of them. River showed up an hour later, a carbon copy of his brother, with the exception of their tattoos. Reese had more, one of them inked across the side of his neck. Otherwise, I wouldn't be able to tell them apart.

Lucas and Reese appeared to have an interesting relationship. It was brotherly, with Lucas digesting the ideas Reese threw at him, and then they went from there. Because that was pretty much what they'd been doing on the other side of the pool. Lucas sat on the edge now, and Reese was in the water. Naked. And they discussed future events and gatherings.

Colt, River, and Madigan were also there, but they were sitting on the steps, having a beer. Not naked.

No, I was much safer in the deep end with Abel.

"Are you feeling better now, by the way?" I asked, refocusing on my friend.

He lifted a shoulder. "A little, I guess. Humiliation is tough for me, but I know why he's doing it. Hell, I've asked him to."

I hesitated. I knew Abel had bipolar, and though we'd spoken about it openly many, many times, I'd learned there was a time and a place. Sometimes, the topic was too sensitive, and it was because Madigan and Abel worked on his insecurities together, leaving the thoroughly pushed buttons extra raw.

I phrased myself as carefully as I could. "Are you two possibly working on a fear right now?"

He dipped his chin and sank under the water briefly. Then his head and shoulders reappeared above the surface, and he pushed back his hair. "I want to be able to tell the difference between humiliation in kink and the degradation I put myself through when I'm going through one of my depressive periods." He paused. "Kinda like a rape survivor telling the difference between rape and rape play." His smile was wobbly and uncertain. "It's difficult not to be triggered when you start."

"I get it," I said quietly. "Does that mean you're doing something with the collar tomorrow?"

"Yeah." He made a face and looked out over the grassy hill. "Down there—he's gonna make me do that obstacle course thing."

Jesus Christ, I felt stupid. It wasn't for dogs. Well...not animal dogs, anyway. It was meant for kinksters who were into puppy play and...stuff. In Abel's case, it was the scene of his next punishment.

Laughter rang out from the other end of the pool. Colt and River were cracking up at whatever Madigan was telling them. Must be a good story. He was animated about it.

"It's never good when Doms laugh together," Abel muttered.

"*Right?*" I shook my head.

"Abel and Kit!" Madigan hollered. "You two up for a little game against Colt and me?"

Uh-oh. Abel and I exchanged a glance.

"A game of what?" I asked warily.

Colt stepped out of the water and walked over to a wicker chest near the patio doors, and he returned with a volleyball. "Rules are easy. We dunk the ball on your end of the pool to score, and you dunk it on this side to score."

"That means grappling," Abel said under his breath. "And we know they're gonna play dirty."

"I'd lose even if they didn't," I pointed out. Sports had never been my stage to shine.

Abel eyed the men as Reese pushed himself up on the edge and took a seat next to Lucas. Still fucking naked.

"Are you sure you're up for it?" Abel called. Why he went there was beyond me. He was basically swatting a stick at a beehive. "I mean...you're looking at 180 pounds of muscle here, and I'm a professional hockey player."

"What're you doing?" I hissed. What was I going to brag about? Being somewhat close to 150 pounds of anxiety?

Colt smirked and got in the water again. "Water ain't frozen. I'll take my chances."

"Your loss, old-timers." Abel shrugged. "What're you, like, fifty?"

I stared at Abel incredulously. Did he have to rile them up? We had no edge here! And he knew very well that Colt was forty-five.

"Why not go higher?" Colt scratched his neck absently. "Why not say sixty or sixty-five? 'Cause that's the old man who's gonna make you watch when I rapefuck your friend's tight little ass later. You know, after you lose to us old-timers."

"Abel, I swear to God," I whisper-yelled.

"Are you sure you wanna keep talking, trouble?" Madigan asked his boy. "I'll give you the same treatment he'll give Kit."

Abel laughed, then pointed at him. "You gotta be able to catch me first, you slow motherf—"

I panicked and slapped a hand over his mouth.

He flinched but made a quick comeback, his eyes sparking up with exhilaration.

Five Doms were having fun at our expense and future misery.

"Don't you get it?" Abel's question was muffled behind my hand, so I lowered it. "Colt wants to see what you got. He's gonna test the limits for the game tomorrow."

I frowned. "He knows I'm not athletic."

"But you can give him more hell than he'll anticipate if you suck even more today," he replied. "We lose on purpose today, Kit. We fumble—*you* fumble, and you lose like the Leafs."

"Are...are they a bad team?" I was fairly certain that was a Toronto hockey team.

He snorted. "Don't get me started. But are you with me?

Because if we make fools of ourselves now, you'll have the added element of surprise tomorrow. That on its own is a powerful weapon, and it can throw Colt—at least for a moment."

Oh wow. My friend was a genius. A diabolical genius. "You're actually giving me a shot." I shook my head in wonder and felt the excitement trickle in. "That thing tomorrow—the game... I've tried not to think about it, because it's ludicrous. Colt is so much stronger and faster than me, but if I pull this off, I might at least take him by surprise a couple times before he defeats me."

"And that's the point." Abel grabbed me by my shoulders. "You don't wanna win. I sure as shit don't wanna win. But we want some fun along the way. We still wanna kick them in the shin on our way down."

I grinned, nervous and, honestly, a little thrilled. Which was nothing close to how I would've described my feelings earlier about tomorrow.

"Thank you for—"

"Hey. Save that for later." He smirked. "There will come a day when I'll need you to save my ass. Probably very soon."

I chuckled. "I've got you."

Okay. Time to lose spectacularly.

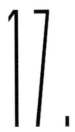

17.

"**K**it, what're you—"

I spun around with my heart in my throat and covered Abel's mouth with my hand for the second time today.

"Be quiet," I breathed.

I was eavesdropping.

I gave Abel a look and pointed upward to the second floor, where Lucas and Colt were currently arguing.

We were supposed to be enjoying our food comas after an amazing barbecue, brought to us by Colt and River, but Lucas had requested "a word" with Colt right after we were done. And I'd had a feeling it would be about me, because Lucas had looked troubled ever since the ball game in the pool.

Abel nodded in understanding, and I turned toward the stairs again but made sure to stay close to the front door in case I had to escape fast.

"Of course I trust you," I heard Lucas say tiredly. "I'm just worried about him. You saw the way he flinched when you came at him in the pool. Imagine how it'll be when you're surrounded by rocks and trees in complete darkness."

"That's the fear I want him to get past," Colt replied. "He ain't weak. He's just held back by fears. It'll take practice, but—"

"And he'll get hurt."

"That's life, darlin'," Colt groaned. "And you know what? Being too scared to take on challenges will hurt him a whole lot more than some cuts and scrapes ever will."

I chewed on my lip, appreciating them both. But as scared as I actually was—and I knew it—I sided with Colt. I'd lived a sheltered life, and I needed to break free from the chains I'd shackled myself with.

Tomorrow night was going to hurt. I was prepared for it.

Lucas sighed. "I'm being the fretting mother, aren't I?"

Colt chuckled quietly. "You make a hot fretter, though. Come here." There was a beat of silence. "I love you. I love that you worry. You know I can take it too far, too fast sometimes—that's where you come in. But I think he needs this. I think we all do. He's still clingin' to that last shred of composure, and I wanna show him that not only will I take it from him, but I'll be there when he's at his worst. He'll be his own sadistic degrader when I beat him tomorrow, and it's our job to nip that shit in the bud. We'll make him focus on his accomplishments and not however far away he might be from a goal."

Abel reached for my hand and squeezed it, and I squeezed back, overwhelmed by the love I had for my Daddies.

"You're right," Lucas murmured. "He's going to be vulnerable when he comes off the adrenaline. I should make plans for aftercare. We'll all need it."

"Definitely," Colt agreed. "Madigan's got plans for Abel, so we'll have some privacy here."

"Okay, good. I'll keep worrying."

Colt let out a soft laugh. "He's our boy. We'll be worryin' for the rest of our lives."

Emotions surged forward, and I had to blink back tears. *For the rest of our lives.* Jesus Christ, I had no words. Abel gave me a quick hug, and I could only grin and wipe my cheeks. I was really their boy, and I had fallen so hard for them. This had happened to me. *Me.*

"I told you," Abel whispered.

I laughed silently and sniffled, then nodded toward the door. It was time to sneak out before I got caught eavesdropping. Again.

We couldn't very well return to the patio right away, because it would be too obvious. Madigan, River, and Reese were sitting there chatting, listening to music, and drinking beer, and they would let Colt and Lucas know in a heartbeat that Abel and I had just come back too. So, I ushered Abel behind the A-frame cabins with an idea.

Abel squinted in the darkness. "Not that I don't enjoy standing in the underbrush when it's dark and snakes are coming out to hunt, but what're we doing back here?"

"Stalling a bit," I replied. "And also, can you teach me some fighting things? Like, some moves? Some techniques?"

Abel was a force to be reckoned with when he played hockey. He had one of those positions where they scored a lot, and he was fast, which meant—as he'd explained to me—that he had players who kept the ice clear for him. From fights. But...he didn't shy away from trash talk and getting physical. Hockey players were hotheaded by default, and you couldn't be some scaredy-cat in the rink.

"I wouldn't say I fight very well," Abel said. "I mean, I just throw my weight around. It's one thing to get into a fight during a game, but if you're studying fighting techniques, you're kind of focusing on the wrong thing and might wanna consider a different sport."

I huffed. "You're still more of a fighter than I am. You heard what Reese and Colt said about these events. They're wild."

And Colt had been up front with me. He wanted me to give him my all. When I went down, it would be because I had nothing left to give. He'd given me permission to kick, bite, grab, punch—all of it. He'd also, thankfully, said he wouldn't go that far with me. He'd undoubtedly seen the horror in my eyes and reassured me, while laughing like the Sadist he was, that he'd never kick me or use his teeth or punch. He was very confident that he wouldn't need to "resort to that cheap kind of fightin'" to bring me down.

I was going for cheap, I guess!

"Kit?" I heard Lucas call. "Baby, where are you?"

"He sounds so worried." Abel pouted.

"We're back here, Daddy!" I called back. "We'll be there soon! We're just talking about world domination!"

Lucas laughed fondly, hopefully put at ease, and I heard chuckles from the others too.

"Okay, fine. I'll teach you some tricks," Abel told me. "But we gotta hurry."

"Is my tongue blue yet?" Abel stuck his out, and I giggled madly.

It was totally blue!

"Is mine red? Oh—wait..." I scowled. My tongue was always red. Red drinks weren't going to change that. Ignoring how the Doms laughed at me, I turned to Colt and gave him my best smile. "Daddy, can I please have a blue drink?"

"Sure," he chuckled. He leaned forward and grabbed one of the little glasses, then reached for the mixers and stuff. They weren't shot glasses; these were bigger, though not by much. Reese had brought them out earlier from what they called the Little Bar. I was going to have to check it out tomorrow, that was for sure. Small glasses, short straws, fun decorations, and brightly colored syrups.

The more time I spent around River and Reese, the clearer it became that they did have some differences after all. Reese was a Daddy Dom too. River wasn't. Both were Sadists and very blunt and unashamed. River was on the quieter side, and he seemed to speak through touch with his brother. They sat next to each other, and he often conveyed his thoughts with a nudge, a tap, or a squeeze. Like when Reese shared a mildly terrifying memory of a masochist they'd played with, and River had just scratched his fingers lightly atop Reese's hand. They'd looked each other, and then Reese had chuckled and added to the story. As if River had reminded his brother of something.

I supposed I would always be a people watcher, even when I was no longer lonely and using people watching to pretend I was part of something. Humans were fascinating, and I had the best view from here. Colt, Lucas, and I occupied the one and only couch around our table, and the other four were across from us. I'd also noticed that Madigan had stopped drinking when Abel started, and his gaze was on his boy most of the time. Always making sure Abel was okay.

"All right, try not to spill this one, baby." Colt slid the drink my way, and my eyes widened with excitement. He'd done the layered thing again! At the bottom of the drink was a layer of dark blue, and it went lighter and lighter closer to the surface.

"Thank you! I only spilled one, though." It was why my T-shirt hung over Lucas's armrest. But it was okay. It wasn't cold out at all, and I liked sitting in just my undies.

I took a sip, and the yummy flavors exploded on my tongue. Sprite, the sweet syrup, lemon, and a little bit of vodka. That was the grown-up part of the drink, and it made everything funny.

"There's more sugar than booze in that thing," Reese said, amused.

"We don't need him hungover tomorrow," Colt chuckled.

"It's delicious." I licked my lips and turned to Lucas. "Wanna try some? It's not gross like your whiskey."

"Blasphemy, dear." He smirked and took a slow sip of his drink. "I think I'll stick to my drink, but thank you."

I scrunched my nose. "Yuck. I like whiskey kisses but hate whiskey. Funny, right?"

"Same he-ere," Abel hiccupped. Then he grinned goofily, and I laughed.

"Okaaay." Madigan raised his brows and let out a little laugh. "I think I'm cutting you off, baby boy."

"I disagree," Abel told him.

I set down my glass and kept my laughter to myself as I snuggled into Lucas's arms.

Colt gathered my legs in his lap, and I smiled at him and blew a kiss.

He winked.

For a while, we had a pleasant time listening to Abel getting bratty with Madigan, whose patience wouldn't last forever. And *River*...he had an interesting approach. Rather than cautioning Abel and showing he was on Madigan's side, he casually said one might argue that vacations were the best places to let go of some rules and have an extra drink.

"See?" Abel exclaimed with a gesture toward River. "He gets it. Why don't you, Daddy?"

"Bless." Colt rumbled a low laugh and took a swig of his beer.

Madigan smiled faintly and shook his head at Abel. "The more infractions you have, the bigger chances he's got of watching me punish you."

Abel's head whipped sharply to face River. "Would you really set me up like that, Sir?"

River smirked a little into his whiskey and took a sip before

he answered. The look in his green eyes was bordering on inde-
cent. "Absolutely."

Yikes, he was scary.

"We like seeing little boys cry." Reese reached for a bag of
chips.

"There's an image..." Colt sighed and sent a look skyward as
he adjusted his cock in his jeans.

"Hey." I frowned at him. "Don't be a meanie. I'm a good boy."

He pinched my toe. "Are you telling me what to do?"

"No, I'm telling you what *not*—"

Lucas covered my mouth with his hand and peered down at
me with a pointed look. "Honestly, boy. Do you not see what
he's doing?"

I scowled and pressed my lips together. He was right. Colt
wasn't much unlike River. Button-pushers, both of them. Hmpf.
More than that, they set traps.

Instinct had me sticking my tongue out at Colt, but as the
realization of what I was doing hit me, I could relax. Lucas was
still covering my mouth, so I'd just ended up licking his hand.

"That means I like you." My words were muffled behind his
hand, and he snorted and wiped himself off on my chest.

"Brat," was all he said.

Phew. Nice save, I thought.

"Nooo, I'm not tired, Daddy," I whined as Colt hooked an arm
under my knees. "I wanna stay here."

"You can't keep your eyes open." He picked me up, my head
landing on his shoulder. "Grab his shirt, darlin'."

I blinked sleepily and yawned. Only Reese and River
remained at the table. When had Madigan and Abel taken off?

"Until tomorrow, gentlemen," Lucas said.

"Sleep well," Reese answered. "It was good to meet you officially, little one."

"You too, Sir," I mumbled and rubbed my eyes. "But you still scare me."

He laughed.

River's mouth twisted with mirth, and he leaned back in his seat and rubbed Reese's neck. To which Reese glanced back at him with a smile and a slight nod.

As intrigued as I was about their dynamic, I had to refocus on my attempts at not looking sleepy. I thought I was doing all right, but my Daddies evidently didn't agree. Colt carried me down from the deck and toward our cabin, and I did my best not to use his shoulder as a pillow. It would indicate I was tired.

"I could go for another drink," I said, stifling a yawn.

"Sure you could," Lucas chuckled.

"I could!" I pouted. And by some weird, dark magic, my head landed on Colt's shoulder again. I had no idea how it happened. "Daddy, do you know what I think?" I blinked drowsily and played with the shell of Colt's ear.

"No, what do you think?" He sounded amused.

There was nothing funny about this. I was dead serious. "I think there needs to be a drink with sprinkles in it. Imagine it. What a big seller."

Colt's shoulders shook with his laugh.

"What're sprinkles made of?" Lucas asked.

"Delicious sugar." I smacked my lips and licked them.

"And what happens to sugar when you put it in liquid?"

But, ohh! I threw him a grumpy look. "You choose to focus on the negative stuff, Daddy. That's on you. I can't help you with that."

He smirked and ruffled my hair. "How lame of Daddy."

"So we're in agreement." My eyes closed of their own volition, and I couldn't open them again. "Sprinkles are the best," I whispered to myself. "Sprinkles and my Daddies. Sprinkles on my Daddies."

Colt laughed through his nose and pressed a kiss to my hair.

I heard a door open, followed by Lucas saying we had to be quiet because Madigan and Abel were asleep.

Once inside the cabin, I managed to crack one eye open to see them cuddled together on the pullout couch.

"They're cute together," I said, super quiet. "Can I brush my teeth tomorrow instead?"

"Shh, baby," Colt whispered. "Yes, you can. I'll need you to take the stairs by yourself, though. Daddy's old."

I grinned and poked his scruffy cheek. "You're perfect."

He smiled and kissed me quickly, then helped me down. Ugh. I had to walk by myself. It was a struggle. I grunted and grabbed on to the railing, and I sort of dragged myself up, step by step.

"Brat," Colt whispered and gave my butt a push. "I thought you weren't tired."

Well. Things could change!

About two very excruciating minutes later, I was buck naked and had face-planted on a cloud. Or mattress, but it felt like a cloud to me. It was so soft, and the pillows were...also so soft. Plus, I had my Daddies crawling into bed with me, and they were naked too. The way it was supposed to be.

"Get in the middle," Colt murmured to Lucas. "When the little one falls asleep, I want your ass."

I yawned and snuggled up against Lucas, who held me to him. "I'm not tired..."

"Just take me, baby," Lucas whispered. "I need it."

"Daddy needs it, Daddy," I giggled, not even fighting the cobwebs of sleep. I welcomed them and stretched and yawned and felt amazing. As I pressed my body against Lucas's fully, wanting to fall asleep to the movements of them fucking, I heard the familiar sound of a bottle opening.

"Sweet dreams, my precious boy." Lucas threaded his fingers into the hair at the back of my head and pressed a lingering kiss to my forehead.

I let out a soft breath. "Night, Daddy. Night, Daddy..."

A moment later, Lucas's body rocked against mine as Colt pushed inside. Lucas held me tighter. His cock grew thick and hard along my thigh, and Colt fucked him. And they came with me into my dreams.

"Don't look that way, Kit."

I made a face and left the edge of our little porch, and I sat down next to Lucas on the wicker couch. He was enjoying a cup of coffee in the shade, and I was worrying my butt off because Abel was currently being punished at the dog course.

"I feel bad for him," I admitted.

"I know, sweetheart." He patted my leg and grabbed the paper from the table. "Hopefully, he'll learn his lesson."

"Brats don't generally do that," I mumbled, squinting at him.

His mouth twitched. "You don't say."

Hardy-har-har. I got it, I got it. I was a brat too. Whatever.

Restless, jittery, and impatient, I stood up again and paced the deck. People had started arriving already. It wasn't even noon, and there were at least six men and women from our community in the pool. Two had come over to say hi to Lucas, and they'd been surprised to learn I was with him and Colt.

I couldn't help but glance down the hill again. Poor Abel. Madigan was making him jump through hoops—literally. I couldn't imagine the humiliation.

"What if Abel's too distraught to partake of the game tonight?" I asked.

"They're not joining," Daddy murmured distractedly. I heard him flip a page in the newspaper. "Madigan was already on the fence, and he told us this morning they won't sign up. Abel's anxiety has been tested quite a bit recently."

Oh. Oh, okay. Then I was glad they wouldn't participate.

I rubbed my elbow absently, running my fingers over the soft skin. My morning routine had certainly changed with my Daddies in charge, and I didn't itch as much anymore. That was nice. Plus, my skin felt crazy smooth.

"Mister West!"

I looked up at the main house and spotted a girl darting across the deck and down onto the lawn. Oh! It was Ivy. Someone I could at least pick from a lineup. Someone I'd exchanged words with before. I was sure Gretchen would be here today too. She never missed events, according to herself. We hadn't spoken much beyond that at munches.

Lucas put down the paper as Ivy reached us, and she gave me a curious smile. Which soon morphed into a wide smirk.

"So, it *is* you, Kit." She narrowed her eyes almost accusingly before turning to Lucas with the biggest grin. "I knew it was him, Sir! I knew it the second part of his hand ended up in one of your pictures on Instagram."

She must have recognized my tattoos.

Lucas chuckled and rose from his seat to give Ivy a kiss on her cheek. "The cat's finally out of the bag, then."

"Am I the cat?" I wondered.

Ivy laughed and rounded the table, and before I knew it, she threw her arms around me. "I'm so happy for y'all! Oh, Kit, I can't even tell you how long Mister West and Mister Carter have been looking for you."

I blushed furiously, taken aback by her quick acceptance.

Lucas smiled at me.

I patted Ivy on the back, and she leaned away, still with that grin on her face. She was very beautiful, all long blond pigtails and dimples.

"There are gonna be some jealous boys once the news breaks," she said.

"I believe you," I replied with an awkward smile. "They make me very happy."

"And I know it's mutual, honey." She winked, facing Lucas once more. "May I tell everyone, Sir?"

Mirth twinkled in Lucas's eyes. "Go for it."

Oh, jeez.

His three-worded green light was all it took for her to bounce off and run back toward the main house.

Lucas came up behind me and kissed my neck. "I'm glad. I want everyone to know you're ours."

I laughed nervously and turned around in his arms. "I'm just going to thank my lucky stars you see it that way. For me, I will always be the one who won the lottery with you two."

He shook his head and touched my cheek. "Don't underestimate Colt and me, sweetheart. We'll make you see what a wonderful young man you are."

Maybe. Maybe he was right. They'd already made me feel better about myself.

For the next couple hours, more people arrived for the event tonight. Lucas knew many, many of the kinksters, and several came over to chat and to ask if it was true, if he and Colt had claimed me as their boy. And each time, Lucas held me close to him on the little couch and confirmed that we were together.

Ivy had been right. Some of the guys had eyed me and offered hollow smiles and felicitations.

It awoke a new restlessness in me, and it made me itch in a

way I'd never encountered before. As if an urge were trying to claw itself out of my body.

At some point, Madigan guided a sobbing Abel up the hill toward the house, and Lucas jogged over to them. He gave Madigan what appeared to be a set of keys, and Madigan nodded in thanks.

When Lucas returned, he explained he'd given them access to a private playroom.

My heart ached uncomfortably, and I hoped Abel would be happy soon. The punishment had to be over.

"Remember this is for Abel's best, dear." Lucas kissed my temple and stopped my fidgeting with a hand over mine. "You know how you feel after we've punished you, don't you? When all is forgiven?"

I nodded hesitantly. It was true. My mind was at peace after a lashing. More than that, I felt littler and younger and more willing to hand over my free will to my Daddies. It was strange, really, but I never trusted them more than when they stood their ground and disciplined me.

"Can I go see him later?" I asked. "I want to make sure he's okay."

Daddy gave me a patient look. "Firstly, they'll probably be locked away most of the day. Secondly..." He paused and kissed the tops of my hands. "Trust Abel's Daddy, Kit. Abel trusts him with his life. Madigan will make sure he's okay."

Crap. He was right again. Fucking hell, I really did need to let go of certain things.

"Okay," I whispered. "You're right, Sir."

A round of laughter rang out from the pool area, and we turned that way and saw Ivy in Colt's arms. He was one of those laughing, the sound warm and infectious. It was impossible not to melt a little. Ivy had probably just shown her excitement at our relationship.

Reese and someone Lucas had pointed out earlier as another founder were there too. Perhaps it meant they were done preparing for tonight? There'd been constant running back and forth, though Colt and Reese had been indoors most of the day. A handful of others, I had no idea who they were, had disappeared into the forest every now and then.

"Ah, good, he has the paperwork," Lucas murmured. "It's going to be impossible to keep the nerves at bay now."

"What do you mean?" I asked curiously.

Lucas was already visibly uncomfortable. "Given the nature of tonight's game, we have every participant sign releases. It's one of the reasons I'm not exactly thrilled about you joining. I'm worried it's going to be too much for your first event."

I understood. I was worried too. But mostly about the fact that I would suck.

Lucas seemed more concerned than I was, though, and I suspected it was because I had no idea what to expect.

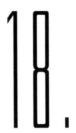

18.

If someone had told me six months ago that I'd sign a waiver and a contract to participate in a primal takedown in the middle of nowhere with one of my two Daddy Doms today...

I wouldn't even know how I'd react, to be honest. It was *that* bizarre.

With Colt standing behind me, he couldn't see how nervous I was.

The place was packed. The entire community was here, it felt like, and everyone was excited for The Games to begin. They sat or stood in groups on or near the deck. A dozen or so were listening from the pool.

Nine Tops had signed up to partake with their bottoms, and we were lined up on the lawn below the pool area.

River and Reese stood out on the lawn, silent, waiting. Well-worn jeans, black tees, and calculating gazes that missed nothing.

The forest loomed ominously down the hill, with lit torches leading the way on both sides.

I caught movement in the corner of my eye and spotted Lucas stepping out of our cabin. Dressed in black dress pants and a matching shirt, along with a severe expression, he came across as strict, if not freaking lethal. He joined Reese and River, as did two others, two women in leather corsets and skintight pants. One of them, a woman with long red hair, had been very nice to me at a munch once, but right now, she looked scary. Just like the others.

Reese paced along his line of friends as he spoke, his voice commanding and rich. He didn't need to raise his voice in order for people to listen to him.

Then he stopped next to Lucas and addressed us all. "Mr. West is going to run through some of the things that were in the contract, so you better listen."

My heart sped up as Lucas took a step forward and cleared his throat.

Hi, Daddy.

"We want to stress the importance of the Predators reviewing the rules and the safety measures with the prey again," he said. "We know you all read the information given to you, but please make sure your prey understands it fully and can repeat it back to you." He paused. "Predators, you may attach the wristbands."

I glanced back at Colt, and he pulled the two wristbands out of the back pocket of his jeans. They looked more like smart-watches, except there wasn't a display. Instead, there was a flashlight of sorts on the front.

"As you know," Lucas went on, "the preys' bands are equipped with an alarm and an emergency light. Hold in the buttons on each side of the light to activate both." There was another pause as the Tops attached the bands. Colt gave me a small smirk and checked that the strap was attached properly. "Prey, you only use this band in the event of an emergency and immediately need to be brought out of the game. Consider it a safeword measure that goes beyond calling red to your Owner. We have monitors in the forest whose sole responsibility is to find you quickly should you need it."

I brushed my thumb and forefinger over the buttons on the side and let out a shaky breath.

"There is an additional function on the Predators' wristbands," Lucas said. "The flashlight is a button on its own, and you will press it when you've captured your prey. Which will send a signal to our scorekeeper. If you do not press it, the clock won't stop, and we can't log your time."

"If you lose your prey after initial capture," Reese filled in, "you have to press the button again." He smirked. "Don't fuckin' lose your prey."

Colt's hands clamped down on my shoulders, and I startled. He dipped down and murmured to me, "I ain't in it to win it, Kit. I wanna play with my food before I eat."

I shuddered and clenched my jaw. He was trying to get into my head.

The redheaded woman took a step forward next, and she studied us prey with her chin held high. "This is for all the little bottoms who think losing quickly will give your Tops a better score to win. It's not going to work, because you'll be graded differently. The Predators will aim for a low score—that would be the amount of time it takes to capture the prey. And the prey... you'll want to hold out for as long as possible. But we're keeping the why to ourselves for the time being."

"We have eyes in the trees," River murmured.

"For more than one reason," Lucas said. "This is a rough game. Please get ready for the mindfucks our Sadists have planned—"

"Not too ready," Reese said with a grin.

"Hear, hear!" Colt hollered.

I gnashed my teeth even harder and resisted the urge to glare back at him.

Lucas nodded with a dip of his chin. No smile, no smirk, just business. "We're going to treat you to a small demonstration." He gestured a go-ahead to Reese. "When the Predators have signaled their success in taking down their prey, everyone will know."

Reese let out a sharp whistle, then cupped his hands around his mouth and yelled down the hill. "Sound the sirens!"

My eyes were glued to the dark forest that suddenly lit up with flashes of blood-red, and the light show was followed by an alarm that sent chills down my spine. It was as if the apocalypse were here and it was everyone for themselves.

The flashes thickened into a red haze with machines shooting smoke into the trees.

I swallowed dryly and glanced around me. My brain kicked into overdrive to take it all in, and time seemed to slow down. With wide eyes, I saw some people cheering, some rolling their shoulders and stretching, some tying their running shoes, some forehead-to-forehead while the Top gave a pep talk, some taking their seats along the deck for the show.

I'd been sort of expecting slave dresses for the girls and underwear for the boys, for some reason. Instead, we were dressed for a hike in rough terrain. I had a long-sleeved T-shirt, jeans, and good running shoes created for this environment. *The best games are the ones we take seriously,* Colt had said, and I could see everyone else was on the same page. The people here, whether they participated or observed, wanted something savage. Something real.

Madigan and Abel weren't around yet. My guess was they were still upstairs in the main house, or they'd retreated to our cabin for aftercare.

I saw a man stepping out onto the lawn. Nondescript cargo pants and a black T-shirt, but the patch around his bicep with a red cross on it sure as hell caught my eye.

As the sirens stopped wailing and the red flashes went dark again, the second woman introduced the man, a Master, who worked as an EMT. He would be ready to assist if anyone sustained any injuries that required attention.

Just as part of me thought this was going to drag on forever, the founders at the front indicated they had covered everything.

"Do we have anything else to say?" Reese looked to his friends, his gaze landing on Lucas.

Lucas offered a threatening little smirk and clasped his hands behind his back. "Ladies and gentlemen, welcome to The Games."

I blew out a nervous breath, and a minor cacophony of chatter broke out across the yard. Colt spun me around and grabbed me by my shoulders, leveling me with a serious stare.

"You're ready for this." It wasn't a question.

I nodded, though. I was ready to try. I was ready to go all in and do my best. I had Abel's advice and tricks running on a loop in my head. I had Lucas's gentle warnings and barely disguised worry playing in the background. He kept me stable. He was my rock.

I had Colt's determination and aggressive faith staring back at me right now.

He kept me wild. He was my fuel.

I never wanted to be without either of them.

"This is only our first time, baby." Colt cupped my cheek, his gaze losing just a bit of its intensity. "We'll come back over and over, and you will see your own progress. You'll feel yourself growing stronger and more confident every time. And..."

"I will surrender to you," I replied softly. "Finally."

I believed him when he said I was struggling. I couldn't put a finger on exactly what I did, only that I hadn't let go of that last tiny piece of control. I noticed it when I tried to interject in decisions it wasn't necessary for me to be involved in making, and I felt it every time I worried about things I should just leave to my Daddies.

I ached to let go of it all.

"It'll work." Colt cupped my cheeks and kissed me fiercely. "Promise you'll fight me with everything you have."

"I promise, Daddy." My heart started thundering, and I sensed the energy around us. Everyone was ready.

"Good boy." He gave me one more kiss, a swift one, then took a step back and surveyed my outfit. "Okay. Let's do this. Watch out for the branches and try not to trip."

I huffed and turned away from him. Some of the other prey had already trekked halfway down the hill to where the starting line was. Reese and the two women were waiting there, and... yeah. It was time. I took deep breaths as I trailed after, and I rolled my shoulders and wriggled my toes in my shoes. They were comfortable even though they were new. No sign of discomfort around my ankles either.

We were going to have a two-minute head start. According to Colt, it was long enough for us to both hide and mindfuck ourselves. Just lovely.

"Kit!"

I knew that voice, hoarse as it was. I glanced back over my shoulder as Abel and Madigan came out from the main house. Boy, Abel looked like he'd been through hell. But he had Madigan and was leaning heavily on him.

"You got this!" Abel called.

Love fluttered its way through my chest. He was such a great friend to me. I nodded once, unable to do much else unless I wanted to let my emotions take over already, and then I turned to the woods again.

Lucas was joining Reese and the women too, and I could tell he was struggling. He'd avoided making eye contact throughout the pregame speech earlier. Now he wasn't.

"Be safe, baby boy," he mouthed to me, a pleading look in his eyes.

"I will, Daddy," I mouthed back.

"All right, we're all here." Reese eyed us. Six guys, three girls. "You'll have two minutes to hide, to get ready, and to let your eyes adjust to the darkness. Try not to look back at the house. The lights up here will blind you."

I blew out a heavy breath.

"On your marks." He waited while we got into position, and one of the women held up a starting pistol toward the sky. The next time Reese spoke, the Predator in him made itself known. It was there in his eyes. "*Run.*" A shot went off, and my pulse skyrocketed.

I took off as quickly as I could and darted down the hill. Adrenaline seeped into my veins, slowly waking me up. I vaguely registered being one of the first who reached the forest, and I broke through the tree line with a jump over a big rock.

In a fraction of a second, my heart went from hammering to stopping. Complete darkness met me like a brick wall, and I blinked rapidly. Sucking in a sharp breath, I left distant hollering and shouting behind, and I veered left to get away from the other prey.

At first, I didn't hear anything other than my pulse rushing in my ears. The adrenaline hadn't reached the important senses yet, and doubt tried to take over. I swallowed hard, my gaze flickering to find a path I could take. *Make your path.* I held out an arm, preventing branches from whipping me in my face, and cut through the thick vegetation.

Someone ran past behind me, panting.

New sounds invaded my ears. Twigs snapping, the underbrush rustling, shoes scuffing against the forest floor. My eyes were adjusting. My footfalls found a rhythm with my heartbeat.

I stumbled into the smallest of clearings and barely managed to steady myself.

A guy whizzed by me, causing my breath to hitch. I decided

right then and there to avoid anyone I saw. There were already going to be mistakes once the Predators were unleashed. I was bound to run into a Top who had to make sure I wasn't who they were hunting.

Time to think strategy. The forest wasn't massive, and it was surrounded by fields. It was big, yet small enough to be certain that the whole area would be utilized for the bottoms' attempts at finding a hiding spot. So I would stay away from the perimeter. I would also get away from the middle and pick a side. Which would give me a fifty-fifty chance that Colt would start searching the opposite side.

I gasped as another shot was fired, letting us know the Predators were coming for us. I scanned my immediate surroundings and went straight for the thicket to my right and picked up the pace.

I saw a babbling little brook straight ahead, and I jumped across it.

"What the—" I hauled in some air and searched the treetops frantically as a weird sound echoed through the forest. It sounded like wheezing laughter. And it got louder and louder.

Get ready for the mindfucks our Sadists have planned...

Lucas's warning came back to me.

The speakers. They had planted speakers all over and were playing sound effects in surround sound. A dark chuckle came from the east, a bark of a laugh from the west.

A woman's scream pierced through the air, and it flooded me with fear and anger. Anger because fuck this fucking shit; I wasn't going to let them take me down with *noises*.

Is that all you got, motherfuckers?

I clenched my teeth and ran deeper into the woods.

"Run, prey, run," came out in a girl's singsong voice. It sounded suspiciously like Ivy. "Run, prey, run. Run for your life, not because it's fun." Her tinkling laughter breezed through the trees. "Run, prey, run. Run because Daddy's got a gun."

The forest was alive.

Adrenaline pumped through my bloodstream, and I came alive too. Hyperalert and more determined than ever, I— "Shit," I panted. The sirens started wailing, and the red flashes pounded on my retinas.

Smoke billowed around me.

The first prey was down.

"I'm coming for you, Tate!" someone yelled.

Too close. I sprinted down a dirt path as the alarm quieted, and I found cover behind a boulder.

An exhale traveled through the forest, turning into a low, drawled chuckle. *Colt.* I'd know that voice anywhere. He'd recorded sounds, too. Then the chuckle died, and he growled, "I'll make you fuckin' crawl, boy."

I let out a shaky breath, half expecting fear to cripple me. It didn't. My hands were steady. My heart kept hammering, but my senses were on high alert, and the thrill had shot into my veins like a heady drug.

"Fuck you!" a girl screamed. "No!"

I hunkered down and kept an eye on my surroundings. The scream hadn't been too close, and I didn't want to run as soon as I heard someone. I had to save my energy for the fight.

For the fight... God, how my way of thinking had changed.

The sirens returned, louder this time. I must be close to a speaker. The red lights flashed, and the mist from the smoke machines grew thicker.

The undergrowth rustled heavily nearby, and I was just about to flee the site when a hand clamped down on my shoulder. Panic set in, and I formed a fist and swung it around until it thudded hard against a chest.

"Ouch," a man coughed.

Oh, thank fuck. It wasn't him. Wrong voice, wrong clothes. "Wrong prey, Sir," I squeaked and ran away.

I ran. I ran too far. I ran past a man fucking a girl into the forest floor, and I jumped across the brook again. Red flashes all around, the sirens bounced between the trees, more screaming, and another recording. A man whispering everything he was going to do to his prey once she was captured.

"Found you."

I screamed and spun around, eyes wide, heart threatening to pound its way out of my chest.

Colt.

Fuck!

He and his sinister smirk stood less than ten feet away, and there was no time to think. I bolted with every ounce of strength and speed I had.

He'd told me he wanted to play with his food first.

I had to lose him somehow—

"Not so fast," I heard him growl, and a second later, he had a grip on my neck.

I screwed my eyes shut instinctively and made a repeat performance, swinging my fist around. Problem was, Colt caught it. *Open your eyes. Focus. You have nothing to lose.* The internal voice sounded a lot like Abel, and maybe that was why I listened.

Holy shit. The feral look in Colt's eyes shot ripples of something I'd never felt before through me. I catalogued the sweat that beaded across his forehead, how his chest heaved underneath his dark T-shirt, and how his fingers curled around my fist.

Fight him. Show him.

I swallowed hard, and then the forest lit up in red once more. And it hit me. I played on my innocence to throw him off. I looked up at the trees as the sirens cried, and when I knew he was glancing up too, I jammed down my foot on his and sent my free hand flying into his stomach.

Colt choked and bowled over, and I hightailed it out of there. Panting, high on adrenaline, fucking grinning, I darted through the woods at high speed, not giving a shit about the branches that whipped at my face. I didn't even feel any pain when I stumbled and fell to the ground. I was up in under two seconds, and I was running again.

"You've been holdin' out on me!" he barked out.

I shot to the left when I heard others straight up ahead.

Four prey were down. Five to go.

It gave me a boost of confidence to know I hadn't been one of the first.

It made me cockier.

Needing to catch my breath for a moment, I stopped at the next boulder I found and hid behind it. Every now and then, I peered around to see where Colt was. There were too many screams and moans, distant or not, real or recorded.

After about a minute, I caught sight of him between the trees.

I watched. For one second, I was the hunter. I stared at him while he came to a stop and lifted his T-shirt to wipe sweat off his face. I hadn't bothered. Perspiration trickled down my neck, causing my clothes to stick to my skin.

He raised his gaze and looked around.

"Time to come outta hidin', little fuckboy," he called. "I know you're here somewhere."

I licked my lips and moved to the other side of the boulder where I could watch him from a safer spot, in the sliver of space between the big rock and a tree.

Was I ready to fight him?

I grew completely still and held my breath when he turned this way.

"You can't hide forever," he said. "If you're a good little whore and come out now, maybe I won't fuck you dry."

I narrowed my eyes and took a slow breath. I could run, but he'd see me. He'd chase after me, and he'd throw me down on the ground sooner or later. Another option, I stepped out right now. He wouldn't expect it. I was sure of it. He fully anticipated he was going to hunt me down, not that I would come out and meet him head on.

As the sirens began wailing again, I steeled myself for the inevitable pain, and I stepped out from behind the boulder.

His stare landed on me instantly, and a slow grin spread across his face.

"Perhaps I'll end up fucking you dry instead," I said.

His grin broadened, and he approached me without any hurry whatsoever. Cocky bastard. "You held back yesterday in the pool."

"Maybe." Wanting to fuck with him for having fucked with me, I crouched down quickly, as if I were about to bolt, and he froze with the Predator's calculating stare. "You afraid I might run, old man?"

His brows rose a fraction. "Careful, Kit."

"Fuck you."

He strode forward to grab me, but I dodged his grasp and came out on the other side of him. He turned with a dark chuckle and rubbed his jaw, a clear sign that he was running out of patience.

"Do you want to sit down and rest?" I asked.

"That's fuckin' it." He glared as he charged at me, and this time, I didn't stand a chance. He rammed into me, sending us both to the ground, and I landed with a wheezed groan. Pain exploded along my back, though I didn't let it control me. I fought back. God, I fought back. I clawed at him, smacked him, and kicked. Something changed. The air around us grew thick, and I saw red.

The second he pressed his forearm across my chest, I knew he was trying to free up a hand so he could push the buttons on his wristband.

Diving into survival mode as Colt held me down with his body to press the buttons, I grabbed a fistful of dry soil and leaves, and I screwed my eyes shut and threw it at his face.

"God*dammit*, Kit!"

I coughed and spat, some of the dirt ending up on my face too, but at least I'd done it. Colt rolled off me and cursed, and I scrambled to my feet as my heart lodged in my throat.

"Don't even try," he growled, grabbing on to my foot.

I fell down on my hands and knees. *Ouch*. A rock cut into my kneecap.

"Let go!" I tried to kick his hand away, to no avail. He either didn't feel pain, or he pushed through it. "Ow!"

His fingers dug painfully into my calf, and he dragged himself on top of me.

Next thing I knew, a sharp smack rang out, and my cheek caught on fire.

I stared with wide eyes. He'd backhanded me, and he looked murderous.

Tears welled up rapidly, blurring my vision, and I didn't move for several seconds. It was long enough for him to straddle my waist and signal to the others that I'd been captured.

"Now I get my fun," he said, breathing heavily. For the sixth time, the sirens and the red lights flooded the forest, and I let out a whimper of defeat. "You were harder to hunt down than I expected, I'll give ya that." He yanked his T-shirt over his head and threw it on the ground.

My eyes grew large again. Oh my God, I'd done that to him. He had scratches all over, and not just on his torso. Now I saw them on his face too. It wasn't only the dirt I'd thrown at him. Blood was smeared across his jaw.

My mouth watered, and I swallowed thickly.

"Now you're all mine." He wrapped his fingers as much as he could around my throat and lowered himself over me. "My feisty little animal, how I'm gonna fuck you."

A proverbial crack split me in two, one half that wanted nothing more than to be taken savagely by him, and the other that still had some fight left in him. I wasn't ready to surrender. Our heavy breathing mingled in the air between us, my blood started pumping again, and a primal need to assert myself slammed its way into my skull and wouldn't be ignored.

I let out a strangled sound as he tightened his chokehold on me, and I glared up at him.

"Don't even think about it," he whispered. "You're done fightin'."

"I've barely started," I snarled.

I latched on to his arm and struggled to loosen his hold. I thrashed against him, frustration building up within, and then I smacked him instead when he wouldn't budge. I struck and scratched him up, the latter pissing him off. With a guttural growl, he flipped me over onto my stomach and planted a hand at the side of my head.

My cheek scraped against the dirt floor.

"No!" I shouted. "Stop it!" I flailed until my hands found his, and I clawed at the top of his hand. *Anything*...to get him to release me.

"Quiet, boy." He grunted and used his free hand to push down my jeans.

Somewhere in the forest, another prey lost their fight. Smoke crept closer, the red lit up the trees, and the alarm thrust panic into the air.

"No, don't!" I screamed. Fury and desperation unfurled,

and I dug my nails deeper into his knuckles. "Let me go!"

I ground my pelvis into the dirt in an attempt to keep my jeans on, but it was futile. Colt wrestled my pants past my hips and down to my knees, leaving only the thin barrier of my briefs between the ground and me. Except my ass. He exposed my butt and spanked me hard.

"Fight me, you coward!" I shouted.

"Don't feel like it." He kneaded my buttocks roughly and spanked me over and over. "What's your safeword?"

"Fuck you, it's red, and I just wanna fight you!" I choked on a sob as the fire spread. "Come on, bastard!" He wouldn't move. I felt something warm and wet around my fingertips, letting me know I'd broken the skin on his hand badly enough that he was bleeding more than a little. And still, he wouldn't let go.

I screamed out my frustration, and all he did was uncap a bottle of whatever he'd brought with him. Oil, lube, what-the-fuck-ever. I couldn't get free. He had me.

Humiliation washed over me when he swiped two fingers coated with something slick over my opening. I couldn't resist whatsoever, and I hated it. He finger-fucked me without mercy. He simply didn't care about what I said or what I did. At some point, he'd freed himself from his own jeans, and before I knew it, he pushed his big cock inside my ass.

He groaned in relief, the sound coming from right over my head.

It hurt so fucking much I couldn't even move. I withdrew my bloodstained fingers, and my hands hit the dirt.

"Please stop," I cried. Tears streamed down my face, mingling with the soil and scratches.

"I can't." He pulled out a few inches and drove in again, and he set a fast pace to fuck me, to own me, to control every inch of me. "You feel fuckin' perfect, little boy. All helpless and ripe for the takin'." He grunted and moaned. There was no finesse to his fucking. He'd hunted me down, he'd wrestled me into submission, and now he was just going to finish. He was going to fuck me and come. "Fuck, I love it when you cry, Kit. You're right there. You hate me, don't you?"

"*Yes!*" I sobbed.

"That's all right," he murmured huskily. "It won't last long."

"You told me y-you wanted me t-to fight," I screamed hoarsely. "*Fight me!*"

"I changed my mind," he panted. "I saw it when you—fuck. Never mind." He rocked in deep, drawing a wail from me. I could barely breathe, and everything hurt. "Tonight—" He sucked in a breath and sped up, ramming his cock in and out of me so fast and hard that I lost my breath. "Tonight, I'm taking it all, Kit, and this is how," he growled in my ear. "I own you. I own the goddamn air you breathe. I own your pain and your *fucking* thoughts."

My lungs burned. Black spots filled my vision, and I gagged when I tried to inhale some much-needed air.

Colt continued fucking me. More than that, his commanding voice laid down the law.

"*When you need something, you will come to us.*"

"*When you've had a long day and need to be little, you won't hesitate.*"

"*We own you, Kit. You're ours. You belong to us—now and for the rest of our goddamn lives.*"

I managed to draw in short, shallow breaths after a while. Other than that, I lay still and stared unseeingly into the dark forest. I stopped hearing sounds. I stopped reacting to the flashes and the smoke around us. The frustration inside rattled as if in a cage, but if I so much as looked at it in my mind, more tears welled up. So, I waited. I waited while Colt used me, while he pushed me down mentally, while he claimed me.

I was utterly helpless.

Colt's thrusts became irregular, and it didn't take long before he groaned and came inside me. His cock throbbed with each shot of his hot release, and his chest rose and fell as if he'd run a marathon.

It was the most bizarre sensation. I felt used, violated, small, worthless, weak, and yet...I was waiting for something. Something told me these feelings weren't necessarily bad. Colt wasn't done with me; I was sure of it. He wouldn't finish like this.

He pulled out shortly after, and I remained motionless.

I didn't know if I was going to explode or implode. I only knew I was going to keep my mouth shut. The tension inside me had never been strung tighter, and anything could trigger a complete meltdown.

Colt tucked himself back into his jeans, then righted my underwear and told me to stand up.

Small sparks of pain fired as I slowly got off the ground. My knee hurt, my cheek burned, my ass was fucking raw. I'd taken hits in places I'd been unaware of until now. I had scratches and little cuts everywhere, and the fabric of my clothes rubbed against them whenever I moved.

"Come on." Colt jerked his chin in the direction he wanted us to go. Presumably back toward the house. To be honest, I wasn't sure I'd find my way out of here on my own.

I was a stranger in my own body on the trek back. Uncomfortable beyond words, I hugged myself loosely and walked in silence. And it didn't escape my notice that Colt kept his distance. He didn't touch me. He didn't call me baby or little one.

He stopped at one point when we reached the stream. Stepping into the water, he bent down and washed his face. Then he straightened and appeared to look up at the sky. No, wait. He was blinking. Then down once again to splash more water on his face.

"My eyes will be bloodshot for days," he muttered. "That was some cruel stunt you pulled. I'm impressed."

What was he t— Oh. The dirt, that was what bothered his eyes.

We were walking again, and I could see the light from the torches like glitter between the trees.

"Don't you have anythin' to say?" he asked.

I shook my head and stepped over a smaller tree trunk.

Colt chuckled through a sigh. "Glad I made the right choice. You'll feel better soon."

Oh yeah? Funny, because none of this felt right. In fact, I recalled feeling this way before, shortly after my parents died. I knew what it was like to shut down, and if you didn't, you'd fall apart. Everything would break. So, I'd kept it bottled up, and I'd set one foot in front of the other and forced myself to go on.

Leaving the woods behind with Colt next to me rattled the cage inside me. People were waiting and watching, and another couple had stepped out of the forest shortly before us. They were almost at the house, and they had friends rushing to meet them.

I shut down further and braced myself for encountering people, even though it was literally the last thing I wanted right now.

I gave no outward reaction when I spotted Lucas leaving one of the seating areas on the deck. But on the inside, I screamed. The pressure built up too fast, and I wasn't sure I could make it. Oh God, I was going to explode.

Lucas signaled something to Reese, who was standing nearby with his brother and a few others. Whatever it was, it made Reese step farther out on the lawn and whistle sharply.

"Let's give the Predators and prey some space, people! You do not approach unless you have permission!"

I exhaled.

19.

Lucas strode toward us with purpose and impatience in each step, and he addressed Colt when he was some twenty feet away. "What does he need?"

"Room four," Colt replied.

Lucas gave him a strange look before he composed his face. "For the shower?"

Colt nodded.

"Okay. Let's go." Lucas eyed me, worry radiating from him. I didn't ask anything. I didn't make eye contact. I didn't touch him. I merely followed them up the last stretch of the hill and then across the pool deck.

I felt eyes on me everywhere.

"Something's wrong," Lucas said.

"Nah." Colt cleared his throat. Maybe he gestured something. Maybe he—whatever. The two exchanged a few words that were too quiet for me to hear.

"Good Christ." Okay, I heard that one. It was Lucas. "Okay, but then we go to our place right after. Madigan and Abel are on the front porch of the main house for some downtime."

The inside of the house was enormous. This was the club area, I deduced. Tables and chairs shared the perimeter with bondage equipment, BDSM furniture, and scene setups, leaving the floor in the middle empty. They must've torn down walls when they bought the place. It was completely open, everything painted black, from floorboards to ceiling. There was a bar in one corner, next to a stage, and I spied two doors on the western wall. Office, one read. The other one didn't have a sign.

We crossed the dance floor and almost-empty downstairs, and we reached the foyer. Two dressing rooms and a small reception desk with a coat check took up the space, along with the stairs leading to the second floor.

Welcome to the haunted house of Virginia, I thought. As soon as we reached the landing and I peered down the hallway, it was like ending up in a horror movie about an old hotel that was haunted. There were no open spaces here, just the corridor, the same black-painted walls, and doors with numbers on them.

Lucas pulled out a card from his wallet that he swiped to open door number four.

I flinched when he turned on the spotlights.

"Sorry, dear." He dimmed them.

More black. Jesus Christ. Black rubber. It was a shower room with every square inch covered in a black rubber mat, including what reminded me of an examining table, two benches, and a shelf to put belongings on. Or maybe your favorite dildo.

The ceiling on one side of the room had several shower mounts, and the water trickled down into the drain in the center of the floor.

"It's mainly used by those into water sports," Colt said.

I stayed near the door, waiting for orders, and said nothing.

Colt turned to Lucas. "I'll go get us some towels and shit from the supply room. Try to get him to talk."

"I will." Lucas touched his arm, and I took a step to the side so Colt could move past me.

Well, now what? I had nothing to say. I had no opinions on

anything. My brain fluctuated between utter apathy and struggling to keep the cage locked.

"Come have a seat, Kit."

I walked over to a bench where Lucas went, and I sat down on it with a wince.

He squatted in front of me and untied my shoes. "How was the game?"

I shrugged.

A crease appeared in his forehead. His worry lines. He set my shoes to the side. "Colt told me you put up a good fight."

My gaze sharpened and was on him instantly. "He didn't let me fight." I barely recognized my own voice; it was raw and scratchy, and damn it, I shouldn't have said anything. The pressure was quickly becoming too much, and something akin to betrayal burned hotly right below the surface.

That was it. It was betrayal. Colt hadn't let me fight, and he'd made me promise to give him everything.

"He didn't let me fight," I whispered. "Why didn't he let me fight?"

"Oh, sweetheart. I'm sure he has something planned." Lucas rose up and lifted my shirt. "Let me take this off. You have scrapes everywhere." And he hated it, I could tell.

I didn't care. My underwear was wet from Colt's come too. Didn't care about that either.

I let Lucas take off my clothes, though, as I battled the internal hell demanding to be unleashed.

Once my jeans and shirt were on the floor, Lucas cursed under his breath. He saw the blotches of fresh bruises forming along my thighs. My torso and arms hid most of the marks with my tattoos, but I still felt them.

The door opened, and Colt walked in with three thick black towels under his arm. He had two bottles of something in his hand too.

Anger ignited in me as his stare landed on me.

Why didn't you let me fight?

"He's upset," Lucas murmured.

"Good." Colt set down the towels and walked over to the shower, where he left the two bottles. "So, I learned somethin' new about our boy tonight. He loves the thrill."

Lucas's gaze flickered to me, curiosity mingling with the concern.

"Which is like winnin' the lottery for me, obviously." Colt pulled his T-shirt over his head, revealing battered skin, much like mine. "We'll have a lot of explorin' to do in that arena, Kit, and I can't fuckin' wait. But it wasn't what we needed tonight."

"You didn't let me fight," I stated hoarsely. "I hate you for it."

"*Kit,*" Lucas admonished, shocked.

"It's okay, darlin'." Colt walked toward me slowly, and he unbuttoned his jeans. "I got him where I want him now."

All the frustration, all the vague comments, and all the rage mixed together and formed an explosive without a fuse, and I was seconds away from erupting. "Why didn't you let me fight?"

"Because you liked it too much," he answered. "You weren't angry enough to flip your shit, so I cut you off. I had my suspicions before, but not like this. There's a primal prey in you that hasn't been allowed to come out and play yet."

I met his glare with a murderous one of my own. "You made me promise," I gritted out.

"And then we both learned something new about you," he pointed out. "I ain't a mind reader, boy. I needed to piss you off so you'd blow, and I could tell you wouldn't do it out there. You were too exhilarated, and the fighting would've given you a release if we'd kept going."

I scoffed. This bastard—unfuckingbelievable. "I wasn't even hard, you fucking idiot."

"Not the type of release I'm talkin' about."

"Guys—"

"No." Colt cut Lucas off. "This is how it's gonna be. He'll get his fight now that he's actually mad—here, where he can't injure himself too much. Unless he's too chickenshit to face—"

He pushed the wrong button. I launched myself at him with a scream, and nothing they did or said could stop me. *I* couldn't even stop me. Completely ruled by fury, I pounded my fists on his chest until he stopped me, and then I switched to kicking at him instead. He couldn't be everywhere.

I became blind and deaf.

I thrashed against Colt, seeing nothing but red, angry swirls of hatred and grief and loneliness and agitation before my eyes. I wanted to punch each goddamn emotion, and I sure as hell tried.

"Let go of me!" I yelled.

There was pressure on my chest, and I realized I wasn't even standing anymore. We were on the floor, and he was on top of me. Something else snapped inside me, and I used all my strength to get on top. I kept hitting him wherever I could reach, and the fucking Sadist was so fast. He dodged most blows and stopped several others.

"You can do more than that, Kit," Colt growled. "Come on!"

His voice sounded far away, almost as if it was underwater.

I toppled over when he got the upper hand again, and I screamed. I fucking screamed, and the images that flashed before me didn't belong. "Nooo!" I saw my parents, I drowned in the uneasy standstill I was at with Vincent, I felt the emptiness of my home. "You shouldn't have left me!" A despaired wail left my body, and gut-wrenching pain tore me to pieces. "I-I don't wanna be lonely again," I sobbed. "I can't. I can't...I can't."

I curled into the fetal position right there on the rubber floor, and I let the screams and breathless cries take me.

"I can't stop weeping." I sniffled and screwed my eyes shut so Lucas could wash the shampoo out of my hair. "Oh... Here I go again," I whined, a new round of tears rolling down my cheeks.

"It'll be a while, little one." Lucas ran the shower head over my head and cupped my cheek lovingly. "You've been carrying the weight of the world on your shoulders for so long. Give it time."

I reached behind me blindly to find Colt, and I grabbed on to his arm. "Daddy, you're not leaving, are you?"

They weren't allowed to leave me.

"Not a chance." He hugged me from behind and stroked my chest. Lucas turned on the rain function on the shower, and I let out a long breath. "We got you, little darlin'."

I giggled and sniffled at the same time. "Darlin' is what you call Daddy. And now I'm little darlin'?"

He smiled against my neck. "It fits, doesn't it? You two are my darlings."

I nodded and started weeping again. I wanted to be his darling forever, but I'd said I hated him. "I don't hate you. I love you," I cried. "I love you both."

"Oh, heavens." Lucas kissed me on the forehead.

Colt hugged me harder and kissed my unscathed cheek. "We love you too, Kit."

"So, so very much," Lucas murmured. "I think we need to make a Kit sandwich."

"Yes, please," I sobbed.

Colt chuckled and moved closer; they both did, until we were a big Kit sandwich with me in the middle. I tilted up my face as the water pelted our bodies, and we came together in a sweet, slow kiss. Until I hiccupped and couldn't hold back the crying, of course.

I cried because I couldn't stop crying. "I'm so tired. I'm sorr—"

"Uh-uh." Colt gave my jaw a little nip. "Don't apologize. This is the whole point, Kit. Let it all go, and we'll take over from here. You're our baby. We'll take care of you."

So I cried, and the relief was so immense that I cried because of that too.

I didn't want to put on my dirty forest clothes after our very long shower, and neither did my Daddies. We wrapped the towels around our hips instead, and Colt grabbed our stuff. I hadn't landed from my meltdown yet, so I stayed close to Lucas, and he guided me out of the rubber room and down the stairs.

"Can one run out of tears, Daddy?" I croaked.

"I don't know," Lucas mused. "We should probably get some water in you, though. We don't want you to get dehydrated."

I sniffled. "There's water in ice cream."

"But not in sprinkles," Colt said and walked past us.

I frowned very hard. "That's not a nice thing to say."

He sent me a smirk over his shoulder. "A Sadist can't be too nice, little darlin'."

I flushed and ducked my head as I grinned. I truly liked my new nickname.

When he opened the patio doors, the noise from the outside made me sneak closer to Lucas and grab his hand. What the outdoors revealed...jeez, pretty much everyone was involved in a pool orgy. A dozen or so sat at the tables, but the rest were either in the big pool or in one of the two Jacuzzis.

"We'll get you some ice cream with sprinkles." Lucas squeezed my hand.

I smiled and got teary-eyed, though it seemed I was all cried out for the moment.

There was a card game going on at one of the tables, and I spotted Reese and River there.

Reese saw me, and I waved shyly.

Even though he offered me one of his smirky smirks, there was something soft in his gaze. This was their lifestyle. Our lifestyle, but...their life. They put so much time and effort into these events. As did my Daddies. It was humbling and wonderful to be able to be a part of their community.

We jumped down from the deck, and I held on to my towel and said, "Daddy, I think we should send a thank-you card to Reese and River. Oh! Maybe I can build them a plane? Do you think they would like that?"

Lucas peered down at me with affection written all over him, and he kissed my fingertips. "I think they'd appreciate anything you send them, dear."

"Great! I know just the way to thank you and Daddy too."

"Oh, really?"

"Yeah, but it's a secret," I giggled.

Daddy laughed softly and hugged me to him. "I love you, Kit. I love it when you're this carefree and happy."

"I love you too," I sang, reaching our cabin. I jumped up on the deck with an, "Oh hey!" and darted after Colt, who entered before me. "Daddy, I have a question." I tapped on his shoulder, and Colt gave me his attention before he dumped our clothes and shoes into a basket. "Do you think it's possible that I lost twenty pounds during the game?"

His eyebrows went up. "What do you mean?"

I shrugged and scratched my nose. "I dunno. I feel lighter."

"Ah." He grinned faintly. "Imagine how light you'll feel after I give you a solid pain session tomorrow."

My eyes widened, and my face fell. "Have I been bad, Daddy?"

"No! Fuck no, baby. Christ." He drew me to his body and hugged my head to his chest. "I swear those puppy-dog eyes of yours will be the death of me." He blew out a breath while I giggled in relief. Then he inched away slightly and lifted my chin. "But I'm sorry to say this—and by sorry, I mean thrilled—there's very much a little masochist in you, and now we've seen what pain does to you. It clears your head." He paused. "That's the release I was talking about earlier. See it as a mental orgasm. It happens to everyone on some level. We all need physical outlets. Some blow off steam at the gym, some go running in the park." He poked my nose, to which I grinned goofily. "Masochists like you get the same release from receiving pain. That's where I come in."

Oh...I finally understood. It was what Abel had talked about. Pain wasn't always what we wanted, but sometimes it was what we needed.

"Thank you for explaining to me," I murmured. "It makes sense now."

"That's my job. And I love it. And I love you." He dipped down and growled playfully against my cheek. "I can't wait to explore all this with you. You've been keeping a lot of trauma and emotions locked up, so we'll be careful. How does that sound?"

I nodded thoughtfully. "I saw a grief counselor after Mom and Dad died, but I guess I'm still sad sometimes."

"Understandable." He touched my cheek. "These things come and go, Kit. Nothin' weird about that. Only difference now is you got two sets of shoulders to cry on, and we'll be there for anything."

I hugged him super-duper hard and closed my eyes. "I love you, Daddy."

He let out a long breath and pressed his lips to the top of my head. "We're gonna have all the fun together. And you know what the biggest bonus is?"

I shook my head and looked up curiously.

"The way you regress after you've suffered," he murmured. "That's twenty pounds of control and worries you just forked over to your Daddies, where it belongs. Adulting builds up pressure, and now I have the best way to relieve it for you."

I snickered. "You said adulting."

He smirked. "Somethin' wrong with that?"

"You're not the type, is all." I put on my best Southern accent and tried to make my voice deeper to sound like Colt. "They keep raisin' them fuckin' taxes—did y'all see the price of gas this week? Where's m'chaw? I forgot my goddamn password to this goddamn computer machine."

Daddy's eyes lit up with laughter. "You fuckin' brat. I'll have you know I even write 'LOL' in texts sometimes."

I laughed so hard. "That's another thing you curse at all the time. Your phone!"

"Because the damn buttons are too small!" He failed to hide his amusement, and I sure wasn't trying to stop my own amusement. I was laughing like silly. "Okay, that's enough outta you, young squirt. Luke promised you ice cream. Then you're brushin' your teeth and marchin' straight to bed."

"I don't wanna wake up yet," I mumbled sleepily around...oh. My thumb. Huh. Whatever, I liked it. I snuggled farther into Colt's arms and waited for sleep to claim me again.

"Our beautiful boy." Lucas trailed kisses along my shoulder and pressed his morning wood against my bottom. "Colt, wake up."

"Mmm..." Colt stirred in his sleep. "What," he uttered groggily. "Jesus Christ."

"No, be quiet," I whined softly.

"I had to take a picture of you two," Lucas whispered. He pushed down the duvet and brushed his hand over my crotch. "My boy sucking on his thumb, lying on my man's chest."

Colt hummed. "Kiss me, darlin'."

Why did they not want to sleep? That's what I wanted to know.

Lucas crawled over me and dropped an unhurried, sensual kiss on Colt's lips, and he never stopped fondling my cock. It was becoming distracting.

Eventually, Lucas rolled me gently onto my back, and he kissed his way down my body. A slow shiver traveled down my spine as he sucked my soft cock into his mouth. My thumb slipped out from between my lips, and I sighed in pleasure. Then I stretched out and yawned and patted Daddy on the head.

"I like it when you suck on me, Daddy."

Colt made another humming sound and withdrew his arm from under my head. "Well, I'm certainly up now. Kit, you know what I think?"

I blinked drowsily. "What?"

"I think you'd like fucking your Daddy too."

"Oh," I mouthed.

Lucas crawled up over me, dropping openmouthed kisses on

his way, until he reached the spot below my ear. "Daddy would like that very much, in fact."

"Okay," I breathed out. Excitement swirled up a storm within me, and I turned to Colt. "Will you help me, please? I don't know what I'm doing."

"Of course I will." Colt leaned in for a quick kiss before getting out of bed. His back showed scratch marks from last night. I didn't know whether to find them incredibly hot or...no, I truly did. But I also felt bad. Slightly. "You can go however hard you like, and you don't have to stop until you come."

I *loved* the sound of that, and I got up on my knees and smiled at Lucas. "Are you also excited, Daddy?"

"Like you wouldn't believe, little one." He met me on all fours and kissed me deeply, his tongue mingling with mine. "How do you want me?"

"Like this, please." I nodded and stared at him hungrily. My cock was getting harder by the second, and I stroked myself as he positioned himself more in the middle of the bed.

Colt helped me lots. Once I was behind Lucas, Colt helped me with the oil, showing me how to guide two wet fingers inside and get Daddy's ass ready. Then he stroked some oil over my cock too, and I really liked that part because it felt so nice.

"I'm so hard now, look." I thrust into Colt's hand and shuddered violently.

"You're perfect." He kissed my temple and guided my hand to the base of my cock. "Hold here and slowly push inside him. A bit closer."

I scooted closer on my knees and pressed the head of my dick against Lucas's opening. "Like this?"

Lucas let out a heavy breath and hung his head.

"Listen." Colt smirked faintly and nodded to the stairs.

I listened curiously and tilted my head—oh! I heard them now. Abel and Madigan were also awake, and they weren't watching TV, exactly. I blushed and peered up at Daddy, who chuckled silently and refocused.

"That's good," Daddy whispered. He splayed his hand on top of Lucas's ass, and Lucas parted his legs some more. The angle became perfect. "Now you push—gently."

I licked my lips and wriggled a bit, trying to enter him just a little. My head popped in, and I gasped and stared up wide-eyed at Colt. Ohh, that felt so good. So, so, so good.

His eyes flashed with desire and amusement. "You like that, don't you? Keep goin'."

I drew a shaky breath and pushed in some more. My mouth ran dry. Daddy was so freaking tight, I didn't know what to do with myself. I couldn't help but moan.

"I want more. Can I have more, please?"

"Take him," Colt murmured. "He's a whore for a good, hard fuck."

"Is that true, Daddy?" I watched myself disappear into Lucas's ass. "Are you a whore for my cock too?"

"Whenever you want, baby boy," Lucas groaned quietly. "Give Daddy everything."

I didn't want to pull out, but I had to if I wanted to push in again, and I really, really wanted that. So I did it quickly, and the sensations that flew through me were unlike anything else. I started fucking Lucas pretty fast, and I stared at the spot where we were joined.

"Look, Daddy," I panted. "I'm fucking him. I'm doing it."

"Yes, you are, little darlin'. You can go harder too."

I went harder.

And faster.

Colt slipped off the bed again and rubbed his cock, and he removed some of the pillows. Then he got in front of Lucas and guided his big cock into a hot, warm, willing mouth. One I'd had my cock in so many times, and I didn't know what was best.

Getting a blow job from one of my Daddies or fucking Lucas's tight ass.

Mine, mine, mine, all mine. They're mine.

I moaned and let my head fall back.

"Oh God." I gripped Lucas's hips tightly and slammed in, hearing how our skin slapped together. I heard him groan around Colt's cock as well, and I felt how his ass clenched around me. "Oh, do that again, Daddy," I pleaded. "Fuck, I can't stop."

Mine.

"You don't have to stop, baby," Colt said, out of breath. "It's gonna be quick for me too."

I whimpered and allowed the pleasure to course through me. It was a luxury to be able to just *take* every now and then. Something I wouldn't want very often because I'd become spoiled and too bratty, but sometimes... I had no words to describe how good this felt. I indulged and I took, and Lucas must've liked it because he was rock hard and stroking himself. Too fucking sexy. And then seeing Colt use Lucas's mouth.

The orgasm loomed close, and I welcomed it. I chased it. I grabbed on to it as soon as it was within reach, and then I was soaring.

I heard Colt curse and growl like he did when he was there on the edge.

Lucas clamped down around my cock, causing me to cry out. It was like fucking the hottest, tightest, softest, wettest vise, and I pumped my orgasm into him, pushing my cock through the ropes of come that shot out of me.

Lucas didn't know the little beast he'd just awoken in me. I was going to fuck my Daddy lots and lots!

"This week went by way too fast," Abel grumbled.

"I know. I think so too." I didn't want to think about their going home tomorrow. It was our last day together in DC, and we were spending it by the pool at home. Except for this morning when we all went out for breakfast.

Now we were lounging in two inflatable pool chairs Colt had bought us. Mine was blue, and Abel's was green.

"Next time, you should come visit us," he said.

I lifted my head, instantly seeking out my Daddies. Colt was inside the house, but Lucas was reading a book on the sunbed. Those reading glasses—gah, he was so hot in them.

"Daddy," I called. "Can we visit Abel and Madigan soon?"

He smiled and inclined his head. "We've already made plans with Madigan, dear. He invited us to a Halloween party their community is hosting."

"Yes!" I fist-pumped the air, and both Abel and I rolled out of our chairs and into the water. Crap! Cold water!

"That's so awesome!" Abel's eyes lit up. "Our community is super small, but they're fun."

Well, I was excited.

Colt and Madigan stepped out on the patio shortly after, and Colt held up his phone.

"They posted the scores from the game, baby. We finished in third place."

"Fuckin' A," Abel exclaimed.

"That's good, right?" I asked, hopeful.

Daddy grinned. "Nine couples participating and it was your first event? Third place is fuckin' fantastic."

I matched his grin with one of my own and let myself feel a little proud.

"All right." Madigan clapped his hands together. "Last barbecue to celebrate our bronze medalists?"

"Let's fire up the grill," Colt said with a nod.

Saying goodbye to Abel and Madigan the next morning was rough. We all saw them off at the airport, and I hugged them both and very politely made Madigan promise that Abel and I could visit each other more often. And he promised! So did my Daddies.

Thankfully, Abel and I still had our FaceTime calls.

Lucas rode in the back seat with me on the way back to Georgetown, and I could admit that *maybe* I cranked up the sadness a tiny bit to resume my quest of turning them into Georgetown residents too.

"Can you believe summer is almost over?" I pouted to myself and stared down at my lap.

"It's July," Lucas answered.

"Yeah, and in a few weeks, your condo will be ready, and I'll be all alone again." I sniffled for effect and looked out the window. "Maybe you'll forget me."

"Jesus Christ," Colt muttered. "Layin' it on a bit thick there, don't you think?"

"But, *ohh*," I complained. "I'm *sad*, Daddy."

"Maybe, but you're also tryin'a play us." He stared at me in the rearview. "Is that nice?"

Damn it! I huffed and slumped back in my seat, and I folded my arms over my chest. "I just love you, is all. I'm not going to say sorry for wanting you with me all the time."

"And we never claimed you should," he replied. "It's your method that needs some work. But maybe you think so little of us that you believe it's okay to manipulate us. Maybe that's how little you love us."

My eyes widened in horror. "No! I never said that! Why would you—" I stifled a scream when I saw his smirk in the rearview. Freaking gah! Why did he have to turn the tables on me?

Lucas chuckled and patted my hand. "Everything will work out. You'll see."

"Okay," I mumbled. "But can we still redecorate the house together?"

"Yes, we can." He linked our fingers together, and relief swept over me. "Daddy and I are working on a few things. You just need to be patient."

"I can be patient, I swear," I said.

"There's a first time for everythin'," Colt laughed.

I stuck my tongue out at him.

He stuck his tongue out at me too.

Silly Daddy!

The following Friday, Vincent agreed to meet me at a coffee shop across the river in Arlington. It was closer to where he lived, and I had an errand there.

Lucas dropped me off in Crystal City after lunch, and he

peered back at me with a sympathetic smile. "You'll be fine, sweetheart."

I nodded nervously and clutched the note with my rehearsed talking points. "You'll be home for dinner?"

"Of course. I'm just gonna head into the office for a few hours."

I nodded again and unbuckled my seat belt.

"Colt and I have a surprise for you later."

A rush of excitement flooded me, and the funny thing was, I'd have a surprise for them too. "I like surprises, Daddy."

"We know." He grinned. "Call Colt if you need him to come get you afterward, okay?"

No, I could do this. I could take the Metro on my own. Using the Metro while Abel was here had helped me navigate the system easier. I was ready. Besides, Colt was busy painting our dining room today.

"I'll call, but I'll be fine," I promised. Leaning forward in my seat, I kissed Lucas on the lips and then opened the door. "Love you, Daddy."

"Love you too, sweet boy. Good luck with Vincent, and let me know how it went. Wait—do you have your money?"

"Yes, Sir." I blushed and patted my pocket where I kept my wallet. This morning, my Daddies told me they were going to start giving me an allowance. Every Friday, they would give me twenty dollars to cover my ice cream needs, and I had to make it last. I couldn't come to them next Wednesday and ask for ice cream because my money was gone.

I was going to learn how to put together a budget.

Tricky stuff.

After saying goodbye to Daddy, I closed the door and joined the late lunch crowd on the sidewalk. The sun was shining on my exposed arms, and I felt good. I had nauseated butterflies flying around in my stomach, but I'd built up enough confidence while rehearsing what to say that Vincent simply had to agree with me. He wasn't allowed to leave me; things just had to change a bit.

I passed an ice cream shop and hesitated for a minute. Why had I not suggested we meet here? *Oh, yikes.* I stepped closer and read the price list in the window, and I couldn't believe what I was reading. Three dollars for one scoop! Without toppings! An ice cream had to have two scoops and toppings—this wasn't news. And in that case...my allowance would be gone in three ice creams.

I'd felt so inspired this morning, sitting there at the kitchen island with a crisp twenty-dollar bill. I was going to use some of it for ice cream, and I was going to save some to show I was a good boy, and maybe I'd buy something for my Daddies. Abel had told me he surprised Madigan like that sometimes. But he wasn't useless with money like I was. I'd never learned to budget!

This was madness.

Sticking my hands down in the pockets of my new cargo shorts, I continued along the sidewalk and tried to come to terms with the fact that there would be less ice cream in my future. Because impressing my Daddies and showing them I could learn how to handle money was more important. It was just... I was a little verklempt.

Vincent was waiting outside the coffee shop I'd found on Yelp, and my nerves made a swift return as he spotted me.

"Who pissed in your cereal?" he asked.

I shook my head. "Hi. I'm sorry. I just found out how expensive ice cream is. Can you imagine? Three dollars for one scoop?"

He gave me the strangest look, for which I couldn't exactly blame him. "Firstly, where the hell is this coming from?

Secondly, the place you like in Georgetown is easily six bucks a scoop."

"Holy shit," I cursed. "I wonder if they set me up to fail."

Vincent stiffened at that. "What did they do?"

"No, no. Not like that." I blew out a breath and glanced around me. "Can we...?" I gestured to the door.

He nodded curtly, and I strode forward to get the door before he could. Because this was the point of today. I didn't want him opening more doors for me. He was done driving me around. No more serving.

Ironically, it was thanks to my Daddies intervening in my life and taking control that I was learning how to stand on my own two feet.

The coffee shop reminded me of a Starbucks, with the exception of another color scheme, white and red, and their specials centered around milk shakes. Milk shakes were *not* ice cream. Therefore, I didn't have to use my allowance.

"What can I get you?" I took out my wallet and retrieved my regular card. The one that had kept me from ever grasping the concept of money.

Vincent frowned. "I can buy my own damn coffee, Kit."

I suppressed a sigh. "Can you please let me do this?" I hated seeing him so rigid around me, and I prayed I could make it better. I wanted him in my life—on terms that were better for both of us.

"Fine," Vincent muttered and rolled his eyes. "Regular coffee—black."

Okay, well, I was getting a triple swirl chocolate milk shake with chocolate sprinkles and chocolate brownie chunks.

It spoke to me from the menu.

After paying for and receiving our orders, we found a table in the back and took our seats. I fidgeted with my straw. It had a little scoop at the bottom of it.

"What's this money thing about?" Vincent leaned back in his chair. Even in July, he wore his leather jacket.

"Well...what would you say is a normal allowance?" I asked. "I know you think it's weird, but it's a kink thing. Colt and Lucas are helping me learn the value of money, so they're giving me an allowance for my ice cream addiction. Their words, not mine. You know I'm not addicted."

He snorted and scrubbed a hand over his jaw. "The only thing you gotta cover with the allowance is ice cream?"

I nodded and fished out a chunk of brownie from my shake.

He shrugged. "I don't know. I'd say ten bucks to most people, but they don't have what you have. And the ice cream you get is pricey as shit."

Fuck, then. So, they weren't setting me up to fail.

"I didn't know it was expensive," I mumbled in my defense.

Vincent slanted a little smirk. "Because you never had to look at a price tag, buddy."

"I do now." I jutted my chin slightly. "I'm trying to learn."

"I can see that." His gaze softened ever so slightly. "Learnin' 'bout money, getting a job, taking the Metro... Shit's sure as hell changed."

I chewed on my lip, uncertain. Then I remembered my note, and I quickly dug it out of my pocket. "I wrote down some thoughts. May I read them to you?"

"Sure." He straightened in his seat again, and I could tell he was on edge.

I cleared my throat. "Hi, Vincent, I—shit. I don't need to say that." I flushed bright red and scanned my note. Was the whole thing going to make me sound stupid? I blew out a frustrated breath and flattened the crumpled piece of paper under my hand. This was Vincent. I shouldn't rely on notes. "I want to start by apologizing for how I've handled things," I said. "You and I have had our routine for a long time, and then I just went and flipped everything around. It wasn't fair to you."

He inclined his head.

"Additionally, I believe we both made a mistake in how we've treated each other," I continued. "I view you as much more than someone who works for me. For the longest time, you were my only friend. But when I met Colt and Lucas, I changed your hours as if you were an employee and nothing more. I barely talked to you about it, and I assumed you wouldn't mind because it would give you time to hang out with your real friends. I treated you the way I assumed you felt about me—that I was just a job. Then you texted—"

He winced at that. "It's my turn, Kit. I set out to hurt you with those texts, and I did."

I nodded hesitantly.

"Things were changing too fast, and I had no control over it," he murmured. "I guess, in a way, before...it was you and me against the world. Except we were both hiding from the world."

Oh. So, he knew now he'd been hiding too? "I've been trying to tell you that."

"I know." He offered a hollow smile. "I haven't been consistent. When something you said didn't fit how I felt, I brushed it off in my head. You was just some sweet punk I worked for. The fuck did you know about the real world, you know? I was a dick. And I flipped it around too. When you cut my hours but continued to pay me, it was like you swept me under the rug." He paused and moved his coffee closer. "Basically, I've treated you like a friend when it fit me, when it meant I could make you feel bad, and I've treated you like an employer when I didn't wanna deal with what you said."

It was as painful as it was freeing to hear him say all this. It was never fun to be hurt, but at the same time, I'd done the same thing. "The lines have been too blurry."

He nodded. "They have. I'm sorry I hurt you, buddy."

I smiled weakly, refusing to get emotional. My Daddies would have to deal with that mess later. They'd made me promise to let them take care of such things, and I was going to obey, dammit. At home, I didn't have to feel bad about crying. I'd be embarrassed like crazy if it happened here.

"We have to unblur the lines," I said quietly.

Vincent's own smile was rueful. "This is the part where I get fired."

Jesus. I shook my head quickly and blinked past the sting in my eyes. "Nuh-uh. It's called reassigned. Richard has a better job waiting for you. One that my dad promised you a very long time ago."

His brow furrowed in confusion.

So I continued. "You're keeping the perks from having worked for my family—your condo and so on. That's what I can do as a thank-you for everything you've done for me. Maybe you see the very few occasions you tried to make me feel guilty, but I am thinking of all the times you stopped by the house and pretended your TV was broken. When, in reality, you knew I was lonely." I dove for my milk shake and gave myself a brain freeze that could explain why my eyes got teary. "Ouch." I rubbed my forehead. Damn it, I could've just faked it. "Bottom line, Vincent, is that I don't want you to work for me personally anymore. I want you at the company where you can live up to your full potential. And most of all, I want you in my life as family and as a friend."

Vincent cleared his throat and looked out over the coffee shop a moment, and I saw his jaw tick. Then he sniffled and chuckled. "Well, damn."

"Are you okay?" I asked worriedly. I hadn't seen his eyes glassy since the funeral.

He winked. "Brain freeze."

No, I was not falling for that. He hadn't even had any milk shake!

"I'm fine, kid. Just didn't see this comin'." He patted my hand briefly on the table.

My forehead creased. "You knew you had job security, right?"

"Sure, but the security is only there until it ain't."

Well. I huffed. "Okay, but now what? Can we be family or not?"

He rumbled a low laugh and picked up his coffee mug. "You're already my annoying little brother, Kit. Sometimes more than my real brothers are."

I smiled widely.

21.

"I'm sorry, Kit. I thought you were on the next train. I'll come pick you up."

"It's fine." Nothing could ruin my good mood as I emerged from the Metro station in Foggy Bottom. "I'll just walk—"

"Oh no, you don't." Lucas wouldn't have that, apparently. "Either you wait for me to pick you up, or you take the bus the last way. We've done it before."

Sometimes I wanted to curse Georgetown for not having a Metro station. "We've also walked this route before," I reminded him. "I'm supposed to face my mom's paranoid fears, remember? It's literally the safest area of DC."

Daddy sighed in the background. "Okay, you're right. We'll compromise. We both start walking now, and we'll meet halfway."

That was fair. It would still give me a ten-minute walk alone. "Deal. I'll keep my phone close."

"Good. See you soon, sweetheart. Love you."

"Love you too." I ended the call and crossed a street, beginning my trek up to Georgetown. Feeling all adult-like. A weird thing to be proud of, probably. Feeling like an adult was also the last thing I wanted as soon as I met up with Daddy. As good as this day had been, it'd also been long and exhausting, and I couldn't wait to go to my Little space.

Much to my joy, Vincent had come with me on my errand today, and then we'd had snacks afterward. Not ice cream! I'd had a big serving of mozzarella sticks in marinara sauce at this place Vincent introduced me to. It was rather affordable, even, and the food there was amazing. I was totally going to bring my Daddies there.

This walk was a good idea. I needed to work up a nice appetite for Colt's cooking. We were having grilled salmon out on the porch for dinner, one of Lucas's favorites. I liked it too, but it didn't beat the buttery garlic mashed potatoes we were having with it! This time, I was going to eat it slowly so my stomach didn't explode.

My steps faltered when I reached a street with two broken lights. It was a short street, and it shouldn't scare me. It was Mom's fears that'd been drilled into my head. Fuck, did it have to be nearly pitch black? No—damn it. The Four Seasons was right around the corner, and there were people everywhere. I wasn't gonna let the fears grab another inch of me.

I kept walking, maybe walking a little faster, and breathed a sigh of relief when I reached a well-lit street again.

Booyah.

It wasn't long thereafter I saw Daddy walking toward me. He hadn't changed from his work clothes, so I was greeted by hotness in a suit.

"Hi! I walked up a street that had, like, no lights."

He smiled a little unsurely and cupped my cheeks, then dipped down for a kiss. "I'm still the worrier in the family, love. Maybe leave out that part."

I snickered and kissed him once more, and then I grabbed his hand, already feeling myself letting go of certain things. Daddy was here now.

"Colt mentioned you had a good day with Vincent," he said.

I nodded lots. I'd called Colt earlier to ask if I could come home a bit later. "Vincent said I'm his annoying little brother."

Daddy grinned. "That might be a fitting relationship for the two of you, wouldn't you say?"

"Yeah," I laughed, "I thought it was funny."

"Well, I'm very glad you worked things out." He kissed the top of my head. "I'll want the details when we sit down for dinn — What on earth happened to your leg, Kit?"

Crap. I'd hoped he wouldn't see it yet.

His eyes flooded with concern, and he scanned my face and arms. "I thought your scratches from the game had healed. Did I miss something?"

"You weren't supposed to notice it yet," I grumbled. "Can you pretend it's not there until we get home? Pretty please? I swear everything is fine."

I'd asked Kirk to wrap the tattoo around my calf as if it were a real wound. With plastic wrap instead of a bandage, my Daddies wouldn't be surprised. But now, well, okay, Daddy got worried, which wasn't awesome, but I wanted it to be a surprise! I had something else too, in a small shopping bag, though that wasn't as big.

"All right," Daddy replied warily. "You didn't fall, though, did you?"

"No, I promise." I dragged Daddy along up the sidewalk again, because he'd slowed down earlier, and I swung my shopping bag in my free hand. "Daddy, did you know how expensive ice cream is? It can be up to six dollars a scoop!"

His gaze gave way to mirth, which was much better. "A bit of an eye-opener, huh?"

"It was better when they were closed, to be honest," I said frankly. "At least when it comes to ice cream. And toppings! You'll never believe it. A dollar for hot fudge—it's an outrage."

He chuckled warmly. "Good thing Colt and I would never deprive you of such things."

"But I have to buy less of it now."

"When you're out on your own," he agreed. "When we take you out for ice cream, life wouldn't be the same if you couldn't put all sorts of weird toppings on there."

I didn't see anything weird about mixing gummy bears with chocolate flakes and caramel sauce.

Daddy was the weird one, though I hugged his arm for being so nice to me about ice cream.

"I'm going to keep my Sunday tradition of having ice cream with Vincent at the Lincoln Memorial, if that's okay," I said.

"I think that's a wonderful idea, little one. You two have a whole new friendship to explore."

I beamed and nodded, looking forward to it.

"Daddy, we're home!" I yelled. Kicking off my shoes, I tightened my grip on my shopping bag and then darted toward—

"Kit! Come back here, young sir. That's not where the shoes go."

"Crap," I whispered.

Once back in the entryway, I gathered my shoes and put them on the shelf. Then I ran into the living room, skidded across the floor, and noticed that the first coat of paint was in place in the dining room. Awesome! Daddy worked fast. It was only a shade darker than what we had in the living room, because we needed them to match and somewhat share a theme since the whole space was fairly open.

Colt was at the grill, and he hadn't put the salmon on yet. Perfect.

"Hi, Daddy, we're home!" I bounced over to him and kissed the grin off his face. "You've done tons of stuff today."

"I enjoy gettin' shit done around here." He set the tongs aside and pulled me close. "How's my boy?"

"He's good. Come, I have a surprise for y'all." I grabbed his hand and tugged him all the way back into the living room.

"Did you hear that, Luke? He said his first y'all. They grow up so fast."

I giggled and peered into my shopping bag. "Okay, this is only new undies." I slapped a pair of light blue briefs to Colt's stomach so he could hold them while I kept digging.

"Cute." Colt stretched them out and held them up. "Fun-sized and all."

"Here." I finally found them. They were so precious, I thought. "Look. Aren't they the best? They're magnets for the fridge." More than that, they were tiny picture frames. I'd used all the photos in my phone that had one or all of us, made them black and white, and had prints made that fit the frames. "There are fourteen in total." I was gonna buy six, but I couldn't decide.

Colt and Lucas stepped closer and inspected the business-card sized magnets with soft smiles.

"I love how you're just moving us in to this house." Colt chuckled and showed one of the magnets to Lucas. "I like this one of you two."

I glanced at the tiny picture. It was me kissing Lucas's cheek. We were in the pool together.

I'd also ordered prints of a few photos from Abel and Madigan's stay here. I wanted them up where I could see them. But I had to buy frames for those first.

"These are lovely, sweetheart." Lucas squeezed my neck affectionately. "If you don't mind, though, please tell us what's wrong with your leg."

Colt took a step back and eyed my leg, then lifted a brow at me.

"I told you, Daddy, nothing is wrong." After stowing away the magnets in the bag again, I sat down on the edge of the coffee table and set the shopping bag on the floor. "I wanted to surprise you." I carefully removed the bandage, layer by layer, until only a fresh tattoo and a sheen of protective gel remained.

Both my Daddies squatted down in front of me and gently examined my leg, reading the tribute that traveled around my calf. It simply read *Their boy*, but nothing Kirk did was simple. He was an artist, and he'd turned it into a three-inch-thick band around my leg, including the classic, cursive letters, the shadow work, and a baby blanket twisted in chains.

I was happy for more than one reason when it came to seeing Kirk today. Because I'd found out that he was officially dating Dr. Cohen at my clinic. According to him, they'd argued heatedly a couple weeks ago, and to "shut her the hell up," he'd kissed her. Then he said the rest of the story was rated R.

"Sweet lord." Lucas's voice was full of awe. "This is exquisite." He brushed his thumb right underneath where small teddy bears were visible on the blanket.

Colt didn't say anything at first. He merely rose slightly to reach me better, and he kissed me hard. Hands under my jaw, fingers tracing back to my neck, he drew shivers from me and made me wonder how one kiss could reduce me to a freaking puddle of want.

"We'll never let you forget who you belong to, baby." He spoke against my lips, his tone low and rich. "Fuck, how you own us."

Possessiveness and love flowed freely through me, and I kissed him back with everything I was.

When Lucas stood up, Colt slowly ended the kiss and told me to follow him to the kitchen.

He took the lead, and Lucas hugged me to him on the way.

"What have we done to deserve you?" he murmured.

For the first time in years, I wasn't going to crack a joke at my own expense. "I think the same every day," I said instead. "I liked getting a tattoo that celebrated something rather than covered something, too."

He squeezed my hand. "You know, when Colt came home after getting injured in Iraq, he told me something beautiful about scars."

"I was on a lot of Vicodin," Colt drawled with a glint in his eye.

I grinned slightly and slid onto one of the stools in the kitchen. "What did you tell him, Daddy?"

"Luke might actually remember that one more clearly," he chuckled.

Lucas smirked and gave a shake of his head, and he took a seat next to me. "I'm paraphrasing a bit, but... Scars are like book covers. They hint at a story. We know the story is there, but we are the authors, and we tell it."

Oh, I liked that. It was similar to what Kirk had once told me. "That's sweet." I rested the side of my jaw in my hand and faced Colt. "You never told me how you got injured."

He lifted a shoulder in a slight shrug and scratched his chest. "Our base took fire during the arrival of a shipment, and one of my buddies got trapped in a Humvee outside the gates. A few of us ran out to get him, and an IED went off nearby." He knocked his hip. "Got enough shrapnel in here to set off the metal detectors every time I go through airport security."

I winced. "I know this sounds lame, but I appreciate everything you've done for us. You're a hero, Daddy."

"Oh, you used the H-word." Lucas smiled teasingly, and I watched how Colt cleared his throat and became visibly uncomfortable. "If there is one single word that makes our man squirm, it's being called a hero. Look at him."

How curious. I chuckled softly and gave Daddy a confused expression. "You call yourself a ten and a living legend, but—"

"No one else is allowed to," Colt stated frankly. "That's correct."

I snickered. "You're weird."

"You're allowed to call me that," he replied. "Now, for the reason we're standing here. We have about—" he checked his watch "—two minutes until the grill is ready for the salmon." He completely ignored Lucas's comment about how quickly Colt changed the topic. "Kit, though Daddy and I suspect you didn't quite know what you got yourself into this morning when you agreed to try the allowance thing, we wanted to tell you we're proud of you for trying."

"And we want to show you that there are options," Lucas added.

"Exactly." Colt hooked his fingers into one of the handles on a cupboard, and he sent me a wink. "You don't have to go out and buy the priciest shit to get what you want." With that said, he opened the cupboard, and my jaw about hit the counter.

"Oh my God!" I scrambled out of my seat and ran around the island to get a closer look.

"Rosa deserves a lot of credit," Colt said. "She helped me put everything together this mornin'."

I was in heaven. It was my very own toppings bar. All the shelves were filled with small bottles of... "Oh my God," I repeated in a whisper. There was *everything*. Gummy bears, Cap'n Crunch, granola crumbs, sprinkles in a dozen different colors and shapes and flavors, edible glitter, tiny peanut butter cups, mini M&Ms, Oreo dust, chocolate chips, nuts, and little bits of fudge.

Overwhelmed by the deliciousness, I sniffled and threw my

arms around Colt's middle. "Thank you, Daddy. This is the best gift ever." Me being me, I had to get weepy about it. I couldn't help it! It was just so beautiful.

"You're welcome, little darlin'," he chuckled. "There are some rules, though. You gotta ask before you take ice cream—because we know you'd have it for breakfast, lunch, and dinner if you could."

Mayyybe.

"You also have to do your chores." Lucas joined us on this side of the island, and I threw myself at him next. He chuckled too and kissed the top of my head. "There will be a list on the fridge every morning. You'll check off the chores, and—"

"I'll do them lickety-split, I promise," I croaked. "Thank you, thank you, thank you, Daddy!"

Colt laughed. "I'm startin' to think we should've made this gift the headliner."

"You and me both." Lucas was amused too.

I sniffled and peered up at Colt over my shoulder. "There's more?"

Colt smiled crookedly. "We'll save the other thing for when we eat."

"May I just point out that we're eating?" I hinted.

I'd waited almost an hour!

"And it's wonderful, isn't it?" Lucas forked up some salmon and mashed potatoes and put it into his mouth. "I do love this meal, baby."

Colt tipped his wineglass at him and then took a sip.

These two misters were testing my patience.

They wanted to talk about work and how their day had been. They'd even taken a minute to discuss the freaking weather and the new bistro lights Colt and I had hung up in the tree above us. *And* they'd just—before I interrupted them—talked about whether or not we should move the sunbeds out here and the dining area to the deck instead.

Why? Why? Why were they doing this to me?

Who cared about where the sunbeds went?

"It does make sense," Lucas said. "To circle back—about the sunbeds. I saw you can buy roof attachments for them and a retractable umbrella of sorts."

"We can't have you burnin' to a crisp in the sun." Colt smirked.

"Not all of us were raised in the Texas desert," Lucas replied mildly. "Besides, if we move the table to the deck, we'd be able to eat outside even when the weather is poor. I like the sound of the rain when I don't have to get wet."

"Yes, yes, we're all fascinated with the flippin' awning." I stabbed a piece of salmon and stuck it into my mouth.

Colt shook his head in amusement and sighed. "Sometimes you're very unobservant, Kit. What've we been talkin' about?"

I waved a fork in the general direction of the deck on the other side of the pool. "What should and shouldn't be under the awning. Exciting stuff."

"And what did we discuss before that?" Lucas prodded.

I scowled. "I dunno. Oh, the bathtub? You wanna install a new bathtub once you've torn down the wall between the two guest rooms." Those rooms were going to be the master bedroom when all was said and done. This house was finally a home again, but I still had a limit or two. For instance, I had no desire to sleep in the room that was once my parents'. So, Colt had come up with the idea that we could turn the two guest rooms into one big master suite.

Colt stared at me expectantly, yet with patience. "I don't

know about you, but I don't make it a habit of plannin' any remodeling in places where I'm only a guest."

"Or where we're only living temporarily," Lucas filled in.

Funny how quickly I grew still. Even my heart stopped for a second.

Colt leaned forward and rested his forearms on the table. "We're gonna keep our condo for a while so we can say we've been patient enough when the day comes, Kit. But Lucas had a meetin' with the bank today."

I exhaled shakily and flicked my gaze to Lucas.

He smiled tentatively and squeezed my leg under the table. "They've looked over our assets and said we qualify for a mortgage that would cover a house in this area once we sell our condo."

"Oh," I breathed. "Does that mean...?" I didn't dare assume.

"We'll be writin' a contract for this." Colt watched me with that serious expression he used when he didn't want me to goof around. "Consider it a prenup—"

"I hate prenups," I blurted out.

His mouth twitched. "It's for your protection, Kit," he explained. "If something were to happen—"

"Nooo!" This was upsetting to me, and I slumped back in my seat and covered my face with my hands. "Why would something happen to us? I don't want you to leave me."

"Sweetheart, no one is saying that," Lucas comforted. "But since Colt and I wish to go all in with you, we'd feel the most comfortable if the three of us owned an equal share of the home that's gonna be ours—hopefully for the rest of our lives."

I sniffled and felt my bottom lip quivering. "We'd own this together? Not me one part and you two together? But like, I don't know if I'm explaining it right—"

"I understand," he assured me. "No, it wouldn't be Colt and

me, for lack of a better word, *against* you. It would be the three of us together, on equal ground."

"*But.*" Colt said the stupidest word ever. "Since it was your home from the beginning, it will stay that way if something did happen. That's really all. And once your army of family lawyers gets involved, I bet you they'll agree."

"Lawyers are stupidheads." I stuck out my tongue.

"Nevertheless, you brat..." Lucas gave me a pointed look. "It's not wrong to make sure everyone is protected. Don't you think Colt and I did this when he and I got together?"

"Did you?" I sat up straighter, feeling slightly better now.

"When we got engaged," Colt replied with a nod. "The only difference now is we'll do it a little bit before we put a ring on your finger."

My lips parted before I quickly shut them and slapped a hand over my mouth.

He rumbled a laugh. "Finally, a not-so-subtle hint you pick up on."

Oh my God!

Lucas leaned over our armrests and kissed my cheek. "How does that sound? Think you can be patient with us a little while longer now?"

I nodded and sniffled and blinked back silly tears.

"Love you, little darlin'." Colt smiled.

"Love you," I whimpered. "More than all the sprinkles."

They both laughed this time, and I was the luckiest boy in the whole world.

EPILOGUE

A few months later

I'd thought meeting Lucas's and Colt's parents was going to be my most nerve-racking experience, but two things had proven me wrong. Firstly, aside from Lucas's parents being slightly more formal, both their families had accepted me. Apparently, according to Colt's mother, they'd long since known "the boys" were into some "alternative stuff."

I liked Colt's mother and sister the most, and they'd put me at ease very quickly and spent a weekend with us at home last month.

It'd been so fun seeing Colt and Lucas with one of their nieces.

Secondly, seeing Colt fly. That was *the* most nerve-racking experience, which I'd just decided.

"He's coming back around." Lucas pointed toward the sky, near the horizon, and I all but held my breath.

Colt had been staying at Langley for the past week, and today, Lucas and I had come down to visit him. I'd been excited and nervous all day, and now I knew why. He flew so fucking fast! And he'd been right the time he'd said he was an aggressive pilot. He was bold and took risks.

I stared with wide eyes as he did a maneuver to get away from the squadron of six fighters chasing him. He shot straight up and made a loop, only to hightail it out of there and disappear from our viewing point.

Lucas and I, along with a few dozen other people—mostly military personnel, but also some family—stood near the taxiway where the planes eventually parked. From here, I could see two gorgeous Raptors, each one with a maintenance crew hard at work. There was also an open hangar with a Super Hercules parked inside.

I was in heaven!

"There he is again!" I almost bounced where I was standing. It was so difficult to contain my excitement.

Somehow, Colt had broken up the squadron, and he was chasing one of the other F-16 jets, with the other five following.

"That would've been a suicidal move in real life," I said matter-of-factly. My guess was, having researched these training missions a little, Colt had probably been given the order to see how quickly he could disband the formation or something like that. And he'd succeeded. However, in a serious situation, Daddy would've been dead. "Any of the other five would've just locked on target and fired. Maybe a sidewinder. They are awesome."

"They are kind of awesome," a man said behind me.

I turned around and smiled politely. It was obviously a pilot standing there, younger than Colt by perhaps ten years.

He smiled back and extended his hand. "You gotta be Kit."

Oh, he knew Colt? I shook his hand. "That's right."

At the same time, Lucas turned around too, and it became clear immediately that he knew the man.

"*Ev*, why— I mean, it's so good to see you. I thought you were stationed in Japan." Lucas brought the guy, Ev, in for a hug.

"Good to see you too, Sir. I came back yesterday." Ev smiled widely. "I had dinner with Top in the cafeteria last night, and I swear he spent the whole meal talking about you two."

I remembered Colt's call sign was Top.

Lucas chuckled and squeezed Ev's shoulder. "I do hope he asked about you too."

Huh. I grew curious. Lucas didn't appear too many years older than Ev, yet he acted that way. Or Ev acted younger. There was something there.

"Well, he did tell me he was gonna pull some strings," Ev admitted, almost shyly. "They want me at Eglin in Florida, and I was kind of hoping for this area."

"Have mercy on anyone who stands in Colt's way," Lucas commented. "Hopefully we can welcome you back to the community soon, then."

I knew it. He was a kinkster. I could sense it.

Ev smiled and inclined his head, then gestured toward the taxiway. "Enjoy the rest of the training mission. I have a meeting, but I wanted to come say hi."

"I'm glad you did, dear. Stay in touch, okay?"

"Yes, Sir." Ev offered a last smile to me and then walked away.

"You'll like him, sweet boy," Lucas said, and we faced the other direction again. "He used to fly with Colt in South Carolina, and they were deployed together when we met." He grinned fondly at something, perhaps a memory. "They're like brothers, those two."

"Should I be worried?" I joked. Okay, half joked.

Lucas snorted. "When you see them in the same room together, you'll know why the mere thought of that is funny. But no." He kissed the side of my head. "I asked that same question once upon a time. Then I met Ev, and…" He shook his head. "He's something else. There isn't a box in this world he would fit into. Shy and submissive one second, cocky and sadistic the next, playing with both men and women." He paused. "Colt actually gave Ev his call sign. Now everyone knows him as Switchblade, but only we know that switch is… well, you know."

I snickered.

"August will be pleased to see Ev's return," Lucas mused. "As will Ivy."

"August is one of your friends, right?" I remember an August being mentioned.

He nodded. "You'll get to know him better soon. He's a bit of a recluse, but he's very nice." He pointed toward the sky again. "Looks like they're getting ready to land."

Oh, but not before Colt made me gasp. He'd told me he would try to do something cool for me, and that was exactly what he did. He flew over us at mad speed, breaking the sound barrier, then did countless spins while I squealed behind my hands.

"Mr. West and Mr. Damien?" someone asked. A man in uniform came over to us. "Please come with me. Colonel Carter asked me to bring you to the flight line."

My mouth popped open, and I stared up at Lucas.

He knew something. It was there in his eyes! He grabbed my hand, and we followed the man past the barricades and out onto the taxiway.

It was really windy here, and fall had arrived with colder weather. I shuddered and hugged Daddy's arm, and I vowed not to leave my beanie in the car next time.

We watched as the training squadron rolled in, each fighter parking under its own ceiling along the ramps.

I was about to see Colt's F-16 real up close, wasn't I? I couldn't believe it.

Daddy was the last to roll in, and I caught him greeting us with an aloha gesture, or shaka sign, something I'd seen pilots do in movies.

"This is so flippin' exciting." I tugged at Lucas's arm and shook it. "Should I mess with him for funsies, Daddy?"

Lucas laughed. "As long as it's the bratting he enjoys, I say go for it."

The man in uniform left us with a nod as soon as Daddy had stopped the plane and the engine was turned off. A maintenance crew was there quickly, and the hatch opened.

Daddy removed his head gear, and I waved excitedly.

It was a beauty, this plane. *Curses*. If only photography wasn't prohibited out here. A small fighter in comparison, yet big and worthy of worship when you found yourself walking under the wing. Thirty-two-foot wingspan, nearly fifty feet long. It was like falling in love all over again.

"Give us a minute, will ya?" I heard Colt say as he climbed out of the jet.

The maintenance crew backed off.

"You were amazing up there!" I exclaimed.

He grinned and dipped down for a kiss. My fighter pilot Daddy. Gah!

"What do you think of my Viper?"

I beamed at the plane—and the perfect joke came to me. Oh, I had to. I couldn't resist. It was the ultimate way to mess with him.

"It's cool," I said. "But have you ever landed on a carrier?"

"Ouch!" Daddy clutched his heart. "Let's file that under, the one thing you don't ask an Air Force pilot."

I giggled madly and hugged him. "I'm kidding! You know I'm kidding, right?"

"Of course I know, baby," he chuckled.

"Yeah, I don't get the joke," Lucas said.

"There are no aircraft carriers in the Air Force," I replied, smirking. "That's the Navy."

The joke was still sort of lost on Lucas, and I couldn't blame him. You kinda had to be a little nerdy—or involved in the armed forces—to appreciate this humor.

"Hey." Colt lifted my chin. "I can't exactly take you for a ride in a single-seater, but do you wanna climb in?"

I froze. And died.

I wasn't gonna cry, I wasn't gonna cry, I wasn't gonna cry. I blew out an unsteady breath and nodded jerkily, unable to speak, and my heart started pounding. Colt helped me up the ladder and reminded me not to touch anything. As if I would dream of such a thing. Holy shit, I couldn't believe this was happening.

A moment later, I sank into the tiny cockpit and sat rigidly in the seat. It was tilted back, the seat, and the cockpit was so small that moving around was nearly impossible. And to think, Daddy was practically twice my size.

I couldn't blink. I stared at the keypad in front of me, at all the buttons, the side-stick controller to my right, the handle between my legs that, if pulled, would eject me from the plane.

Daddy grinned, resting his forearms on the edge where I'd just climbed in. "You're allowed to breathe, boy."

I sucked in a breath and stared at him. "I'm sitting in a fighter jet," I whimpered.

"Pretty cool, huh?" He touched my cheek.

I sniffled and nodded. "Help me out, please. I don't want to blow it up somehow."

He let out a laugh and offered me a hand. "Okay, the easiest is if you hike up your foot so you stand up in the seat."

I carefully lifted my foot to the seat and hoisted myself up, and then Daddy descended the ladder so I could climb out.

"I got you if you fall."

I didn't fall, thankfully, but he still captured me when I had a step or two left to the ground, and he spun me around once before setting me down.

My stomach had the biggest butterflies.

"I am going to blog about this so much." I wiped at my cheeks. Another day, I would ask Daddy for pictures. I knew they allowed it at air shows. "Thank you, Daddy. Thank you, thank you, thank you."

"You're welcome, little darlin'." He draped an arm around my neck and kissed the top of my head. "I have a debrief in ten minutes, and then we're outta here. For today."

"Do you think you'll come back for more training missions? I wanna see you in the sky a thousand times."

He laughed a little. "There will definitely be more, but I can't promise you a thousand."

"Okay." I pouted, but not really. "Do you know something?"

"What?"

I smiled up at him. "You'll always be my king of the sky."

He smiled back and stole a hard smooch. "Music to my ears. I love you."

"Love you more, Daddy," I sang.

"Why's the kid tired?" Colt asked.

"It's been a long day, I suppose. A lot of excitement." Lucas helped me buckle my seat belt in the middle instead. That way,

I could use my Daddy as a pillow. "He's been working a lot this week too."

"I've barely had time for my Little space," I said, disgruntled. "Can you believe that, Daddy? So awful."

Colt was driving as usual, and his companion in the passenger's seat consisted of a massive bag of candy his mother had packed for him. He was a mama's boy.

Lucas and I had received our own, though. She was the best.

"We'll have to do somethin' about that, won't we?" Colt asked.

I nodded sleepily and got comfortable against Lucas's chest. He wrapped an arm around me.

"I'm glad you're not gonna be at Langley for a while," I said, then yawned. "We missed you lots, Daddy."

"I missed you guys too. We'll catch up good and proper on the trip."

I smiled and sucked my thumb into my mouth. I couldn't wait. We had a munch tomorrow, and then I was going to go see a movie with Cameron and Tate. The day after, I had lunch plans with Vincent and a quick meeting at work, before my Daddies and I flew to Seattle for a kinky Halloween with Abel and Madigan.

"Rest up, sweet boy." Lucas held me close and pressed his lips to my hair.

"Wait," I mumbled. Something was missing. "Daddy, did you bring my stuffie?"

"Oh shit, yeah, sorry. Let me just change lanes." Colt moved over to the right lane and then leaned toward the floor of the passenger's side.

I'd let him borrow my teddy bear, a gift from a few months ago, when he headed down to Langley last week. So he could pretend I was there with him when he went to bed at night.

"Here you go, baby." He snuck his hand between the seats,

and I grabbed my stuffie and cuddled back into Lucas's embrace.

"Do you want us to wake you when we stop for dinner?" Lucas murmured.

"McDonald's?" I wondered.

He nodded. "Probably."

"Yes, please." I closed my eyes and sucked my thumb into my mouth again. "I want the toy."

He chuckled softly. "How could I forget? Sleep now. I love you."

"Love you more, Daddy," I whispered and drifted off to sleep.

MORE FROM CARA

Next up in The Game Series is Breathless
Shay & Reese & River

Cara freely admits she's addicted to revisiting the men and women who yammer in her head, and several of her characters cross over in other titles. If you enjoyed this book, you might like the following.

Power Play
MM | Daddykink Romance | Age Difference |
Mental Health | Standalone

Love sucked. Correction: it sucked when you were in love with your parents' closest friend and he didn't feel the same. Madigan had always been there for me, from when I was a kid to when I got drafted by the NHL. Then I made the mistake of confessing my feelings for him... I was such a loser. My bipolar disorder was already difficult to manage as it was; add high anxiety and, most recently, as the cherry on a shit sundae, a suspension from the team. Why couldn't he see that I was perfect for him? We even had kink in common! Not that he knew that...

Breathless
MMM | The Game Series, #3 | BDSM | S/M | Daddykink | Standalone

"Will you beat me without knowing why I want it?"

I'm used to rejection by Sadists at this point. No one wants to beat me or skip aftercare; they wanna talk and get all up in my business—where they don't freaking belong. But I give it one more try when I spot River and Reese Tenley at a kink party. The only thing bigger than them is their reputation as hardcore Sadists. To the memories of grief and why I'm seeking punishment, I ask them to hurt me.

"Sure. It's your funeral."

Touch: The Complete Series
MF, MFM, MM | BDSM | S/M | Daddykink

Seven novels and novellas, several outtakes and future takes, and one epilogue. *Touch: The Complete Series* is your not-so-little black book of kink. Meet Nicholas Ford, club owner and Daddy Dom, who can't resist Kayla, the forbidden fruit. Mark Cooper is a Master and works the bar, and in his story he's tasked with introducing two subbies in the lifestyle. He just might keep them both to himself. Rio Kelly, a high-protocol Master, sees a ghost from his past in the club one night. A girl he's never been able to forget. A girl on a mission to serve. And Cade Kingsley may be a rough-around-the-edges Daddy Dom who scares off some subbies, but he wears his heart on his sleeve, and when two Little hearts need mending, he's there.

The series originally consisted of six kinky love stories: *Look but Don't Touch, Twice the Touch, A Touch to Surrender, Comforting Touch,* and *Touching Ink.* Now they've been reworked and prettied up, and they're published together with a dozen outtakes as well as the new novella, *Touching Truth,* that follows masochist Greg, sadistic Daddy Ryan, and switchy baby girl Angel.

Check out Cara's entire collection at www.caradeewrites.com, and don't forget to sign up for her newsletter so you don't miss any new releases, updates on book signings, free outtakes, give-aways, and much more.

ABOUT CARA

I'm often awkwardly silent or, if the topic interests me, a chronic rambler. In other words, I can discuss writing forever and ever. Fiction, in particular. The love story—while a huge draw and constantly present—is secondary for me, because there's so much more to writing romance fiction than just making two (or more) people fall in love and have hot sex.

There's a world to build, characters to develop, interests to create, and a topic or two to research thoroughly.

Every book is a challenge for me, an opportunity to learn something new, and a puzzle to piece together. I want my characters to come to life, and the only way I know to do that is to give them substance—passions, history, goals, quirks, and strong opinions—and to let them evolve.

I want my men and women to be relatable. That means allowing room for everyday problems and, for lack of a better word, flaws. My characters will never be perfect.

Wait...this was supposed to be about me, not my writing.

I'm a writey person who loves to write. Always wanderlusting, twitterpating, kinking, cooking, baking, and geeking. There's time for hockey and family, too. But mostly, I just love to write.

~Cara.

Get social with Cara
www.caradeewrites.com
www.camassiacove.com
Facebook: @caradeewrites
Twitter: @caradeewrites
Instagram: @caradeewrites

Made in the USA
Columbia, SC
19 February 2025

54073334R00170